Kane couldn't s⬚⬚⬚
familiarity in th⬚ ⬚⬚⬚⬚'s voice

"I'm not here to kill you. I don't even want to seriously hurt you, because my real contention is with the errant young Sam."

"He likes to call himself Enlil, now," Kane corrected. He struggled to focus his eyes, but the shove of a warm, human-feeling hand left him swinging. "You want Enlil, so you do what...lure us out here to hang us up like beef?"

"The enemy of my enemy is..."

"Let me see your damn face!" Kane growled.

"Touchy, touchy," the Thrush-thing replied. He stepped back and, finally, Kane's vision was clear enough and focused enough for him to see that the metallic-toned voice had come from his own face. Hard, predator-sharp blue eyes glinted to match the cruel smile on the doppelganger Kane's lips. It was identical to him, right down to the amount of scruffy beard growth on his jaw and the faint remnant of a scar on his cheek.

Other titles in this series:

Parallax Red

Doomstar Relic

Iceblood

Hellbound Fury

Night Eternal

Outer Darkness

Armageddon Axis

Wreath of Fire

Shadow Scourge

Hell Rising

Doom Dynasty

Tigers of Heaven

Purgatory Road

Sargasso Plunder

Tomb of Time

Prodigal Chalice

Devil in the Moon

Dragoneye

Far Empire

Equinox Zero

Talon and Fang

Sea of Plague

Awakening

Mad God's Wrath

Sun Lord

Mask of the Sphinx

Uluru Destiny

Evil Abyss

Children of the Serpent

Successors

Rim of the World

Lords of the Deep

Hydra's Ring

Closing the Cosmic Eye

Skull Throne

Satan's Seed

Dark Goddess

Grailstone Gambit

Ghostwalk

Pantheon of Vengeance

Death Cry

Serpent's Tooth

Shadow Box

Janus Trap

Warlord of the Pit

James Axler
Outlanders®

REALITY ECHO

A GOLD EAGLE BOOK FROM
W✷RLDWIDE®

TORONTO • NEW YORK • LONDON
AMSTERDAM • PARIS • SYDNEY • HAMBURG
STOCKHOLM • ATHENS • TOKYO • MILAN
MADRID • WARSAW • BUDAPEST • AUCKLAND

Recycling programs
for this product may
not exist in your area.

First edition February 2010

ISBN-13: 978-0-373-63865-9

REALITY ECHO

Copyright © 2010 by Worldwide Library.

Special thanks to Doug Wojtowicz for his contribution to this work.

Printed in U.S.A.

How many crimes, how many wars, how many murders, how many misfortunes and horrors, would that man have saved the human species, who pulling up the stakes or filling up the ditches should have cried to his fellows: Be sure not to listen to this imposter; you are lost, if you forget that the fruits of the earth belong equally to us all, and the earth itself to nobody!
—Jean Jacques Rousseau
1712–1778
On the Inequality among Mankind

The deadliest weapon I've ever seen used is a lie. It can crumble nations and slay hundreds without effort. Only knowledge and truth can dispel a lie's wrongs, yet it is a battle to spread the facts, and no truth can revive those who have fallen.
—Brigid Baptiste, scholar and warrior

The Road to Outlands—
From Secret Government Files to the Future

Almost two hundred years after the global holocaust, Kane, a former Magistrate of Cobaltville, often thought the world had been lucky to survive at all after a nuclear device detonated in the Russian embassy in Washington, D.C. The aftermath—forever known as skydark—reshaped continents and turned civilization into ashes.

Nearly depopulated, America became the Deathlands—poisoned by radiation, home to chaos and mutated life forms. Feudal rule reappeared in the form of baronies, while remote outposts clung to a brutish existence.

What eventually helped shape this wasteland were the redoubts, the secret preholocaust military installations with stores of weapons, and the home of gateways, the locational matter-transfer facilities. Some of the redoubts hid clues that had once fed wild theories of government cover-ups and alien visitations.

Rearmed from redoubt stockpiles, the barons consolidated their power and reclaimed technology for the villes. Their power, supported by some invisible authority, extended beyond their fortified walls to what was now called the Outlands. It was here that the rootstock of humanity survived, living with hellzones and chemical storms, hounded by Magistrates.

In the villes, rigid laws were enforced—to atone for the sins of the past and prepare the way for a better future. That was the barons' public credo and their right-to-rule.

Kane, along with friend and fellow Magistrate Grant, had upheld that claim until a fateful Outlands expedition. A displaced piece of technology…a question to a keeper of the archives…a vague clue about alien masters—and their world shifted radically. Suddenly, Brigid Baptiste, the archivist, faced summary execution, and Grant a quick termination. For

Kane there was forgiveness if he pledged his unquestioning allegiance to Baron Cobalt and his unknown masters and abandoned his friends.

But that allegiance would make him support a mysterious and alien power and deny loyalty and friends. Then what else was there?

Kane had been brought up solely to serve the ville. Brigid's only link with her family was her mother's red-gold hair, green eyes and supple form. Grant's clues to his lineage were his ebony skin and powerful physique. But Domi, she of the white hair, was an Outlander pressed into sexual servitude in Cobaltville. She at least knew her roots and was a reminder to the exiles that the outcasts belonged in the human family.

Parents, friends, community—the very rootedness of humanity was denied. With no continuity, there was no forward momentum to the future. And that was the crux—when Kane began to wonder if there *was* a future.

For Kane, it wouldn't do. So the only way was out—way, way out.

After their escape, they found shelter at the forgotten Cerberus redoubt headed by Lakesh, a scientist, Cobaltville's head archivist, and secret opponent of the barons.

With their past turned into a lie, their future threatened, only one thing was left to give meaning to the outcasts. The hunger for freedom, the will to resist the hostile influences. And perhaps, by opposing, end them.

Chapter 1

Sitting on the rock, his long legs drawn up to his chest, Grant's hulking frame bore a passing resemblance to a large gargoyle carved from jet-black obsidian. Though Grant was silent, Brigid Baptiste could tell that the ex-Magistrate was on edge. Too often, opponents of the Cerberus warriors had mistaken the phenomenal power of the massive man's limbs for a lack of intelligence, underestimating him at their own peril.

As a Magistrate in Cobaltville, one of the fortified baronies that rose from the wastelands of postapocalyptic America, Grant and his partner, Kane, developed the resourcefulness to deal with nearly any crisis. Grant also honed a set of observational skills that complemented Brigid's keen intellect and Kane's nearly preternatural instincts. That sharp mind had also made the big warrior one of the best pilots that Brigid had ever seen, adept at flying all manner of aircraft and capable of getting a damaged ship up and running with a minimum of tools.

The turmoil presently consuming Grant stemmed from the fact that Kane had been sent off on a solo quest to satisfy the Appalachian witch Epona and her cadre of mountain scouts. Grant had been opposed to such a handicap situation, but Kane conceded for the sake of diplomacy.

"Damn fool," Grant's deep voice grumbled, startling Brigid from her reverie.

"He can handle himself," Brigid argued.

Grant's dark eyes swiveled. The glare of momentary annoyance faded as he regarded her in his peripheral vision. "We all can. But I can still say this situation sucks."

Brigid nodded in agreement. She turned back toward where Granny Epona sat with her protective cordon of mountain folk. The term "Granny" was a misnomer, as the water witch had the body of a woman in her twenties, lean and tight corded muscles beneath her protective furs and leathers. Her face, windburned to a deep tan by the cold mountaintop winds of this stretch of the Poconos in what used to be known as Pennsylvania, was relatively unlined, making any determination of her age difficult, though Brigid guessed that the woman was between forty and sixty. A breeze plucked at Epona's black hair, tugging it aside like a curtain so that Brigid was able to see the water witch in profile.

This was the second time that Brigid had met the woman. Their first meeting was when Brigid, Kane and Grant had arrived via interphaser to negotiate for the release of a small team of Cerberus explorers who had stumbled upon the mountain folk. Initially Epona and her people had been suspicious of outlanders, but their fear of outside interference was tempered by enough reason that the Appalachians didn't execute them on the spot. It was a reprieve from the usual first contact that the three outlanders encountered, one of cold peace, both sides afraid to trust each other but too smart to make the first hostile move. Something had changed about Epona since then, and the flame-haired former archivist couldn't quite place it. Given her observational skills and eidetic memory, the incongruence nibbled at her, but there was nothing concrete to quantify her suspicions.

Epona looked up, as if she had noticed the attention locked on to her. "Has Kane appeared at the tree line?"

"No," Brigid answered.

Grant's lips curled in a sneer, but he kept his voice low so only Brigid could hear him. "You know, with our Commtacts, those primitive screwheads wouldn't hear Kane even if he did turn his on."

Brigid sighed and fingered the Commtact attached to her jaw. The tiny unit was a two-part man-machine interface developed by Cerberus techs with the help of the scientists of Manitius. The little comm unit worn on the outside hooked up to implanted steel pintels and allowed Brigid to communicate with her partners, as well as keep in touch across the globe with the Cerberus redoubt, which served as their home. Thanks to a series of satellites controlled from the redoubt's depths, the Commtact signal was strong and clear almost anywhere on the face of the Earth.

The insert implanted on her mandible was voice activated and utilized vibrations in the bone mass to allow her to hear without anyone else listening in. She could also speak so softly that someone only a few feet away wouldn't hear, but her jaw would transmit the sound to the Commtact in a way that it would be clear and audible to anyone with a proper receiving unit. More than once, since the addition of the Commtact to their regular gear, Brigid and her allies had been able to covertly communicate with one another, even under all but the closest scrutiny.

"I'm going to have to teach that boy to turn his Commtact on," Grant said.

"That would be breaking the spirit of our deal, stranger," Epona answered.

Brigid whirled, surprised at the silence with which the witch woman had moved, but only momentarily. Epona traveled with mountain scouts who were as stealthy a group of hunters as Brigid had ever seen, rivaling even Sky Dog's tribe.

Epona continued after both Cerberus explorers took note of her presence. "Would you rather your friend dishonor your people by being a liar?"

Grant's eyes narrowed. "It's funny you should mention honor, witch. Where I come from, it's considered an affront to let your friend walk into a fucking trap just because you want to impress the natives. Something about loyalty and concern for those who've watched out for you. Know anything about that?"

Brigid bit her upper lip, both to kill the smile that threatened to cross her face and to bite back an apology for her friend's rudeness. Sometimes Grant forgot the adage that you could draw more flies with honey than vinegar, but that was the big ex-Magistrate's way. Kane had often joked that Grant wasn't happy unless he was complaining about how miserable he was.

Epona smirked. "Your loyalty does your friend honor. Just remember, we are the ones who invited you here. And I am the lawmaker of my people."

Grant rolled his eyes and turned his attention to Brigid. "She must be confusing us with some other group of travelers."

Brigid smiled. "Behave, Grant."

Grant managed a grin. "Where's the joy in that?"

He settled back down, staring toward the tree line.

The rules of this particular engagement were simple. In order to open up diplomatic channels between the Appalachians and the Cerberus redoubt, Kane had to go into the forest of this particular valley. Hidden among the trees lurked a race of genetic mutations that had taken to calling themselves the Fomorians, claiming to be the descendants of the beings who menaced the Tuatha de Danaan.

Nothing in Brigid's studies of the interactions of the panterrestrial entities she knew as the Tuatha de Danaan suggested that the Fomorians were anything but Annunaki, whose roles in the history of humanity had been misinterpreted after years of permutations of the original stories. Brigid was aware that according to the creation legends of the Celts, the Fomorians were allegedly the predecessors of the more human-centric god entities, a parallel tale to the relations between the Hellenic pantheon of Olympian gods and their forebears, the Titans. According to information that Brigid had gleaned from various sources, the Tuatha de Danaan and the Annunaki had warred terribly, thus giving her the impression that those recorded as the malformed and misshapen Fomorians were actually Annunaki, or rather, one of their servant races, which were currently known as the Nephilhim.

Only after the two godlike races had come to peace, and chose to create a supervisory hybrid race known as the Archons, did they fade from the forefront of interaction with humanity. The Archons had been crossbreeds, possessing genetic material of both great races, as well as the stuff of human DNA in them, serving as a bridge between the three species. The hybrid creatures had been charged with retarding human potential, keeping humankind from growing too powerful, lest they grow strong enough to resist the panterrestrial overlords as they slept or lived out their retirement in other dimensions.

Brigid decided to throw a few questions at Epona, as long as she was present. The mystery of what the Fomorians actually were had weighed too much for her to keep her tongue still.

"Your enemies claim to be actual descendants of the

Fomorians of Celtic myth?" she asked the Appalachian headwoman.

Epona glanced sidelong at Brigid, as if weighing her response. "You doubt our assertion?"

Brigid shook her head. "I'm just trying to fit this in to what we know about the Tuatha de Danaan."

"Our forebears," Epona stated.

Brigid's brow wrinkled. According to what she knew about Appalachian granny magic in the wake of the Cerberus explorers' first encounter with Epona and her people, the arts of magic they used were supposedly imported with the Scottish and Irish immigrants who had first arrived on American shores back in the late 1700s. Given the region that they had originated in, it was likely that the isolated and secretive water witches and witch doctors who practiced the arts had links extending back to the Tuatha de Danaan. The only thing that stuck awkwardly in Brigid's evaluation of Epona's veracity was that the practitioners of granny magic tended to locate farther south than the Pennsylvanian Poconos, the original territory stretching from the Virginias down to Georgia, where the remote location of their territories allowed the immigrants to retain the ancient Irish and Scottish songs, dances and recipes far more easily than their island predecessors who were dragged into modern society by being made part of Great Britain.

"You seem doubtful of my story. Is it because we're not in our traditional homelands?" Epona asked.

"That's part of it," Brigid said.

Epona smiled. "We migrated in the wake of the great war. Rather than displace people in valleys that weren't affected by the nuclear bombs, we wandered until we finally settled here. However, if you wish to check our genealogy, we first originated in Georgia. I assume you explorers have traveled there."

Brigid nodded. "Radioactive fallout zones in Georgia would have forced a migration to more hospitable climes. But what about the Fomorians?"

"The Fomorian warriors who hound the mountain folk were often like us. It was the touch of Bres the Beautiful that awoke the true power within those we thought were merely men," Epona explained.

Brigid's eyes narrowed. She didn't particularly like the reverence that tinged the Appalachian woman's words. When Epona's gaze focused on the worry in her features, Brigid pressed on. "Bres the Beautiful, who was the son of Balor, the leader of the Fomorians, correct? He's still alive after all these millennia?"

Epona smiled unnervingly. "You came to us seeking information on whether Enlil, one of the Sumerian gods, was using one of the many valleys in the Appalachians as a potential hideout. An Annunaki can live for thousands of years, but a son of the beings who fathered the Tuatha de Danaan cannot?"

"In our defense, Enlil and his kin were stored inside of the genetic codes of their descendants until they could be awakened by a signal from their great ship *Tiamat*,"

Brigid said. "They hadn't been awake the whole time. However, we have encountered another Tuatha, the being known as Maccan."

"Aengus," Epona corrected. "His true name is Aengus, son of Dagda, high king of the Tuatha de Danaan and Boann."

A smile crossed Epona's lips. Brigid anticipated the source of the granny witch's humor as her studies of the Tuatha de Danaan sprang to the forefront of her infallible memory. "Boann, who has among her other identities the goddess Brigid."

Epona nodded knowingly. "It is good to speak with an outsider who knows of our faith."

Brigid returned the smile. "It's more a case of occupational necessity. The figures you worship are still alive and well in some form or another. They and their Annunaki counterparts are precisely the reason why making an alliance with you is so vital."

"Even with the aid of every mountain scout among my people, the Appalachians stretch for thousands of miles. We have not been able to locate the heart of the Fomorian base of operations—what makes you think we would be any more useful in ascertaining whether Enlil and his kin have taken refuge in one of our valleys?" Epona asked.

"Because at least you are a set of eyes and ears in this area. Indeed, you contacted us simply because the Fomorians seemed to be increasing their intelligence and the quality of their equipment," Brigid pointed out.

"Otherwise, you would not have made use of the radio we left behind for you."

"Well played, Brigid," Epona said. "There are some things we are not capable of handling. The Fomorians were balanced against us because we at least had the advantage of homemade rifles crafted by our gunsmiths while they relied more upon their brute strength and natural endurance. However, things have shifted."

Brigid glanced at one of the mountain scouts. The man sat on a rock, a five-foot-long rifle resting between his knees. Though she was not one who took much interest in the minutiae of musketry, it didn't take a firearm fanatic to realize the quality and art involved in the production of the long weapon, nor was it any surprise that the rifle's bore was designed to fire cartridges that were meant for more than any normal person. Externally, the arms that the scouts carried were hand-carved wood and steel, the wooden furniture painted and adorned with runes to bless them. The steel barrels were set into heavy firing mechanisms, single-shot bolt action by their appearance, and there was no mistaking the half-inch cavernous hole at the end of the long tube. Taking the opportunity to get a closer look at one of the long brass fangs that were stuffed into a belt loop around the scout's waist, she recognized the .50-caliber cartridge that was the same type that Grant used for one of his favorite weapons, the M-85 Barrett.

The fact that the scouts chose this as their primary rifle caliber when it was likely that they would encounter their hated enemies meant that the Fomorians were not simply deformed humans, but creatures of phenomenal strength.

"You said that Kane would recognize them when he saw them," Brigid said. "Unfortunately, I don't recall any past lives as he does. How did you, er, recognize him?"

Epona chuckled. "I would be a poor water witch if I could not identify the modern embodiment of Cuchulainn."

Brigid's lip curled at the mention of that name. It was what Fand, the half Tuatha de Danaan and half Annunaki daughter of Enlil, had insisted on calling Kane. She claimed that he was her destined lover, reborn in order to reunite with her. Though Brigid's affection for Kane wasn't of a lustful nature, the thought of Fand sinking her claws into Kane was repulsive. He wasn't particularly interested in the long-lived demigoddess himself, a surprise considering that Fand was a statuesque being who could have been a Greek sculpture come to life.

"Don't tell me you've got some kind of link to Cuchulainn," Brigid spoke up.

"No, but you can't begrudge me a girlish crush on such a hero, can you?" Epona asked.

Brigid clenched her eyes shut. She finally opened one eye, glancing out of the corner toward Grant, whose face was split with a broad smile.

"You'd think Kane was some kind of immature wish-fulfillment fantasy, all the women he gets," Brigid complained.

"Maybe this time you'll get some interest," Grant said.

Brigid raised an eyebrow. "As good-looking as Bres the Beautiful sounds, I don't think I want to be genetically manipulated to become a Fomorian. From what I've heard, my options are missing limbs, missing eyes or the head of a goat."

Epona studied Brigid for a moment. "You would not be changed. There is nothing of the blood in you."

"Your granny-witch sight, lady?" Grant asked, raising an eyebrow.

"I can see Cuchulainn in your friend. I can see Fomorian tendencies, or the lack of, in you two," Epona said. "Do not fear, large one."

Grant waved her off dismissively. "Whatever."

Something crackled in the distance, and Brigid's and Grant's ears instantly picked it up as the sound of gunfire.

"Kane?" Brigid asked as the Sin Eater snapped into Grant's grasp.

Chapter 2

When the crackle of gunfire cut through the quiet mountain air, Grant sprung to his full height, his Sin Eater deploying instantly, launched by a flex of his forearm muscles. The microelectric motors attached to the machine pistol's holster allowed the weapon to be readied instantly, but the demanding weapon required six months of training before a Magistrate could be trusted with a loaded Sin Eater. Grant kept his trigger finger straight as the gun unfolded, grip deposited right into his grasp. Had the digit remained crooked, then the weapon would have launched a 240-grain specially loaded 9 mm bullet, a powerhouse round designed to penetrate the most durable of body armor, even the cockpit of a Deathbird assault helicopter

To Brigid Baptiste's credit, the woman had pulled her TP-9 pistol and was ready a heartbeat later. Grant wondered how the beautiful, flame-haired former archivist would take his amazement at how she went from a quiet, bespectacled academic to a confident, adventure-hardened explorer of a hostile world. She had never settled into the overly macho, paramilitary mind-set that had surrounded Grant and Kane in the barracks while they were still Cobaltville Mags, but despite that, she'd forged herself into a warrior. She didn't rely on false pride and bravado rather than genuine courage to face barbaric or powerful opponents.

Indeed, Grant often wondered at the quality of the Magistrate corps had not the hybrid barons not segregated the ville societies and allowed women to be part of the armored warrior caste that formed the core of their power. That thought evaporated as soon as it struck the light of his logic. The barons had been corrupt, and their sexist segregation had been designed to keep humankind on its knees. To combine both strength and intellect in a person, and to break the limiting bonds of a caste hierarchy, would have made humans less likely to assent to being slaves of a little seen, secretive society of hybrid beings. Grant had only one name, as did Kane and all the other Magistrates, a move calculated to strip the black-armored warriors of any individual identity. It was exceedingly rare for Magistrates to develop intense bonds of friendship and loyalty to anything other than the barons, which was probably why the two partners had so readily slipped the bonds of their orders.

Kane made Grant a little more human, and the reverse was true. That little touch of compassion, a link to another person, had given them both the strength to see the corruption of the villes and break loose. Brigid had been part of that process, as well, giving Kane another anchor of human emotion that the rulers of the baronies had sought to crush. Grant had expanded his own world-view in the form of a friendship with the feral child of the Outlands they knew as Domi. At first, Grant and Domi had been opponents, the young outlander employed by a smuggling ring under the Pit boss Guana Teague. However, an act of compassion on Grant's part for Domi, as she was wounded and abused by the sluglike Teague, had formed a bond between them. For a long time, Domi had acted as if it was something inspired by sexual attraction, but the bright young feral woman and Grant finally realized that their bond was more along the line of surrogate father and daughter, especially when Grant became romantically involved with Shizuka, the leader of the Tigers of Heaven. The love between Grant and Domi was as strong as ever, but it had found its true form, rather than the sexual tension that had first developed.

Returning to Brigid, Grant realized that though he and Kane often joked about Brigid's predilection to launch into an educational lecture, her relentless pursuit and sharing of knowledge was infectious. Both Kane and Grant had been spurred to learn about the world before civilization was burned to ashes in nuclear fire, and to seek out lore that extended far beyond their old world-view as dictated by the barons. Where Brigid became physically adept and skilled in the arts of war, Kane and Grant saw their intellectual horizons broadened.

Rounding out the three aspects of mind, body and soul, it didn't escape Grant's notice that Kane's presence in their lives had been an escape from a single-minded existence. Brigid Baptiste could have spent her entire life poring over historical artifacts and records without seeking human companionship, and Grant could have been condemned to a life where he relentlessly soldiered for Cobaltville until he died. The compassion and friendship that Kane had added to their lives was the agent of change that made everything possible.

It was Kane who had the curiosity to seek out the strange matter-transfer device utilized by Teague's smugglers. It was Kane who questioned the authority that told him to look away. It was Kane who saw that there was something more than just what was in front of their eyes. Certainly, Kane himself was a physically adept and capable warrior, and he had a keen perception that at times bordered on psychic sensitivity, but the man who had gone alone into the valley at Epona's request was not just a warrior or a seeker of knowledge. He sought out what was right; he was a man with a moral core that had chafed under orders to kill and crush rebellion, who felt more at home being a defender of those who couldn't fight back, or helping those in need. Kane's strength and intellect were slaves to a spirit that was driven to the service of others.

The smart thing for Kane to have done would have been to turn his back on Epona so the Cerberus explorers could have returned to the redoubt without a second thought of risking themselves. The *right* thing, however, was what Kane chose. The Appalachian mountain folk were under siege by a cruel and implacable enemy that had been given an edge by a mysterious foe. Allowing the Fomorians to continue unabated would result in suffering and unchecked evil.

In his readings, Grant came across a line by Edmund Burke. "For evil to succeed, all that is needed is for good men to do nothing."

Grant wondered, with all those women who saw Kane's "soul," if any had ever read those words tattooed across his heart, because there was never a more defining quote for his friend and partner.

It was five hundred feet downslope to the edge of the pine forest that clung tenaciously to the mountainside, which was just outside of the range of his Sin Eater's normal deployment parameters. With another flex of his forearm, the electric motors retracted the machine pistol, folding it from its active thirteen-inch length to only six inches, lying flatly against his forearm. The motorized holster clicked as the Sin Eater returned to its resting spot. It was time to make use of something more appropriate for the situation.

Grant opened his rifle bag and drew out one of his favorite pieces of equipment, the five-and-a-half-foot-long Barrett M-85 .50-caliber rifle. Designed in the twentieth century as a means of allowing a ground soldier to stave off armored fighting vehicles short of a tank, the Barrett could hurl its missiles over two miles. Though it was only a single shot, it utilized .50-caliber Browning machine gun ammunition and held eleven rounds when fully loaded. A smaller man would have had trouble hauling around the thirty-pound rifle, but it fit comfortably in Grant's massive hands.

Grant had wondered if it had been overkill to bring such a handheld cannon to this mission, but when he saw that the Appalachian scouts had their own .50-caliber long rifles, he knew that he hadn't overreacted. Whoever the Fomorians were, they were creatures of impressive strength and durability, requiring more than standard small-arms fire to stop conclusively.

All of that information only served to worry Grant more about Kane and his fate. The Sin Eaters were powerful side arms, having proved their worth against heavily armored foes such as the Nephilhim drones in the service of the Annunaki, or Magistrate stormtroopers in their black, impregnable polycarbonate shells, but as the mountain folk had all manner of calibers at their disposal to deploy against the man-eating mutants that tormented them, their choice of arm was telling. The riflelike power of the Sin Eater might wound, but only the steel-smashing force of a .50-caliber round was sufficient for the Appalachians to trust against the Fomorians.

"You cannot move until Kane is in plain sight!" Epona said.

Grant glared at the witch woman, his rage only barely under control. "Do I look like I'm getting off this fucking rock?"

"Mind yourself, stranger," Epona warned.

Grant turned away, pushing the aggravating witch out of his thoughts. It was time to do everything he could to watch over his best friend in the world. That meant pulling up the hood folded into the collar of his shadow suit. The fabric sheathed the big man's head, conforming to it snugly as if it had been grown as a second skin for him. In truth, the high-tech polymers of the shadow suit were pliant enough to fit anyone who wore one, stretching or contracting, yet giving up none of its environmental protection capabilities.

But Grant hadn't donned the hood to keep out a chill. Instead, he drew the face piece of the shadow suit, a rolled-up mask kept in a flat pocket, and affixed it to the edges of the hood. An electrostatic charge gave an in-audible crackle before the unit was sealed to his skull. Though the mask was opaque to outside viewers, as soon as the charge hooked the mask in place, Grant was able to see through the circuitry laden fabric.

Though Grant had hated squeezing into old Magis-trate armor suits, he had enjoyed the advanced optics and communications abilities built into the Mag helmets. It had taken months of experimentation with the shadow suits to convince the veteran Grant that they offered the same sensory enhancements as the Mag helmets, except in a far more compact and portable form. As well, with the hood tucked into the collar and the face piece folded away, the shadow suits were far less imposing than the ominous black helmets and poly-carbonate armor shells of old. Grant still pulled a jacket and pants over the shadow suit sometimes, to give himself some pockets and a modicum of modesty. The skintight uniform conformed to every contour of his body, so while he might have been able to walk through an Antarctic blizzard without feeling a single chill, he wore pants to keep his sense of decency.

Grant focused his eyes, and the remarkable technology built into the mask interpreted his eye movements and magnified his vision. Suddenly, it was as if he was only five feet away from the tree line, and Grant swept the forest, looking for signs of Kane. Gunshots cracked, and the magnification dropped back to zero, a green heads-up circle showing in Grant's vision. He adjusted his gaze to that spot where the suit had picked up the sound. All he could see were trees, but now Grant had at least an idea where Kane was on the slope.

"Can you see anything?" Brigid asked, unfurling her own hood and drawing out her face mask.

"No, but apparently the suits can pick up the origin points of loud sounds," Grant said.

Brigid nodded, affixing her face mask into place. "Like that last gunshot."

The former archivist turned to Epona. "This isn't violating the letter of your law, is it?"

Grant smirked behind the safety and anonymity of his faceplate. Though environmentally he wouldn't even feel the iciest breeze, a chill ran through him at the sound of Brigid's question to Epona. Diplomacy and courtesy were all fine, but right now, Kane was shooting at something, and from the sound of things, he wasn't having an easy time.

Epona shook her head in response to the barbed question. "Just remember, you can only go to Kane's aid when he is in *plain* sight to us. Who knows how far you can see into the forest with your technology, but we are not gifted like you."

Grant's fist clenched around his Barrett, tendons creaking under his polymer glove. "Trust me, witch. If I could see him right now, I'd tell you hillbillies to go piss uphill."

"Behave," Brigid admonished, though this time her heart wasn't in the warning. She gripped the handles of her Copperhead submachine gun with as much tension as Grant felt. He couldn't see her knuckles through the black polymer of her gloves, but he knew that she was as white-knuckled with concern for Kane as he was.

Grant stared, as if trying to command the shadow suit to spontaneously develop the power of X-ray vision to peer through tree trunks and other foliage as if they were made of glass. He rested the Barrett's steel girder like stock on his thick, powerful thigh, because even his powerful shoulders couldn't hold the heavy rifle aloft forever. Crouched deeply, resting on his haunches, Grant was poised to explode, but the fuse burned far too slowly for his taste.

He activated his Commtact, opening a connection back to Cerberus redoubt, where Lakesh, Bry and others were watching the events of this mission as closely as they could.

"Bry, you there?" Grant asked.

"Nah. I'm in the middle of a Three Stooges marathon and eating bonbons," the computer expert replied with his typical, laid-back sarcasm.

Grant rolled his eyes. "Do you have anything that could make this wait a little more bearable?"

"There's only so much I can do with a virtual reality girlfriend for you," Bry answered, but Grant could hear the clatter of his fingertips across a keyboard as he commanded the network of satellites from his computer console. Bry's acerbic, bored tone was the young genius's armor against a world of panic and emergency.

"Kane," Brigid said over the communications link. "Where is he now?"

All the Cerberus personnel had been fitted with subcutaneous biolink transponders that, among other things, allowed Cerberus redoubt to monitor their whereabouts.

"Range?" Grant asked, rising off his haunches. "Bry, give me—"

"He's 4200 feet from your position, which means 3700 from the tree line," Bry answered. "He's getting closer."

"But still not in plain sight," Grant growled.

"Where is he?" Epona asked. Anxiety and concern had crept into her voice. Whether it was genuine worry for Kane and the people standing watch for him, or it was fear of reprisal from an angry Grant, it was a disarming change.

"Still a long run from the tree line," Grant told her. "It's a two-way shooting match now, so that means one of the Fomorians has an assault rifle."

"More than one," Epona warned. "That's why we called you for help."

"So you've got mutant freaks who need 50-caliber rifles to kill them now armed with assault weapons, and you told us to send one of our own after them while he's outnumbered and outmuscled?" Grant snapped. "You've got to be fucking kidding me!"

"Kane told us that he was as silent as the wind and twice as hard to capture," Epona said. "We figured that he would be stealthy and not end up on the run from a superhuman horde with high-tech weapons!"

Grant was tempted to rip his face mask off his hood, but he needed its advanced optics to keep an eye on Kane. Luckily, his hood's sensors picked up the chatter of more automatic weapons. "What's Kane's range to the tree line, Bry?"

"Now 3400 feet. He's not making much progress, and according to the audio pickups on your hood, there are four hostiles shooting at him," Bry informed him.

"Four," Grant grumbled. The bark of a Sin Eater was amplified by the hood's sensors. He shouldered his rifle, even though there was no way that someone could see through 1100 yards of tree trunks. The rifle was something solid to hold on to, a firm piece of reality that was an anchor when all he had were electronic ghost images thrown against his eyeballs. Intelligence hurled at him was not a substitute for his personal senses. Sight, hearing, touch—he trusted those much more than some anonymous computer setup. He wanted tactile feedback.

Instead, all he could do was wait and hope for a single glimpse of Kane, if he somehow managed to fight his way past a quartet of superhuman mutants.

Chapter 3

Brigid Baptiste glared at Granny Epona, then made a decision. She wasn't one given to brash action, but right now she knew that something was wrong with the whole situation. Epona had gone from stating that Kane's scouting mission was one of honor to stating that he was sent because he could move with ghostlike grace among the trees in order to determine the machinations that had been involved in the upgrade of the Fomorian raiders' equipment. At the very least, Epona was hiding something.

Brigid swiftly went into Grant's war bag, drew out a .45-caliber SIG-Sauer P-220 pistol and its spare magazines strapped together in a shoulder holster sized for her slender, athletic frame. The big ex-Magistrate spotted the activity, and she could imagine his eyebrow quirking underneath the opaque black hood of his shadow suit. The .45-caliber pistol had been something that Brigid had asked Grant to carry for her ever since their encounter with the mad cybergoddess Hera in New Olympus, a decision reinforced by a subsequent battle against the nanotechnologically enhanced Durga. Her little TP-9 pistol might have been more than enough to deal with ordinary threats, but against superhuman beings, she'd developed the opinion that bigger was indeed better. Since the TP-9 couldn't fire the same kind of superheavy slugs that the Sin Eater ate like gumdrops, the only way to deal with armor plating was to go with a bigger, more powerful gun.

"Granny Epona, you can tell your men to go piss uphill," Brigid said, tightening the SIG's holster straps. "Kane needs us."

With that, she turned and began to sprint down the slope toward the tree line.

"Brigid!" Grant's voice bellowed over her Commtact.

Brigid wished that she had the ability to talk, but at the moment, she was concentrating on keeping her balance and avoiding obstacles. She'd hoped that she would reach the tree line and that a pine tree would stop her headlong progress, but now even her intellect raced, throwing up a series of possibilities that ended up with her encountering an impact that would overwhelm the shadow suit's protective capabilities.

"Brigid, stop now!" Grant bellowed over the Commtact.

The force of Grant's order, transmitted through her jawbone, made it seem as if he had taken control of her body. She shot her feet out, ramrod straight, and her heels sank into the soft shale. She'd passed down the slope to a point where the ground had softened into soil and areas of mossy scrub. By extending her legs, she'd applied the brakes and slowed enough that she could control her descent.

"Thanks," Brigid said.

She could feel Grant's smile, even over the radio. "Anytime, Brigid."

Brigid stopped only twenty feet from the edge of the trees. Looking back, she could see where she'd first straightened out and the furrows her heels had cut through the slope as she'd slowed. She pulled her .45 from its holster. "I don't see anything yet down here, Grant. Do you?"

"Not a damn thing," Grant responded. "Nothing on the suit optics nor through the Barrett's scope. You go into the woods too far, you'll be on your own."

"Not going to try my way down?" Brigid asked.

"I'll be along," Grant responded. "Just a little slower."

Brigid scanned uphill and saw the big ex-Magistrate running, jumping and dodging to avoid boulders. She could see why he was reluctant to turn himself into a human avalanche, as the Barrett was not as easily portable as the heavy pistol she carried. The rifle would either serve as a brutal clothesline that would catch on something and do its best to cleave Grant in two, or the weapon would shatter important parts, leaving it useless as a firearm and left only as a clumsy, unwieldy club.

"I'll stay in touch," Brigid said, and she charged into the trees, relying on the heads-up optics in her faceplate to plot Kane's last known positions by the sound of his Sin Eater.

"Just remember, that .45 is nowhere nearly as potent as the rifles the scouts and I are carrying," Grant said. "If you have to shoot, aim for the face, not the forehead. The area around the nose—"

"Yes. The area around the nose has the weakest maxillofacial bone structure, enabling the surest incapacitation on a head shot," Brigid replied. "You act like I don't have a photographic memory."

"Well, it's not as if I'm feeling particularly useful jogging down a mountainside five hundred feet behind you," Grant growled. "Leave me something to feel worthwhile."

"Sorry," Brigid said. She remembered that Kane's Commtact wasn't activated. Calling out loud might draw Kane's attention, but that might serve as a distraction that would allow the Fomorians to fall upon him and crush the life out of him. Furthermore, a shout would just as likely turn Kane's attention from survival to concern for her.

Brigid had spent years forging herself from an academic into an equal partner to her two warrior allies. She refused to put herself in the position of a walking disaster, the role of someone whose presence only served to expose the team to more dangers. She operated a control interface on the forearm of her shadow suit, and the black polymer suddenly shimmered and took on the pattern of the surrounding forest floor. The real-time, adaptive camouflage, while it wouldn't offer true invisibility, would turn the Cerberus explorer into a shadow among the trees. If Kane was in trouble, her sudden arrival wouldn't break his concentration, and she'd have the element of surprise against any creature endeavoring to tear the man limb from limb.

"I've gone camouflage, Grant," she said over her Commtact.

"Remember to stay out of the cross fire," Grant offered. "And don't forget, your shoulder harness isn't camouflaged."

Brigid looked down at her shoulder, seeing the nylon-and-leather holster strap visible against her optic digital camouflage. She wrinkled her nose. "Noted. Thank you."

She padded off into the pine trees, heading toward where she'd last heard the sounds of battle.

Brigid scrambled through the woods, keeping herself close to the trees but avoiding branches so that she minimized the commotion of her passage. There were more factors at moving unnoticed than having an electronically enhanced fabric adapt like a chameleon to its background, and she was fortunate to have a teacher in Kane who had schooled her in the arts of stealth. Up ahead in a clearing she spotted Kane, stripped naked to the waist and battling a tall, gangly monstrosity. The cyclopean beast screeched in untamed fury as it struggled with the half-naked Cerberus warrior in its arms.

Brigid considered taking a shot at the Fomorian warrior, but Kane thrashed violently, twisting to keep the deadly bear hug around his torso from tightening. The deceptively slender hunter's forearms were cabled masses of muscle and sinew that looked to have the strength of anacondas, and the moment his adversary had a solid grasp, Kane's ribs and spine would be subjected to a lethal crushing force. With the two opponents wrestling fiercely, there was no way that Brigid could take a clean shot without the possibility of hitting Kane.

She stuffed the handgun back into its holster and scanned around for something that would be more useful. She spotted a thick branch on the ground and scooped it up. Still practically invisible as anything other than a blurred wraith, shc lunged toward the Fomorian, swinging her wooden club at the back of the its knees. The creature's long, strong legs buckled in instantaneous reaction to the impact. Despite the superhuman physique and size of the mutant, it still had basic human anatomy, and Brigid had reasoned that it also had basic human reflex. The crash of the branch across the back of its knees inspired an automatic bending of the creature's legs. That, combined with Kane's struggles on top of it, forced the Fomorian to crash to the ground.

The Cerberus warrior hammered his fist violently into the monstrosity's throat, punching again and again with every ounce of his strength. Kane's physique had placed the bulk of his muscle mass in his upper chest and shoulders, and now, as if he were some beast-reared jungle lord, he unleashed that power. His back and shoulders flexed and rippled with each downward stroke, the smack of his fist on the mutant's vulnerable face and throat cracking through the forest. There was no grace, no art in this beating; the time for unarmed combat finesse had disappeared the moment Kane had been stripped of weaponry and forced to fight tooth and claw. The Fomorian hunter's nose was a bloody pit in the center of his skull, and twisted lips coughed up a torrent of gore from where Kane's fist had crushed its windpipe. Its arms flailed helplessly, trying to block the maddened assault, but in the end, it was useless.

Brigid knew that Kane would never die easily, and this day, he'd fought off the hounds of death seeking his soul.

"Baptiste?" Kane asked, bursting from his opponent's grasp.

"Yes," she said. She tapped her forearm, canceling the camouflage effect. Brigid looked the man over and saw that his forehead had been split open, a ragged gash that seeped blood into his eyes. His legs had a wobble to them, but he fought against the urge to collapse, shoulders rising and falling as he breathed deeply to regain his composure. "What happened?"

"I was jumped," Kane murmured. "Everything since then's been kind of blurry. I don't even know where my weapons went."

Brigid slid out of her shoulder harness. "Take this, then."

Kane blinked, looking at the pistol and spare magazines in their holster. He looked confused for a moment, but slid his arms through the shoulder loops and drew the handgun. "When did you start carrying this?"

"I've had Grant keep a spare gun for me in his war

bag," Brigid said as she knelt by the dead Fomorian. She quickly took a strip of its ragged vest and tore it free, creating a long bandage. "No reason why you'd know anything about it. Come over here."

Kane obeyed her command without fuss, so Brigid could tell that something wasn't completely right with him. Her best guess, given the minimal blood loss and his uncertain stance, was that he'd suffered a concussion when he'd been struck in the head. Kane was fortunate that the heavy curved bone of the skull had made his forehead one of the most difficult structures to break on the human body. Still, with the blood seeping from the wound and pouring down over his brow, he'd have a hard time seeing. She tied the bandage around his head, but didn't knot it too tightly. Too much pressure would only aggravate any head trauma that she couldn't see right now.

"Thanks, Baptiste," Kane muttered. Brigid offered her shoulder to allow him to stand back up.

"You're going to be freezing to death in a few minutes unless we get you to shelter," Brigid said.

Kane grimaced. "I can deal with the cold for now. It's not as bad as it is higher up on the mountain. But we should be able to borrow a blanket or some furs from Epona's scouts, shouldn't we?"

"I'm not sure we can trust her," Brigid began. "Even if she is on the up and up, I broke the rules and came into the forest after you."

Kane smirked through the pain. "I'm a bad influence on you. Big guns, and wrecking diplomacy…"

"Cut the criticism," Brigid admonished, "and activate your Commtact."

Kane nodded and reached behind his ear to activate his comm device. "Grant, we're trying to concentrate here. Shut it!"

"Well, it's about damn time!" Grant cursed. "If I hadn't shaved my head bald, I'd be a mass of gray hair by now."

"Listen…my head's a little fuzzy right now and I'm trying to climb a steep mountainside while half-naked," Kane complained. "You throwing a fit on your side of things is not making my skull ache any less, got it?"

Brigid kept an eye on Kane's progress. His body was already shiny with a sheen of sweat, gleaming off his rippling muscles as he fought against the incline. The steep slope was an effort for her, as well, her legs burning with each push. Brigid at least had the shadow suit to regulate her perspiration and body temperature as they climbed. Once they hit the open slope, which was at six thousand feet more or less, Kane's wet skin would be exposed to a freezing wind. Hypothermia would be inevitable, and frostbite a distinct possibility.

"All right. Did you find out anything?" Grant asked

"Yeah. I found out that the Fomorians have some old friends of ours working with them," Kane said. "The Thrush Continuum."

"What?" Grant grimaced.

"I'll explain later," Kane answered. "Right now, I can barely make heads or tails out of anything. What kind of explosives did you bring along?"

"The usual assortment of grens and plastic explosives," Grant replied. "You got anything special in your war bag?"

"No, but I'm thinking that we can at least drop an avalanche on the Fomorian camp on this mountainside," Kane said. "It's not going to be a long-term solution, but we can retreat and regroup while they're digging themselves out of the rubble."

Brigid and Kane continued ascending, both of them thankful for the pine tree trunks that allowed them good handholds as they fought their way uphill. Kane's knee buckled, and he slumped against the bark of a pine, eyes clenched in momentary pain.

"Let me help," Brigid said.

"I'll be all right," Kane answered breathlessly. He rummaged around in the cargo pants that he and Grant took to wearing over the lower halves of their shadow suits. Finally he ripped open a pocket and found a foil envelope within. His fingers trembled as he tore into the packet, withdrawing a rustling mass of shiny metallic sheeting. Taking the corners of the thermal blanket, he wrapped them around his neck, tying the blanket into an improvised cloak that draped around his shoulders.

"Allow me?" Brigid asked.

Kane blinked, his eyes unfocused. "Better idea?"

"Somewhat," Brigid answered. She untied the thermal blanket and pulled a utility knife from her belt. She sliced a slit in the center large enough to fit Kane's head through. Then she patted through his pockets until she found a roll of cord. Gathering the blanket at Kane's waist, she left plenty of room for his arms to move freely, but cinched the blanket so that he now possessed a shiny metallic parka to shield him. "You forgot that you had this?"

"I took a whack to the head, damn it," Kane reminded her. "Plus, I thought I could last a little longer against the cold."

Gunfire bellowed below and Brigid whirled. "Damn it, they've caught up to us."

Kane fisted the handgun that she'd lent him. "It'll take a lot to put them down."

Brigid shook her head. "Give me that and my magazines back. You keep climbing."

"Damn it, Baptiste."

"You're injured, and you're the brightest, shiniest target on this mountainside," Brigid returned. "I'm in one piece, and the shadow suit makes me harder to hit. And if they do shoot me, I'll be harder to hurt. Get moving!"

Kane glowered at her. "Just be careful. The Thrushes didn't just give them rifles—"

"Talk later. Run now!" Brigid snapped.

Movement rustled among the pines, and she whirled to face it, bringing up the big .45. A one-armed monstrosity lurched into view, holding a SIG AMT rifle in its hand. Brigit aligned the sights and fired two shots from her pistol, aiming at the troll-like face of the Fomorian hunter, her shadow suit's faceplate optics enabling her to focus the handgun's point of aim as if she had a laser targeting device on the pistol. A mass of cheekbone exploded off the Fomorian's face with the first hit, the second round carving a ghastly furrow along the creature's bald temple. The mutant dropped its rifle and clutched its wounded face with its sole hand. Brigid cursed the haste with which she'd fired her shots, wasting ammunition and making the man-eater suffer. It may have been a murderous beast, but unnecessary cruelty had never been part of any of the three Cerberus warriors.

As it was, she had bought herself some time, and glanced back to see Kane furiously scrambling up the hill. A large form in black leaped down by his side, and Brigid nearly whirled her pistol around to fire on it when she recognized the unmistakable bulk of Grant, hooking one hand under Kane's shoulder.

"Move it, Brigid!" Grant bellowed, hefting his massive Barrett with one rippling arm. The .50-caliber rifle bellowed authoritatively to punctuate his command. "This slope's going to be a no-man's-land in a minute!"

Brigid spun back and saw that Grant had put the creature she'd shot out of its misery. Muzzle-flashes flickered among the trees, but the .30-caliber rounds found only dirt and tree trunks. Two of the Fomorian hunters were back in the forest, trying to finish the job they started. Brigid stuffed her gun into her belt and clawed at the mountainside on all fours, her lean and athletically toned limbs helping her to eat the distance between herself and the two ex-Magistrates near the tree line. A tree root for a handhold here, a leap off the trunk of a pine there, and mad pawing at the dirt were what she needed to climb as she'd never climbed before.

Grant continued to thunder away with his mighty rifle, bolts of blazing hot lead slicing down to cover Brigid against the advance and harassing fire of the Fomorians. Like some form of obsidian storm god, Grant cut loose. A tree trunk shattered under the impact of one monster .50-caliber slug, and the pine tree crackled, groaned and toppled, crashing to the slope and skidding toward the Fomorians. One of those mutated hunters let out a wail of horror as the tree toppled toward him like a massive emerald spear. Its long limbs sprang and hurled it out of its path, branches shearing off against other tree trunks, producing deep gouges in the bark. The impact of the plummeting pine broke another apart, but one shank of wood held on tenaciously, so that the tree was only bent, its top half dangling like a pendulum in the wake of the one-log avalanche.

Brigid scurried up to Grant as he reloaded the Barrett. She could see the tree line just past him. Grenades and explosive charges were wired together, nudged against tree trunks and two large, flat masses of granite that broke up the incline of the slope, giving the trees something level to stand upon. Though she wasn't an explosives expert, she knew that Grant had set the explosives in such a manner as to shear off this particular chunk of forest and hurl it down the slope like a massive guillotine of stone, dirt and wood.

"We've got to move," Grant said as he slung the rifle over one broad shoulder. "Take the detonator."

Brigid took the box, and Grant scooped up Kane as if he were a rag doll. She followed Grant as he charged uphill, cradling his injured partner and held off pressing the trigger for the mass of charges planted at the tree line. Once they were a safe distance from the blast area, Grant would know. Brigid didn't want to make that guess. If she fired the detonator too soon, they would be swept up in the torrent. If she waited too long, more Fomorians would scurry into rifle range and dozens of rifles would chop them to ribbons.

"Do it!" Grant ordered.

Brigid thumbed the stud, and the whole mountainside heaved violently. Behind her white-hot fire faded instantly into a plume of blackened smoke and airborne ash and dust. The air crackled with the sound of rock and soil peeling off the slope under a sharp wave of energy released by Grant's explosive setup. The crackle deepened into an all-pervasive rumble, the thick clouds sucked down along with the avalanche as the rapidly descending mass of the mountainside created a vacuum. Trees snapped and exploded under the shock wave, but as much as Brigid focused on the receding landslide, even with the telescopic optics in her shadow suit, trees she knew to be four and five feet in diameter resembled nothing more than twigs and pencils as they toppled and pinwheeled through the turgid mass. The avalanche's height was not the only thing that grew. It widened, spreading like a fan of rocky devastation. The rumble became less of a constant storm of sound engulfing them as the mass tumbled down to the valley below, but Brigid could still feel it vibrating up through her legs.

"Was that good enough?" Grant asked Kane.

Brigid turned and looked at her partner. His steely eyes held a cold rage in them that she had rarely seen before. Whatever evil they had inflicted upon him, it had inspired a similar fury in him. The rage faded as the landslide crashed to the bottom of the valley, settling a thick fog of debris over the floor. He nodded slowly, tentatively so as not to aggravate the pain of his head injury.

"For now," Kane said. "Now put me down. I can walk the rest of the way back."

Grant sighed and let Kane stand on his own two feet. Brigid could see traces of his earlier wobble, but the brief respite had steeled the man's determination to walk on his own power.

Epona and the scouts waited in a line, just farther up the slope. Epona remained silent, the shadow suit's telescopic vision showing her features cast in dread awe of the power that Grant had unleashed, carving a horrendous scar along the side of a mountain. The scouts, on the other hand, had their rifles raised in the air, cheers for the thunderous blow struck against their Fomorian enemies echoing from on high.

"For now?" Brigid asked.

"I said these things are incredibly tough," Kane answered, his voice taut and brittle with annoyance and pain. "We might have killed some of them and wrecked whatever equipment the Thrush Continuum provided for them, but this isn't over yet."

Grant sneered. "Shit. If a black hole couldn't kill that android freak, dropping a mountain on him won't be more than a minor inconvenience."

"Something's really eating at you, Kane. What's the big worry?" Brigid asked.

Kane grimaced. "Because the Thrush that's down there, working with Bres and Balor and the rest of those monsters, he's wearing my face."

Grant and Brigid shared a glance, then stared at their wounded comrade.

Kane held out both hands to Grant, a near universal symbol of surrendering himself into restraints. "And just so we're sure that I'm not some kind of preprogrammed fake that just thinks I'm the real deal, I want you two to bind me up and make damn certain I'm not some android infiltrator sent to murder everyone in Cerberus."

Standing on a silent, gouged mountainside, watching Grant seize Kane's wrists roughly to put a plastic cable tie around them, Brigid Baptiste felt as if the avalanche were just a rug, pulling her whole world out from underneath her.

Chapter 4

Reba DeFore looked over Kane in the observation room of the Cerberus redoubt sick bay. In silence and darkness, Mohandas Lakesh Singh, Domi, Brigid Baptiste and Grant sat on the other side of one-way glass. No one wanted to speak as DeFore took blood samples, fingerprints, retinal scans and cheek swabs with practiced precision.

DeFore was a stocky woman with tanned skin and ash-blond hair, which she usually wore in braids. This day it was pulled back into a bun beneath her surgeon's cap. She had served as the redoubt's chief physician ever since its inception by Lakesh. Her knowledge of anatomy had been bolstered by years of all manner of practical application, from meatball surgery to delivering the half-human spawn of a Quad Vee hybrid in mid-transformation. While the redoubt's personnel had all been trained in first aid, DeFore's scientific knowledge of the human body and how it worked was remarkable. Of course, if DeFore's talents hadn't been impressive, Lakesh wouldn't have recruited her for his rebellion against the tyranny of the baronies.

Kane rested on the table, poked and prodded, subjected to all manner of probes in DeFore's collection of equipment. Lakesh and the others sat on the other side of the glass, not speaking, barely even breathing loudly as they awaited word on whether or not the man on the table was or some transdimensional construct sent to infiltrate their base.

"You know, there is the possibility that Thrush could have mentally reprogrammed a Kane from a different casement," Brigid spoke up at the end of the second hour of examinations.

DeFore had been consistently handing off samples to her staff, Manitius base medical experts who had been upgrading and redesigning technology since relocating from their station on the moon. Where in the late twentieth century processing genetic markers could be measured in months, the new machinery they had developed pared the analysis to hours. She'd called up a readout on the screen, and the preliminary testing showed identical matches for several gene pairs, though the process had only been forty percent complete. "They'd be identical down to a genetic scale, but—"

"We know what we're dealing with when it comes to Thrush, dearest Brigid," Lakesh said, cutting her off. Lakesh rested his chin on the knuckles of his fist. Though born on the Indian subcontinent, the scientist had entered his third century of life with blue eyes, replacements for his original orbs, which had failed due to their advanced years and the rigors of the cryogenic sleep that had extended his existence. More than 250 years old chronologically, the brilliant scientist had been restored to the relatively youthful age of his early forties, thanks to the incredible technology of the Thrush Continuum, wielded by Sam the Imperator. With a touch and an infusion of nanotechnology robots into his physical system, the ravages of age, countless surgeries to replace failing organs with harvested or cybernetic replacements, and the stresses of surviving under the iron rule of the hybrid barons had been erased.

The one thing that hadn't been returned to "normal" as he'd seen it, was the fact that his eyes were still blue. It was because they had their own genetic code from an unknown donor. The cataracts that had started to develop, however, had been eaten away, nanites transforming the damaged tissues into healthy, vital, young tissues.

If Sam had the power to undo two centuries of aging with a touch, constructing a living man, an exact duplicate with memories and behavior patterns to match the original, wasn't outside of his capabilities. DNA, blood testing, fingerprinting, all of that would only prove that the Kane they were looking at was biologically human, not a cleverly built android duplicate.

Lakesh turned to Grant. In the darkness, his dark bronzed features looked particularly grim, illuminated by the light filtering through the window. Grant's brow was wrinkled with the same worries that Brigid had just voiced. Of all the people in the room, though, Grant had known Kane the longest. The two men were as close to brothers as could possibly be without sharing a single parent.

Grant was probably riddled with worry over not being able to tell if his closest friend on the planet had been subverted by a doppelganger. Sure, as they came through the mat-trans chamber, Bry had stated that the three signatures were nonanomalous, but that was merely a machine. Grant had been a Magistrate, and he lived his life dependent on senses and instincts that weren't susceptible to the whims of electronic failure or alteration of computer code. Being told by Kane that he himself doubted the veracity of his existence had cast the same shadow over Grant's observational abilities.

"All right, Kane. I've checked everything in our medical file on you," DeFore said. "There are no artificial constructs within your body, except for the Commtact implant on your mastoid. Your retinas and fingerprints are identical. I checked with Brigid, and your hair and beard growth are identical to what they were when you first headed off into the woods. Your bones are normal. Your reflexes are suboptimal, but that's to be expected with a concussion. Blood chemistry shows no variants from before."

"What about the contents of my stomach?" Kane asked.

"There aren't any, but I looked at your throat, and you had vomited earlier today," DeFore said.

Kane grimaced.

"You got hit on the head hard enough to be knocked

out. And you stated that the Thrush duplicate and the Fomorian had taken you captive after rendering you unconscious," DeFore said. "When you woke up, you puked, emptying your stomach."

"Yes," Kane added, annoyed. "You get knocked out, you wake up and vomit. It's happened enough times to me…I think."

"What I can tell is that you suffered a mild concussion. Your skull, thick wonder that it is, hasn't been fractured," DeFore said. "You're not a cyborg. You're not an android. You're as real as can possibly be."

Kane touched his forehead, feeling the nylon sutures that had closed up the gash. "Another scar."

"If there is, I'll be disappointed," DeFore told him. "That should heal up nicely."

Kane looked at the one-way glass, as if trying to see past the mirrored surface on his side and look into the faces of his friends. "So, I'm me. I'm Kane, right?"

"You tell us," Grant spoke said into the microphone in the observation room.

Lakesh felt his gut tighten at the pronouncement. Yes, they were dealing with a pandimensional being with access to technologies that even the brilliant scientific knowledge amassed at Cerberus couldn't even dream of. But would Thrush go so far as to make an unwitting duplicate that actively voiced doubts of its own veracity? Or would the fiendish hive mind be so crass and subtle as to engage in a series of obfuscating maneuvers to plant a cunning and savage entity in their midst?

Lakesh's brilliant mind went over every single iteration of the ruse that had seemingly thrown their friend into such paranoia that he had had himself taken prisoner and subjected to a wide suite of physical, chemical and genetic scans. He tried to apply Occam's razor to each of these plots, but realized that, given the history of their brutal encounters with Colonel Thrush and his continuum of alternate selves, carving away the improbable was impossible. Which ended up with another potential outcome that the pandimensional menace could have sought. By inserting a poisonous doubt into Cerberus, a doubt affecting the man who, essentially, was the heart of the entire war against the Annunaki overlords and all others who would enslave Earth and humanity, had Thrush taken the wind out of their sails? The android multiverse traveler had just made it so that they couldn't trust one-third of the triumvirate of heroes who had formed such a confluence that they could accomplish the impossible.

Without that perfect team at the core of Cerberus, savagely undercut by doubt, the whole of the rebellion against Enlil and his kind, and by proxy, all the other superpowers seeking Earth's domination, had been instantly defanged.

"Friend Kane?" Lakesh asked. "You're the one who brought this crisis to our attention. What do you feel?"

Kane closed his eyes, concentrating. When he finally opened them, he sighed. "I feel bruises all over my carcass, a splitting headache and I'm getting nauseous from lack of food and drink. Beyond that, it's anybody's damn guess."

Grant studied his friend's face as he spoke. He turned to the others. "Sounds as authentic as ever to me."

"No variations from Kane's normal form of speech," Brigid added. "Right now, we've got one hundred percent verification on retinal and fingerprint analysis, dental records are identical right down to the wear factor and, after forty percent of the data has been analyzed on his genetics, there is not a single variation. Healed scars match photographic record of prior wound recovery, as well, except for the new injuries he picked up in the battle with the Fomorians."

Kane looked at the mirrored glass separating him from the rest of the leadership of the Cerberus base. "So does that mean I can have a cup of coffee and a pot roast sandwich? Or just crackers and water?"

Grant leaned to the intercom. "Edwards, give Kane his damn lunch before he starves to death."

The hulking ex-Magistrate under Domi's command in Cerberus Away Team Beta strode into the operating room carrying a tray. Edwards was almost the same size as Grant, and Lakesh marveled at the rippling power emanating from the ex-Mag as he handed the meal to Kane.

"Edwards," Domi spoke up, "you couldn't intimidate the real Kane. You can unclench your muscles now."

Edwards looked down at Kane, then snorted. "If you're just a fake, I'll take your head off."

Kane rubbed the crown of his head, as touching his forehead would obviously unleash whole new waves of pain. He glanced up to the physical monster in the room with him and sighed. "You know, you'd actually be doing me a favor."

DeFore put a small cup on the tray before Kane. "You step off the mat-trans all grim and determined not to show an ounce of human weakness, but after a few hours, you're bitching that I'm not giving you some ibuprofen. If that's not a sign he's the real Kane, then I'll eat my thermometer."

Lakesh cupped his hand over his mouth. He wanted to tell DeFore not to make promises she might have to keep, but for now, he didn't want to cause any conflict. He fought down the doubt from his voice and spoke up. "So now what are we going to do regarding the Thrush presence in the Poconos and their mutant assistants?"

"I dropped a mountainside onto them," Grant said. "So for now, they'll be off balance. Epona has moved her people to an older settlement before their expansion closer to the valley we hit with the avalanche. It will give the Appalachians some room and leave the Fomorian raiders nothing to attack."

"Why couldn't they just stay in the older valley?" Domi asked.

"Pride. The fact that the Fomorians would eventually track them down," Brigid said. "As well, the hunting and water supplies are plentiful in that area, not exhausted like the area they'd abandoned. Right now, all Epona's people have only a few days of supplies that they were able to move into the older shelters."

"We could transport extra stuff to them," Domi suggested.

"Really? Because we've got a redoubt full of people here," Lakesh interjected. "I'm all for a little bit of charity, but we have our own needs to take care of, and the Appalachians don't strike me as the type of people to willingly resort to welfare from people they barely trust."

"It's a temporary solution," Grant concluded. "But between Cerberus Away Teams Alpha and Beta, we'll be able to deal with whatever the Fomorians and Thrush can recover from the avalanche."

"And if not, we can always request assistance from Shizuka and Aristotle," Brigid said, mentioning the respective leaders of the Tigers of Heaven in New Edo and the Pantheon operating out of New Olympus. "Between a force of samurai and a squad of gear skeletons, we can hit the Fomorians with a lot of fighting skill and technology."

Lakesh frowned. "Or give Thrush information about the extent of our allies. He knew about the Tigers of Heaven, we assume, since it was around the time he returned to Earth as the Imperator Sam that we first encountered them. Whether Thrush retains the knowledge of Enlil and the related technology is unknown for now."

"And who's to say that Thrush, being a robot himself, really would worry about the relatively primitive combat suits of the Olympians?" Grant asked. "It'd be like throwing a Deathbird after one of Enlil's scout ships."

Kane rapped his knuckles on the mirror. Lakesh sighed and turned on the lights in the meeting room, then retracted the one-way glass. "Yes, friend Kane?"

Kane swallowed his mouthful of sandwich. "I'd like to point out that while we know one form of Thrush, native to our planet, became Enlil, I don't think that they share all the same technology. The Orb is as different from an Annunaki scout ship as you can get. Otherwise, Thrush would be sending his android copies after us in squadrons of craft, and the Orb would be parked in orbit, throwing down as much firepower as *Tiamat* could have brought to bear."

Lakesh looked to Brigid for confirmation.

"He's got a point, and this time it's not the one at the top of his head," Brigid said.

Kane winked at her, then chomped another bite out of his pot roast sandwich. DeFore gave him a mock slap on the shoulder.

"This isn't your personal dining room," she grumbled.

Kane nodded in agreement and rose to join his colleagues in the meeting room. DeFore handed him the rest of his meal tray, then barked orders for her interns to clean up and sterilize the observation room.

For the moment, things had returned to normal, but Lakesh kept his eye on Kane throughout the strategy meeting.

And from what he could tell about Grant and Brigid, their suspicions remained, hidden just below the surface.

Chapter 5

Grant spied Brigid take Kane out of the side door of the meeting room, and she gave him a quick nod while he was distracted. She was going to do her best to minimize any problems with him, whether he was genuine or fake. Limping and battered from hand-to-hand combat with what appeared to be the product of Tuatha de Danaan mutation technology, the Cerberus staff had a valid reason for sidelining the man who was, by record, reputation and the blood he'd shed, the star player for the human rebels. If anyone deserved a chance to throw himself back into a comfortable bed and get some rest after the battering he'd received, it was Kane.

Brigid, with her close relationship with Kane, took the task of escorting him out of the meeting room and assuring him that this was one crisis that Cerberus could handle without his assistance. Of course, that meant that Grant was going to be the only member of Cerberus Away Team Alpha immediately ready for action. He caught Domi looking mischievously at him.

"CAT Beta is ready to go," Domi told him.

Lakesh's forehead wrinkled with the statement.

"We're not even certain that friend Grant's avalanche was sufficient to cripple the Fomorians and their Thrush liaison."

"*If* the liaison is still in that valley," Grant said, his voice low, as if he were tempting fate.

Lakesh looked toward the hallway, then cleared his throat.

"Come on, Moe," Domi protested. "We'll have Grant with us...."

"It just doesn't seem to have the same confluence of fate that would be available if it were Kane, Brigid and Grant," Lakesh said. "My apologies for any disrespect."

Grant shook his head. "None taken."

"Listen, if Kane is back at the Poconos, then we're going to have to have people in the area to find him," Domi said. "And outside of Sky Dog's people, I'm the best wilderness tracker in this hemisphere."

"She's got a point," Grant said. "And if Kane catches me sitting around Cerberus while we've got Thrush and mutant man-eaters running around and working together, he'll want to get back out into the field."

"Which could aggravate his injuries, leading to real problems if he's the real thing," Lakesh spoke up. "Or if he's fake, give him the opportunity to return to the Thrush Continuum after accomplishing whichever task he was sent to do."

"Even if it were just to throw doubt onto one of our own," Domi added.

"We have to keep Kane here and under wraps for

now," Grant said. "Anything else is just an invitation to disaster. Lakesh, maybe you should start thinking about exactly what Thrush would want to do with the resources we have here at Cerberus that he couldn't do from his Orb."

"I've been running everything I could in my mind," Lakesh said.

Grant nodded. "All you need to do is keep an eye on Kane to figure out what he's trying to do here and put it up against what you've suspected."

"Precisely," Lakesh answered. "Be careful, darlingest Domi."

"I'm going to have to say the same thing," Domi returned. "Edwards, go get Sela. We're suiting up for the field. Grant, you might—"

"I'm already on the way to the armory to pick up some spare gear for Kane," Grant cut her off.

"And more restraints," Domi added. "What we run into might look like Kane, but what if that really is the fake, and we've been stuck running around and picking up the infiltrator when we brought the real guy home?"

Grant grimaced. "DeFore, could you spare a couple painkillers for me? All this shit's giving me a headache."

"You're not the only one lost here," DeFore responded. "But I'm going to give you my educated opinion. I've been over that man easily forty times in the past. If he's a duplicate, then whoever kidnapped the real Kane stripped him naked and looked over every inch of his body, then utilized some pretty impressive technology to copy every bit of scar tissue around."

"That's not saying much," Lakesh returned. "Sam regressed my age. Remolding a patch of skin to look like healed tissue shouldn't be beyond that level of biological engineering."

"Or we could just be too damn paranoid for our own good," Grant said. "Domi, did you get anything wrong about him?"

Domi shook her head. "It's not as if I have the sense of smell of a dog or shit like that. I'm a good tracker, but the only superhuman ability I have are the soles of my feet. They're harder than armadillo shells."

Grant shrugged. "I just thought you'd spot something the rest of us didn't think of. You've proved to be pretty perceptive on more than enough occasions."

Domi sighed. "Sorry. I'm not thinking straight."

"Which I believe could be Thrush's plan," Lakesh said.

"Whatever the plan, the more time we spend jawing about this shit, the closer it comes to succeeding," Grant growled. "Come on, Domi."

The pair was as physically different as could be, one tall, muscular and seemingly cast out of bronze and obsidian, the other small, wiry and looking as if she were crafted from porcelain. Yet the two people shared an identical intensity and determination as they left the meeting room.

BRIGID ACCOMPANIED Kane to the canteen, where he finished his meal. She watched as Kane threw away the remaining trash from his lunch. He sighed and picked up his plate and utensils, carrying them to the washing basin. "I know, don't make more work for the kitchen staff. You'd think with all the extra bodies around, we'd need something to keep them busy."

Brigid raised an eyebrow. "You mean that digging through the garbage for your fork and knife is a good utilization of some of the most brilliant minds left over from the twentieth century?"

Kane shrugged. "Look at the world they left behind for us. All that genius and…"

"You're putting the blame for skydark on them?" Brigid asked. "Especially when we saw Colonel Thrush himself pull the trigger that blew up the Russian embassy?"

Kane shook his head and grimaced. "Thrush took advantage of the tensions those big brains created. I'm not absolving that freak. He's the one who jumped me and set a bunch of Fomorian mutants on my ass. Right now, I'm just realizing how antisocial I feel with all these people crowding around."

Brigid took a deep breath and nodded. As compassionate as Kane was toward the plight of others, ever since the Manitius personnel had been evacuated and relocated to Cerberus redoubt, privacy and peace and quiet had been curtailed. Beset with a pounding headache, and not at the top of his physical condition, his impatience couldn't be cast aside by strolling off into the surrounding hills and spending time in the relative tranquility of

Sky Dog's village. Brigid had often joked that she'd keep an eye out for little Indian papooses with blue eyes, but the truth of the matter was, Kane was much like Domi in that they were at home in the wilderness. The trappings of the redoubt were cold and sterile, no matter how brightly lit or colorfully painted. With the addition of more people, Brigid could see that Kane's momentary musings were not an endorsement of Thrush's destruction of humanity.

Still, Kane winced internally. "I'm not doing much for my case by being so misanthropic."

Brigid shook her head. "I'll bring you some coffee. We'll start over."

Kane rolled his eyes. "I wouldn't overlook that kind of a rant if I were you."

Brigid rested her hand on his shoulder. "Why? It *is* a sentiment you'd voice if you were too hurt and too tired to get back into the fresh air. In fact, I'd be afraid if you didn't let some of your rough edges show. As much as we get called heroes, we're still just normal people who are allowed to be grumpy and hold some loathing for others."

Kane took a deep breath. "Maybe...but you don't have to disguise the fact that you're babysitting me because I haven't been officially cleared."

Brigid nodded. "Find us a table, okay?"

"Sure," Kane relented.

Brigid cursed herself for being too quick to disregard Kane's rant, but that was an emotional reaction. She went over the pure logic of the situation and she stood on her decision. Everything she knew about the man pointed to someone who'd make a glib statement, a joking condemnation. Throw in the effects of physical trauma he'd experienced, including one tortuous bit of combat that occurred before her eyes, and she really had nothing to flag in Kane's behavior or speech.

She prepared their coffee mechanically while her intellect threw up a flow chart of possibilities in her mind's eye. The benefits of having a photographic memory allowed her to visualize a thousand different things at once. In one part of the flow chart, she ran before and after imagery of Kane from multiple angles, looking for details that didn't quite match. Nothing showed up, which frustrated her. On another part of the flow chart, she remembered the details of the Thrush Continuum's transdimensional Orb ship. The great ark was staffed by copies of Thrush from across a multitude of universes, though they all bore only minor variations of appearance.

Brigid brought up her memories of the young boy into whom Thrush had implanted his mind. The child had been birthed by Erica van Sloan, and had seemed entirely human, except for an intellect that dwarfed anything Brigid had ever seen, and access to technologies such as the Heart of the World and the nanomachines that rebuilt Lakesh so adeptly. She concentrated on young Sam's face, processing its similarities to the more adult versions of Colonel Thrush. Thanks to her eidetic mental imagery, she was able to compare facial bone structure, eyes, jaw profile and ears. She ran those pictures through her mind's eye and sighed in disgust. If she hadn't recognized the boy Sam as a younger version of Thrush with her infallible memory, then why would she be able to pick up such alterations and similarities now?

"Because you're being thorough," Brigid whispered to herself.

"Thorough about what?" a familiar voice asked. A scientist from the Manitius base stood by the table that Kane had selected. Daryl Morganstern gave a small wave to her. "Hi, Brigid. I wasn't expecting you guys back so soon."

Brigid's cheeks burned. "Well, you can see Kane took a knock to the head, so we're letting him recuperate before we go running back into the field."

Morganstern nodded.

"I know that he's from the moon base, but I for one can't place this guy," Kane said.

Brigid sighed. "That's because I hadn't introduced you two yet."

"Introduced us?" Kane asked.

Morganstern shrugged. "Well…we're sort of dating."

Kane shot a glance toward Brigid. "Dating?"

Brigid set down the coffee cups. "Have a seat, Daryl."

"Thanks," Morganstern replied. He sat next to Brigid but turned his chair to avoid eye contact with Kane. He'd lowered his head, hunching his shoulders in a turtlelike defensive posture.

"Straighten up, Daryl. I'm not going to bite your head off," Kane said. "Dating?"

Brigid rolled her eyes. "Listen, I'm not sure if you can remember past that head trauma, but just because you seem to have been happy to learn from Sindri that we're married in some alternate future, I'm not buying it."

Kane took his cup of coffee and took a sip. "We undid that timeline, didn't we?"

Brigid nodded. "And aren't you the one who's always fighting fate?"

Kane lifted a hand to hold off Brigid. "Hang on, Baptiste. I'm not complaining. I just didn't realize that you'd found someone worth dating from Manitius."

Brigid didn't have to look back at Morganstern, who had put a hand up to his eyes to hide his wince. The lunar scientist was a theoretical mathematician and part of a new team that Lakesh had assembled to rework the quantum equations to further enhance and refine the interphaser and mat-trans system. He was also another person who had been gifted with a near perfect memory, and while Brigid was helping out with Lakesh's interphaser program, they had started talking. Physically, Morganstern was average, and his eyes and hair were a plain brown, though he had a sweet smile and dimples. Still, the pair had developed a rapport.

"There are quite a few nice people who came down to Cerberus," Brigid stated. "Plus, he's been a great chess opponent."

"I've played chess with you," Kane said, sounding almost hurt.

"We don't need the board," Morganstern said, voice low and brittle. He looked at Brigid. "Oh. I have you in check on board two."

Brigid nodded. "Game five, though, I'll mate in six moves."

Morganstern winced. "I was hoping you hadn't taken queen's pawn into that equation…."

Kane gave a low whistle. "Okay, maybe I haven't played chess with you that well. How many games do you have going?"

"We've tied and drawn so many times, we've expanded it to seven concurrent games," Morganstern admitted.

"And how many moves until mate?" Kane asked.

Brigid glared at Kane. "Excuse me?"

Morganstern flinched at the flare of anger on Brigid's part. "I don't—"

"Oh, I know what he meant," Brigid replied.

"You bust my chops over little blue-eyed Indian babies," Kane said.

"That doesn't mean you can be a prick and put poor Daryl on the spot," Brigid said.

Morganstern swallowed. "I think I'll go get myself a soft drink."

"I'm not letting Kane drive you off," Brigid said. She narrowed her gaze at the man as he took another sip of coffee. "That's why I didn't introduce you—because I knew you'd be a pig."

"Really, Brigid. I'm just thirsty," Morganstern said, his voice rising an octave with obvious nervousness. "I'll be right back."

Brigid puffed out her cheeks. "You've got a minute."

Morganstern nodded, a little too rapidly to be anything but on edge. He scurried out of his chair and headed toward the drink station.

"I'm sorry, Baptiste," Kane said. "He's an okay-seeming guy."

"Yeah," Brigid grumbled. "It's nothing big for you, Mister Hero-man, to lay a slick line on one of those bar-barian trollops you encounter on days ending with the letter *y,* but it's not easy for women. He told me there's a dozen moon base scientists who are afraid to talk to me because I'm out of their league."

"You are," Kane admitted. "Guys are intimidated by pretty girls," Kane continued. "Throw in the fact that you're a resident superheroine, able to walk across di-mensions by concentrating on funky rugs and regularly prance about in skintight uniforms…"

Brigid grimaced.

"I'm not going to rain on your parade," Kane said.

Brigid squeezed her eyebrows. "Just drop it, Kane."

"Consider it dropped," he answered. "Besides, what's that you called us once upon a time?"

"Anam-chara," Brigid said. "Soul friends. That's if I buy into that jump-dream memory you had of rescuing one of my other incarnations. We're bound together, but nothing you've told me says that we're some kind of

cosmic lovers. Good grief, I'm trying to apply logic to reincarnation."

"Enlil reincarnated. Fand and Epona recognize my old soul," Kane offered.

"Where's Daryl with his soda?" Brigid muttered.

"The nozzle popped on his soft drink," Kane said. "He and a couple of the other members of the geek squad have the dispenser disassembled and are arguing over how best to rebuild it."

Brigid looked over her shoulder and saw Morganstern. The young scientist shrugged, looking pained at the brown, soaking stain on his chest. Brigid gave him a smile that she wasn't particularly feeling at the moment, and he waved at her before walking toward the table.

"Sorry. It looks like we've got our emergency to counterpoint whatever crisis you're dealing with," Morganstern told her.

"Who says we're in the middle of a crisis?" Brigid asked.

"Kane's injured, and CAT Beta is preparing for a jump back to the Poconos," Morganstern noted. "Grant's going with them."

Kane nodded. "I know. I hate being sidelined, but DeFore told me I have a concussion."

Brigid sighed. "I'm sorry, Daryl."

"That's all right. We still have our date scheduled for tomorrow night. Running into you and Kane was an unexpected surprise for the day," Morganstern offered.

Kane nodded toward the soft drink machine. "It looks like one of your buddies is upset."

Morganstern looked back, horrified. "Wynan! No, we are not going to waste valuable platinum on diet soda! I'm sorry, Brigid."

She reached up and grabbed Morganstern's shirt, kissing him on the cheek. "Thanks for understanding, Daryl."

Morganstern chuckled nervously, his dimpled smile glowing beneath blushing cheeks. "Brigid, I want to thank *you*."

Brigid turned back and saw the smirk on Kane's face. "You say another word, and I will peel the flesh from your bones and tell everyone that I was certain you are a death pod person from Dimension Fifteen. And they'd never blame me."

Kane covered his mouth to hold back his laughter. Brigid hoped that in her mock rage, she hadn't given form to a dangerous prophecy. The man's stifled amusement seemed to echo in a haunting taunt to her doubts.

Chapter 6

As Grant went over the gear stuffed into the pouches of his web utility belt, Domi remained silent. The two had come a long way since their first meeting in the Tartarus Pits of Cobaltville. Originally Domi had fallen deeply for the dark ex-Mag because he was the first person ever to show genuine concern and affection for her. Since then, both had found the true loves of their lives, and their relationship had matured. Domi herself had matured, and the love she felt for Grant wasn't something that was based on sexual attraction.

If anything, Grant was a nurturing father figure that she had grown up without, which was why Grant had felt so uncomfortable with her fleeting advances, and then her campaign to scandalize and make him jealous. More than once, she had wanted to apologize for giving him such an awkward time, but Grant wouldn't hear anything about it. They had both found partners, and now with that stumbling block out of the way, Grant no longer felt aloof toward her.

They could have these comfortable silences together. Though Domi could see a million questions and doubts storming through his mind, Grant focused on preparing for the mission back to the mountain range. It was enough that Domi was there, and though her vocabulary had grown greatly since her arrival at Cerberus, her silence spoke more deeply than anything else. Grant strapped his Sin Eater onto his forearm last of all, and he tested the holster mechanism. A quick whirr and the machine pistol snapped into his palm, then withdrew.

He looked at Domi who was ready for action. Her big, ruby-red eyes, startling globes of crimson, searched his face.

"If that's the wrong Kane, we'll find the right one," Domi said softly.

Grant nodded. "He's lucky like that. To have us come in as the cavalry and rescue his sorry ass."

"He's done it for us enough times."

Grant took a deep breath and slid a Kevlar-lined load-bearing vest over his shadow suit top. The photocell camouflage of the remarkable uniform wouldn't be needed, and Grant wanted plenty of pockets and some extra armor to augment the protective abilities of his uniform. The vest's bullet-resistant fabric was reinforced with lightweight ceramic trauma plates. He'd heard the kind of firepower that the Fomorians were packing, and the AK-47 fired a notoriously difficult round to resist with conventional body armor. "'Course, it would be like him…"

"Shut up," Domi whispered.

Grant's eyes flashed with annoyance, but he remained

silent. It may have been silly superstition on Domi's part, but she was not the kind of woman to tempt fate by talking about the worst that could happen. The loss of Kane from Cerberus would be a crippling blow on so many levels. It was his courage and compassion that had redirected and refocused the fight against the barons after Lakesh's years of quiet, desperate machinations. Kane had forged the bond with the local Native American tribe, and had been instrumental in rescuing societies from corruption. He'd saved everyone's life a dozen times over.

Domi remembered how Kane had, in a moment of desperation, plucked her from the brink of annihilation with the technology of Thunder Isle. It had been during a fierce battle to escape Area 51. Domi had helped Kane escape a forced breeding program where he sired a new generation of children with superior genetics and all of Kane's phenomenal physical and mental attributes. In the battle to break loose, Domi had been trapped in the path of an implode grenade, a powerful weapon that by all rights should have turned her into a smear of plasma.

Instead, Kane had discovered the Thunder Isle temporal matrix. He pushed the staff to lock on to her position at the moment just before the grenade's detonation. In Domi's mind, she had simply blinked, leaving behind the underground complex and appearing in the time scoop. She'd lived simply because Kane had not given up, because his supersharp perceptions noticed that her supposed death was not how it should have been from a grenade detonation. His faith, his willingness to defy the laws of physics and consequence enabled Kane to wrench her from the jaws of death.

That same undying loyalty had been the impetus to save others. Kane would never think that someone was dead and lost. He'd fight with the Grim Reaper himself to protect those he loved. Without him, the glue that united Cerberus would dry, crack and come apart in a spray of brittle crumbs. Domi would never admit to any possibility that Kane was dead, and she wouldn't allow others to even breathe that doubt into existence.

It was stubborn and superstitious, but Kane had been too bullheaded to allow Domi to be murdered.

Grant swallowed hard and recovered his ability to speak, but this time, he skirted the issue. "You might want to take some extra equipment."

Domi patted her crossbow, a large steel one with a reel crank on the side. It was an upgrade of the small pistol bow model she often carried. "Shot through tree trunk with this."

Domi blushed as she realized that she'd dropped back into her abbreviated outlanders speech. Grant smiled, then pretended that he couldn't detect the nerves made all too obvious when she spoke.

"This crossbow's rated at 416 feet per second for a bolt," she said, fighting down her clipped verbosity. "And the crank allows for fast reloads."

"But it's not going to be ideal if a Fomorian comes

into close combat," Grant said. "I'm not so much worried about me or Edwards—we're as big as they are."

"I know," Domi said. "But I've got my Detonics .45." She patted the small pistol on her hip. "There's a MAC-10 in my bag, too."

"I hope that's enough." Grant sighed. His mind had already let go of the logistical issues of their upcoming trip and had returned to his best friend. It had been a feeble effort, trying to distract Grant from his true fears by delving into the musketry necessary to bring down Bres's mutants. Still, it was a moment or two where he had been distracted from worries.

Domi took Grant by the hand and gave him a quiet, loving embrace. Her slender arms squeezed around his shoulders with far more strength than they would have appeared to, and Grant responded with a gentle tap on her back.

"Go get the rest of your team," Grant said. "I want to make one last check with Brigid and him."

Even as she left him alone in the locker room to check on the status of her CAT Beta Team, Domi noted that Grant couldn't bring himself to say his friend's name. Though she remained skeptical of "supernatural" abilities, she'd survived in the Outlands and the slums of Cobaltville utilizing instincts that couldn't readily be defined. Grant's instincts refused to allow him to call the man everyone recognized as Kane by that name. The bonds of friendship were strong, and they ran deeper than simple blood chemistry and genetics. There was a hint of falseness, an imperceptible doubt that shouldn't exist after retinal scans and fingerprint matching.

Domi hated that her own hunter's senses didn't pick up anything worthwhile, except that she could tell that Grant didn't quite trust the version of Kane they carried back through the mat-trans. Whatever the menace Thrush had placed within their ranks, it was something that had been an absolutely perfect duplicate, right down to healed scars and a jawbone implant to attach a Commtact. The similarities were so fine that even Brigid Baptiste's eidetic memory couldn't find enough incongruity to give more than a vague doubt on her own.

The balance of the three Cerberus heroes had been altered, and they weren't certain if it was due to head trauma. Brigid herself had suffered a skull injury before and had taken a while to recover. For a brief period, the three people weren't at their top game on missions, part of what had inspired Lakesh to form a second Cerberus away team to take up the slack. Domi had done her best to emulate the kind of team formed by her friends, but Kane, Grant and Brigid were a magical combination, a one-in-a-million act of emotional and mental chemistry that went far beyond the sum of intellect and raw muscle. Lakesh had pointed out many times before that their union as a team allowed them to defy the laws of probability and defeat threats that loomed so large, they could swallow the entire solar system.

Domi simply had to rely on skill, knowledge and well-applied brute force for CAT Beta. It had carried them through a few missions, and they'd even been able to contain the rage of a technogoddess gone mad before she utilized an ancient Threshhold device to teleport her from a stony tomb in which she'd trapped the bitch. Even then, though, they'd had Brigid Baptiste's aid while Kane and Grant battled a rival god and his army.

Together or apart, the three of them in coordination had been a focused force, and any goal they sought to achieve usually ended in victory. Bittersweet ashes from a Pyrrhic win were rare; for the most part, a win was a win.

She didn't want to think of the torment and horrors that would lie ahead if the three heroes of Cerberus were ever to split up. Kane liked to point out that the core of the human resistance was formed by everyone's free will, an indomitable spirit. He'd even brought out the old American flag to wave as a banner in the face of the Annunaki when Enlil sent his forces for the first open warfare that had broken out after *Tiamat*'s return to Earth. The cloth had meant much to the people of the moon base, but Domi's loyalty wasn't to a striped piece of fabric. She'd bled and wept with Kane and his allies. They were family. And with family came a fealty that couldn't be broken.

Edwards raised an eyebrow at Domi's approach. The big former Magistrate was clad in a shadow suit, like all the members of the away teams, but like Grant, he also wore a Kevlar-and-ceramic-laden load-bearing vest. Sela Sinclair also had one over her shadow suit, but she didn't look as bulky as the two former Magistrates.

"Trouble, boss?" Edwards asked.

"Just worried about what we'll find in the mountains," Domi said. She checked her wrist chronometer, still a little uncomfortable with the device that threw off the balance of her hand somewhat. She had never really taken to wearing chrons, but as commander of a team, it helped her to be more precise at telling time and coordinating with her subordinates on the team. "And don't call me boss."

"You're the boss," Edwards answered with a mischievous grin.

Domi opened her mouth to say something, but realized that the big man's joke formed a logical loop that started to make her head hurt. "Remind me to kick your ass in the next sparring practice."

"Again?" Edwards asked.

Domi's eyes narrowed. "You do not want to get on my nerves today, Edwards."

Sela rested a hand on Domi's shoulder. "What's the deal with Kanc? Why's everyone acting so weird?"

At first, Domi wondered at the logic of having a woman, especially a freezie from another century, as a member of her away team. It wasn't a matter of sexism on Domi's part; in her experience with strong and capable women like Brigid, Fand and Shizuka, among dozens of others, being female wasn't a detriment to ability. However, Domi had started out at Cerberus alienating other women because of her blatant sexuality. She had also experienced a brief bout of intense jealousy against Shizuka when the lady samurai and Grant first became involved. Domi didn't know if she'd be emotionally compatible with a woman as a teammate, but now, Sela seemed to have a way of sensing her distress, and actually be able to talk about it.

Edwards was more perceptive than he'd seemed, hence his needling over calling her boss. Right now, Domi preferred the understanding approach of Sinclair, but Edwards's sarcasm was comforting, as well.

"Just watch your fire when we get to the Appalachians," Domi ordered. "And don't trust your eyes, okay?"

Sinclair and Edwards shared a conspiratorial glance, then nodded to their field commander.

"And watch each other's back. Right now, we can't trust just anybody," Domi continued. "Me and Grant, and yourselves."

"This isn't anything like those ghost things we had trouble with a while ago?" Edwards asked.

"Not that, no," Domi answered.

"Okay," Sinclair replied. She checked her weapon, an M-16 with an underbarrel grenade launcher. If the assault rifle, loaded with armor-piercing ammunition, wasn't enough to handle the Fomorians, then the 40 mm packet of explosives that the launcher fired would definitely do the job. It was a bit heavy for a rifle, but still under ten pounds. Edwards, by comparison, went for a cannon. A large multichambered revolver-style grenade launcher and pouches for spare shells adorned his uniform, in addition to his traditional Sin Eater machine pistol in its forearm sheath.

"And the Fomorians are really that bad?" Edwards asked.

"Grant saw them. He shot at them. They're not invulnerable, but they are tough enough to pound Kane pretty badly," Domi said. She wished that she could have said Kane's name without the word sticking in her throat. Her teammates noticed that pause, the pained halt in her speech.

Given how cryptic she had tried to be, Domi cursed herself for dropping the ball. She didn't want doubts about Kane's identity to cloud their minds.

"All right, what is going on?" Edwards asked bluntly.

"We returned with Kane," Domi said. "Kane informed us that when he was down among the Fomorians, he encountered an impostor. We ran a check to confirm his identity, and he's the same person we have medical records for. We're heading to deal with the Fomorian mutants and to catch up with this duplicate Kane."

"But you want us to check our fire," Sinclair said.

Domi nodded. "We'd like to take the Thrush-made fake—"

"Thrush, that android dude who time travels and shit?" Edwards asked.

"Yeah," Domi answered. "Big time scary, with technology that's almost magic."

Edwards nodded.

"It's so much easier in *Star Trek*." Sinclair sighed. "If you're a duplicate from an evil universe, you've got a funky sharp goatee."

Domi raised an eyebrow at the twentieth-century woman's reference, not because she didn't get it. Indeed, Sinclair had made her sit through the ancient television show for a few episodes. It was a form of bonding. To Domi, the snacks were the real draw, and anything that showed up on the video screen was far removed from the real wonders she'd encountered. She'd been to space, she'd traveled to other times and dimensions and she'd encountered aliens and gods. The reality she'd slammed into made those old stories seem hokey, although some of the tales and the basic themes still had resonance. "Duplicate from evil universe. Time and dimension traveling android. Do own math."

Sinclair swallowed hard, and Domi grimaced as she realized that stress had crept into her voice again, her speech having devolved once more.

"So who's babysitting our hurt little friend?" Edwards asked. Domi had to applaud the normally undiplomatic Magistrate's choice of words.

"Brigid," Domi answered. Her Commtact plate hummed to life.

"Did someone just say my name?" Brigid's voice came over the unit.

"We were just talking about you," Domi said. "How's everything?"

"Except for a breakdown in the mess hall, everything's simply glowing," Brigid answered. She sounded a little perturbed.

"So what's gotten under your skin?" Domi asked.

"Kane's needling," Brigid said. "He just met the guy I'm dating."

"Oh, the nerd? Daryl?" Domi asked.

"He's a scientist," Brigid countered. "He's smart."

"I'm dating a nerd, too, if you haven't noticed," Domi said. That elicited a chuckle from Baptiste and her teammates. "So Kane's busting your chops over that?"

"A little," Brigid answered.

"Honestly. All the women he's been with, and he's begrudging your relationship with Daryl?" Domi asked. "Remind me to kick him in the balls next sparring session."

There was a moment of silence as Edwards and Sinclair picked up on a certain unreality of the conversation they were listening in to over the Commtact. Brigid's perceptions, coupled with an infallible memory and a magnificent intellect, tended to be sharper than most people's. And when they'd reached that point of the conversation, there was enough of a shade of doubt in Brigid's voice to make them suspicious that things weren't quite right.

"You do that," Brigid stated. She'd regained her composure, but that could have been because Kane—or his impostor—was now watching her. "Just checking on how you guys were doing, actually. You about ready to leave?"

"We'll be jumping out in about fifteen minutes," Domi answered.

"I'm sorry I won't be joining you guys, but DeFore

says I should heal up a bit," they heard Kane's voice say over the Commtact.

"You already went a few rounds with the Fomorians. Why would you want to hog more of the fun?" Edwards asked. "Let the second-stringers get their chance to shine."

Kane's laughter met their ears. "Be careful, okay?"

"Will do," Sinclair said. She cast a glance toward Domi, who frowned. Sinclair was only a recent addition to the Cerberus staff, so she and Edwards were not familiar with the same Kane that Domi was.

"*You* behave and heal up, Kane," Domi said, smiling to avoid having her glum mood darken her tone of voice.

"I will, thanks," Kane responded.

Domi was glad that the Commtact only transmitted audio and not video. The sound of the impostor was just too good, his concern too genuine. It was torture trying to keep a cap on her doubts and suspicions, even if he'd passed every test put to him.

So far, both Grant and Brigid had pointed out that though they got the wrong vibe from Kane, the man's behavior was above suspicion. As far as anyone knew, he was the real Kane. Even the note of worry he had for the people that, as an intruder, he should have been fooling, felt right. All Domi had to go on were the instincts of Grant and Brigid, people who should have known conclusively whether or not they were dealing with an imposter. The doubt that Domi sensed was not just to Kane's existence, but to their own perceptions.

Were they amplifying little tics that they simply had ignored and avoided scrutinizing before? Were they giving in to paranoia?

Domi thought back to Scla Sinclair's "mirror universe" scenario. What if this was Kane, right down to the smallest particle, but simply from elsewhere? It seemed far-fetched, but Domi had traveled to other casements, parallel dimensions, and her psyche deposited into the bodies of her counterparts there. It wasn't far-fetched; it was simply an easier means of traveling across universal divides. The story of an exact duplicate in the field could have been a ruse, as the real Kane *was* the impostor.

"You okay?" Sinclair asked.

Domi shook her head. A knot of pain pulsed behind her ruby-red eyes. "I'm really no fucking good at this."

"You've kept us alive every mission so far," Edwards said. "What, so you're trying to wrap your brain about exactly what we're dealing with, right? Even Brigid doesn't sound sure."

"Thanks, you two," Domi said.

"Anytime, boss," Edwards told her.

Domi settled one glaring red eye on him. "Did I tell you to remind me to kick your ass in sparring practice earlier?"

"I can neither confirm nor deny, ma'am," Edwards replied with a grin.

Domi snorted. "I'd say you're not as stupid as you look, but that'd be impossible."

Edwards elbowed Sinclair, gently. "Victory is mine!"

Sinclair rolled her eyes. "Come on. Grant's probably wondering what's keeping us."

Domi sighed. "If that's the only thing he's worrying about, then I'm happy for him."

The members of Cerberus Away Team Beta made their way to the mat-trans chamber for their jump to the Appalachians.

Chapter 7

Thrush-Kane was surprised when he saw that Brigid Baptiste had an interest in someone other than the being he was duplicating. Sure, he acted the smart-ass, ribbing her about the nature of the young man she'd chosen as her "date." It was what Kane would have done, wouldn't it? But his chiding was directed toward her, not the man he should have been jealous of.

That was what perplexed at least one section of the plasma matrix brain that housed his enhanced consciousness. While Brigid was busy talking with Domi about the albino woman's upcoming trek to the Poconos with Grant, the cybernetic intruder was conducting his own preparations for war. The redoubt had been cutting-edge technology, powered by a nuclear reactor and utilizing a remarkable computer system that had been modified for wireless computer connection capabilities. It was something that the current tenants had much use for, other than operating portable tablet PCs to run inventory. Thrush-Kane, however, had seen a similar Wi-Fi in a dozen realities where it was used to connect to a global intercomputer network resource that had made research and communication much easier. Without an Internet to run on, at least not since January 2001, such wireless technology was purely a business application, not a time waster as Thrush had seen. However, the plasma matrix brain he had was powerful, and it had a wireless modem built into it, capable of transmitting and receiving.

Thrush-Kane gently prodded the system, looking for infiltration prevention protocols. The designer of the system, presumably Donald Bry, had assembled a powerful blockade of "black ice," nearly invisible hacking countermeasures designed to keep the mainframe safe. Thrush-Kane's canny cybervision picked up new constructs, countersurveillance bots that patrolled the system searching for interlopers. The infiltrator cyborg saw the footsteps of other, previous intruders, which were being tended to by blocks of assembly code, repairing old injuries to the mainframe. This changed a few of the cyborg's plans, but the obstacles were not insurmountable. Utilizing computer hacking lessons from several realities, the Thrush Continuum had designed Thrush-Kane's plasma matrix brain to be able to defeat any human-designed countermeasure. Still, the doppelganger had to admit some respect for the brilliance of the humans involved in setting up their cybernetic defenses. He could see the fingerprints of several geniuses, including a tiny bit of code identifying Daryl Morganstern—Brigid's boyfriend—as one of the mathematicians who had created the encryption algorithm.

Thrush-Kane looked at the algorithm, attempting to decipher it, and realized that the human had to have been operating on mathematical principles that lay outside even the Thrush Continuum's conceptual capabilities.

"No wonder she's interested in him," Thrush-Kane muttered to himself as Brigid was speaking over her Commtact to Domi.

The flame-haired beauty glanced at him, wondering at Thrush-Kane's mouthing. However, it was only a momentary awareness as she returned to speaking with them. The secondary team was hooked up with Grant, dividing the remnants of CAT Alpha.

It had been Thrush-Kane's plan to split up the two remaining Cerberus defenders, Grant and Baptiste. The pandimensional entity knew from earlier encounters that dealing with them together was too much of a risk. The separation of the team, and casting the shadow of doubt into their minds, was calculated to undo whatever odds-defying equation the trio had assembled. His ploy at causing them to doubt, ever so slightly, his veracity, gave Thrush-Kane an added advantage.

The three people who had worked so closely together were suddenly no longer a cohesive unit. The emotional and spiritual core of the group, Kane, was the key to their effectiveness. Taking out their heart, suddenly the Three Musketeers template of Cerberus had been erased. By his introduction of doubt into their equation, Thrush-Kane had altered their dynamic. Now, no matter how capable they were, they had been effectively sundered from the unit that had been much more than the sum of its parts. The god-defying, world-beating trio no longer existed, shattered completely by a brazen act of impersonation.

The situation would not last long, especially if Grant managed to come across the real Kane back in the Appalachians, but that was why Thrush-Kane was hard at work, trying to penetrate the mainframe's command structure. There was simply one barrier between him and control of the system, and that was a single mathematical equation that befuddled the android mind resting within its polymer-reinforced skull.

All this was going on in a higher plane of thought and consciousness, and Thrush heard "Kane's" genuine love and concern for Domi and her team spoken aloud. He'd withdrawn just a little too much from his external disguise after his momentary faux pas, but that wasn't a problem. The normal conversational mode he'd established for Kane worked perfectly. He could see in Brigid Baptiste's face the torment of her doubts.

She was most likely asking herself if she was truly too paranoid, dismissing the potential that the man standing before her was the real deal. It was a cleverly played ruse, one designed to strike at the woman's intellectual core. Logic and hard facts were her strength, and right now, they all seemed to be in Thrush-Kane's favor. He'd verbally expressed doubts about his own reality, and inspired a long session of medical tests that were useless in the wake of the efforts the doppelganger had taken. A laser scalpel had duplicated every minor laceration that still remained as scar tissue on the original Kane's naked body, every imperfection. A needle filled with saline had created minor skin tags that had formed due to friction with clothing. A heating element built up calluses exactly where they had formed on Kane's hands and feet from hours of martial-arts training, hiking and marksmanship refreshment.

Thrush-Kane had gone over the original with far more than a fine-tooth comb, and utilized all manner of tools to create the exact likeness, down to the diameter of a hardened shell of shin on Kane's left toe, or the precise dimensions of his fingernails, trimmed to perfection by the laser scalpel, measured to the micron. Nothing physical had been left to chance, and mentally, Thrush-Kane's "concussion" allowed for any oddities and variations in behavior, even after hours of watching Kane with Grant and Brigid.

Observations of every subtle vocal inflection and facial tic Kane made as he spoke had been burned into the deep terrabyte memory core set side for duplicating his behavior. It would never be forgotten, and any energy force that could erase the plasma matrix brain cells would incinerate Thrush-Kane, or rend him asunder due to magnetic pressures that would turn the iron in a normal human's blood into an explosive, anyway.

A second and third memory core had been dedicated to wireless computer operations, and these two cores were working in coordination, yet independently. The two-pronged mental assault on the redoubt's defenses was intended to break through the antiviral defenses without setting off intrusion alarms. Through the development of diversions and feints, they were keeping the defensive programming busy, but not enough to send an alert to Bry or any of the computer technicians running the mainframe. As it was, there was still the problem of the encryption algorithm, which would make everything easier for Thrush-Kane.

There was one way that he could get to Morganstern, but it would involve making Brigid Baptiste much more paranoid about his motives.

Or would it? For all of his chiding, as Kane, wouldn't it be in the man's character to make amends and to just talk with Daryl in order to prove to Brigid that he was all right with their relationship, regardless of how intimate it was?

In doing that, Thrush-Kane would be able to find a way to speak with Morganstern in his office, or quarters, or wherever, and perhaps by getting a glimpse of the man's lifestyle, he'd find insight into the mathematical inspirations for the genius's concepts. Then, it would only take his plasma matrix a few million cycles and calculations to actually decode and decipher. Barring that, there was always the option of breaking the schmuck's neck after torturing the information out of him.

Thrush-Kane wondered where that thought came from, and he realized that those were Kane's actual emotions. If the real man wasn't jealous of Morganstern, then something had to have been wrong with him. Brigid Baptiste was a beautiful, vivacious, athletic woman. Though he was derived from an artificial being, the basic concept of carnal relations was still tied into the Thrush Continuum. Having her body against his, long, strong limbs embracing his hips and shoulders, the heat of her sex as she slid onto him—

Thrush-Kane blinked the continuation of that thought away. How much of that was from his observation? None of it, really. Kane had acted professionally, aloof even, toward Baptiste. There was a conspiratorial moment where they had made fun of Grant for some triviality, a bonding.

I want Baptiste, the android brain realized.

Here was a woman who actually was on an intellectual level with him, and he was wrapped in the flesh of a handsome, powerful figure who regularly had his pick of the most beautiful women in the solar system. Unbidden, an analogy bubbled to the surface. Kane had the tree of knowledge in his very own private garden, with the most delicious, nourishing and enlightening fruit in the whole universe, and yet he rooted around in distant orchards, looking for something nearly as tasty, but available only through increased risk and torment.

"Fucking idiot," he said aloud.

Brigid turned and looked at him. "Who is?"

"I am—" Thrush-Kane quickly covered for himself "—I'm an idiot because I'm not making an effort to be nice to someone you care about."

"Calling yourself an idiot is also insulting someone I care about, Kane," Brigid countered.

The android tilted his head, stricken by the curious turn of words. "A little self-deprecation never killed anyone, but Daryl looked as if he were going to pull his head into his own chest like some kind of human turtle."

Brigid raised one eyebrow. "So?"

"He's probably not with the game plan of how we are," Thrush-Kane said.

"And just how are we?"

Thrush-Kane paused, measuring his response. This was walking a razor's edge, and while he had gigabytes of data on hand, nearly all of it was useless in terms of emotional context. "We're us."

Thrush-Kane reached out a hand for her. Brigid haltingly took it, and he gave her a gentle squeeze. "I'm pretty much a brute. You're a genius. And while we complement each other, we care about each other, we would die for each other, we've had years together to make some kind of move toward intimacy. And we haven't. Why?"

Brigid shrugged. "Because for you, it'd be the end of your line. You wouldn't be able to enjoy a girl in every port."

"Or, you're right about us being soul friends. Partners and equals," Thrush-Kane continued. "And when we've got that going for us, putting sexual intimacy into that equation just ends up diminishing one or the other of us. And it alters things dramatically in Grant's and my relationship."

Brigid rolled her eyes. "Grant's been with Shizuka for how many years?"

"Yeah, but Grant and I have never had sex," Thrush-Kane replied. "And neither have we."

"So where is this all going?" Brigid asked.

"I'd like to make amends for my crudeness toward Daryl earlier," he explained.

Brigid frowned. "Like how?"

Thrush-Kane shrugged. "I'll give him the little speech. Yes, I love you, but like a brother. And as your big brother, if he hurts you, I'll beat him silly. Outside of him messing with your heart, I'm fine. We're family, like Domi keeps saying."

Brigid bit her upper lip, and for a moment, Thrush-Kane wondered if he'd overplayed his hand.

"Bonus to this, while I'm chatting with Daryl, you'll be free to help Lakesh and Bry support Grant and Domi in the field," he added. "I know that you're just keeping me out of trouble, whether I'd been brainwashed, or just knocked goofy with head trauma, or replaced. What kind of harm could I do just talking to a theoretical mathematician?"

Brigid's eyes were alight with thousands of thoughts. Thrush-Kane knew that her perfect memory would spot one glaring reason why talking to Daryl Morganstern would be problematic, and he picked up just when she remembered that the mathematician had programmed the algorithm for the supplemental encryption defenses for Cerberus. While that would have been common knowledge for her, as well as the real Kane, would a doppelganger know that? It was an offhand piece of information that otherwise would be buried in terms of telepathic probes, and an evil Kane from another universe would, if he was some kind of lover for another world's Brigid Baptiste, simply have killed anyone looking to mate with his flame-haired goddess. Right here and now, Baptiste had no knowledge of the wireless modem that allowed Thrush-Kane to penetrate the mainframe's defenses, nor the powerful semiorganic computer that nestled in his reinforced skull.

After all, those medical tests had recognized him as truly human.

"Hurt Daryl, and there will be no place in the universe safe for you, got that?" Brigid asked.

It was a harsh threat, but said in a mocking manner. The plasma matrix ran calculations on her mood in an effort to determine how serious she was, and how much she was trying to undercut her potential rage with an injection of humor into her tone.

Thrush-Kane lifted his hands in mock surrender. "I'm just going to talk. I don't even have my weapons with me."

"That wouldn't stop you," Brigid said. "You were bare-handed fighting a Fomorian to the death."

The odds that Brigid was deathly serious rose considerably. Thrush-Kane put on his best hurt expression in hopes of disarming her suspicions.

"I'm not going to ever hurt you," he told her. "And

if that means protecting Daryl, then I will literally take a bullet for the guy. What kind of a monster do you think I am?"

Brigid's features flickered between several emotions. The chess-game turmoil of doubt running through her mind had been upset, the table jarred, shifting all of the pieces. The infiltrator's cold strategy left her reeling over a myriad of possibilities as to who he truly was, and what his true intentions were. In the end, however, this was a wild gamble. Women were wild, unpredictable forces, no matter how logical their intellect held them. Emotions and perceptions would seem to be clear-cut and cast in stone for a male point of view, and Thrush-Kane realized that he was indeed truly masculine, given his reaction to the woman's subdued sexuality. For a female mind, however, things could be seen in whole new levels. They saw everything in layers of subtext and hidden meaning, which meant that right now, the multifaceted game Thrush-Kane played with his impersonation had to be perfect, or else everything was lost.

One error, and the secret of his existence as only a construct would be peeled away, exposing him as a monster who probably murdered the real Kane with an avalanche.

All of this cycled through the plasma matrix supercomputer between his ears, taking less than a second. The two-heartbeat pause before Brigid spoke again felt like an agonizing eternity, and Thrush-Kane felt as if he was dangling naked over a pit of hungry, carnivorous mouths.

"I'm sorry," Brigid finally said. She gave him a slap on the shoulder. "It's your own damn fault for making us think you could have been replaced or brainwashed or whatever Thrush wanted to do."

"Yeah," Thrush-Kane answered. "I put my foot in my mouth. But, hey, when is that news?"

Brigid smirked. "Be nice. Okay?"

Thrush-Kane put his hand over his heart. "I promise, *anam-chara.*"

"Don't be making fun of me," Brigid said, pointing at him.

"Listen, Grant and the others are going to be leaving in ten minutes or so," Kane grumbled. "You can help them a lot more than watching over me talking to a math dude in the mess hall."

Brigid looked around, as if seeking some form of support, then nodded.

One step closer, Thrush-Kane thought as she left for the command center.

Chapter 8

The Appalachians, minutes before the avalanche

Certain anatomical facts become intrinsically apparent to a person who is one of the premier adventurers in a postapocalyptic world.

Even before he opened his eyes, Kane was familiar with the effects of having been knocked out, and the unique sensation of being suspended by his ankles, upside down. The Cerberus explorer had become inured enough to no longer vomit every time he regained consciousness, though he had been struck by the frustrating queasiness that assailed his stomach. His inverted state contributed to the vertigo-induced sickness, and there was no avoiding it. Kane craned his neck and allowed the muscular spasms to empty the contents of his gut.

The purging hadn't made him feel any better, and very little would allow him to penetrate the fog of memory that interfered with his recollection of the events that had brought him to this sorry, captive condition. On top of that, acidic bile overwhelmed his taste buds, though he had the will and self-control to repeat his initial eruption. He blinked and tried to clear his vision, but it was dim in the forest, and whatever had rendered him unconscious colluded with his upside-down state to keep his vision blurry, at least for now. Kane was able to make out his feet above him, but not the kind of bindings that suspended him nearly four feet off the forest floor.

Kane felt a cool breeze and realized that he had been stripped to the waist. Whoever had partially disrobed him had at least given him the courtesy of a tucked-in shirt, a ragged tank top, and he could tell that he had his cargo pants on. The shirt had to have been tucked in; otherwise it would have hung down over his face. He tested his dangling arms, and they were not only restrained by a slender leather thong, but they were also sluggish and unresponsive. Straining his eyes, he saw that he had long scratches down both forearms. They weren't deep, but they trickled blood.

In a flash of memory he remembered seeing bear tracks when they first appeared at the parallax point. The sight of the tracks had spurred a conversation with Brigid Baptiste, whose eidetic memory had produced a fact that several of the ten largest black bears shot in America had been hunted down in Pennsylvania in the nineteenth and twentieth centuries.

Kane grimaced. That memory wasn't lost. The only thing fuzzy was the moment immediately preceding his lapse into unconsciousness. In all likelihood, Kane wouldn't know who had taken him down because he had been actively attempting to avoid a stalker in the woods. The hunter had caught up and taken him down. The cuts on his forearms weren't defensive injuries; they were precise and deliberate, meant to put the scent of blood into the air. Through the tingling numbness of his limbs, he could tell that he hadn't been in a fight. No sensations of tender, bruised flesh or lacerations from deflecting weapons or lashing claws. His blood chilled at the idea that someone had most likely caught him unaware enough to put him in a sleeper hold. The headache currently rampaging through his brainpan wasn't from a sudden trauma akin to a blow to the skull.

He stifled the urge to curse himself for listening to the water witch when they had rendezvoused with the Pennsylvanian mountain folk. It was difficult to tell how old Granny Epona was, even to Kane's trained eye, but living in the rough, but relatively pristine stretch of Appalachian Mountains known as the Poconos had left her with the physique of a woman in her twenties, if a little weathered. Epona was unlike other self-appointed crones by being relatively young for such a task. Her skin was windburned and deeply tanned from her decades of wilderness life, and her eyes were a shockingly bright green that burrowed into Kane as if seeking the depths of his soul from beneath a curtain of silken black bangs.

Kane grimaced as he fought to sort out his jumbled memories. Granny Epona had peered into the depths of his reincarnated spirit on the first meeting months before when the explorers were seeking out allies in the mountain range. The Appalachians in Pennsylvania had rebuffed the initial offer of allegiance with Cerberus, seeing their independence threatened by such outside contact. The mountain folk said that they had their own internal problems, which could only become complicated with the addition of Kane and his allies' war with the beings seeking to control all of humanity.

Months later, however, the mountain folk had made use of the communication equipment left behind on the off chance that they would change their mind. The electronic summons to meet had been accompanied by dread news, the results that the Cerberus rebels had feared when they first came. Someone or something had been improving the ability of the cannibals to conduct their raids against the mountain folk's settlements.

Granny Epona and her cadre led the three explorers to one settlement that had been attacked by the cannibals. There was evidence of rocket-propelled grenades as well as automatic rifles, more than matching the centuries-old weapons production of the Appalachians.

"This kind of brute force is what we did not want to deal with," Granny Epona had said. "You told us of the Annunaki and their ilk, but we wanted to avoid their notice."

Kane remembered picking up wreckage of a rocket shell, turning it over and sighing in disgust. "It may not be Enlil. There are other factions at work in what used to be America."

"Yes, you had mentioned the Millennial Consortium," Granny Epona said. "But the cannibals would see mere men as food, not benefactor. This is why I am erring on the side of accusing the aliens."

Kane threw the shard of rocket to the dirt. "That crossed my mind, as well."

"You have a destiny, Kane," Granny Epona said. "I see it draped over your spirit like a cloak. Perhaps it was inevitable that we would need your aid against the beasts who threaten us."

Kane had quirked an eyebrow at that statement. "Destiny. In other words, I don't have a choice. I don't enjoy having things ordained about my future."

"When you are such a nexus individual as yourself, such things are common, Kane," Granny Epona replied.

"Just what kind of people are these cannibals?" Kane asked.

"Some say they are the Fomorians, the children of Balor of the Baleful Eye. Indeed, one prides himself on his cyclopean visage," Epona explained. "He calls himself the new Balor. They have long sought out the descendants of their enemies."

"Those who still follow the old ways, even across the great ocean," Kane said, gesturing toward the east and the Atlantic. "When did they first appear?"

"A hundred years back," Granny Epona replied. "And they've been relentless, if somewhat simple."

"That's a long time," Kane said.

Granny Epona smiled. "You are a chosen hero. But you are also destined to have a long and storied life ahead of you, Kane. Fear not."

"Long life ahead," Kane grumbled. He tried to flex his body again. Aches racked his lean, muscular frame and he cursed his weakness. If only he could reach the bindings around his thighs and shins, he could wriggle out of his restraints before whoever had hung him up like a side of beef came back with carving utensils. He tried to bend at the waist, but sore abdominal muscles failed him for now. His skull throbbed as if it had its own pulse that pushed acid through nerve centers.

"You have a destiny this day," Granny Epona had explained to the three explorers. "It is to seek out the man-monsters infesting our land. If he is successful, then my people will speak more openly to the outlanders from your caverns."

Kane had been tempted to tell the old broad to stuff the offer sideways up her craw when Brigid reminded him of the fertile expanse of hiding spots along the great Appalachian mountain ranges. Considering the Tuatha blood that was strong within the water witches, the mountain folk would be an invaluable asset in locating the scattered overlords should any of them choose the coast-spanning valley as a hiding spot.

"Just me?" Kane had asked Granny Epona.

"Indeed. We are not expecting you to win a war on

your own. But if you can survive a trek into their lands, then you have proved that you are a worthy ally."

Kane couldn't resist the logic. The mountain folk had been pressed hard of late. Somehow, the mutant man-eaters had gotten hold of improved technology, specifically in the form of communications.

It had been so easy looking back to see that Kane had been led into a trap. He swore that if he had seen Granny Epona again, he'd put his fist through her tanned face. The flash of anger preceded a splitting headache that left his eyesight blurry once again.

His vision cleared further and he saw, in the shadows, a pair of legs.

"Looks as if you've gone and made a mess," a mocking, metallically hollow voice spoke.

Though the inflection behind the robotic speech was new, Kane recognized the mechanical rumble itself.

"Thrush?" Kane asked, croaking. His throat was still raw from vomiting. "I thought we'd seen the last of you when little Sam grew up and became Enlil."

"Wishful thinking on your part, Kane," the figure standing before him said. The feet moved, and Kane tried to focus on Thrush's face. Instead, his vision swam, nausea welling in his stomach.

Kane ground his back teeth in concern. Kane and his fellow outlanders had encountered Thrush in his various incarnations on multiple occasions. Chronologically, their first encounter with him came January 20, 2001, when Thrush, posing as a member of the KGB, ignited the nuclear bomb that sparked the megacull nuclear war that drove humanity to the brink of extinction. The cybernetic being had no concern for the destruction of one body, as it had been evidenced that it was a pantemporal, pandimensional being. If anything, there was a continuum of Thrushes, hundreds of whom had been based on a reality-spanning Orb craft that had served as a central base. The "leader" of this horde of dimensional travelers had been swallowed by a singularity, an event that had presumably left the rest of the continuum without an individual motivator. Kane and the rest of the Cerberus rebels felt that they could rest easier with one less enemy to hound them as they sought to retake the Earth for humanity.

Unfortunately, Erica van Sloan had been restored to youth and vitality and impregnated by unknown means. She'd soon given birth to a being who would become the new imperator of the baronies, Sam. Eventually Kane and his allies had learned that Sam was the embodiment of Thrush's intellect. When the time came where the fragile, alien-like barons transformed into the overlords, Sam had evolved into Enlil, the original leader of the Dragon Kings on Earth. Only the greed of the Annunaki's dark goddess Lilitu had shattered the unified threat of the secret masters of the world and removed their powerful, living starship *Tiamat* from the equation of battle between Enlil's forces and the Cerberus warriors. While Enlil and the other overlords had withdrawn in recent months, their absence from the battlefield could not be considered permanent.

And now, here was a being identifying itself as Thrush once more.

Kane winced as another wave of nausea rocked him. "You're from another casement?"

That elicited a chuckle. "I am part of an infinite consciousness, Kane. It is more likely that I will see your end than you would see mine."

"Especially since mine is hanging in the air," Kane grumbled. He spit in a futile effort to clear his mouth of the sharp, bitter tang of bile.

"You look a little uncomfortable there, Kane," the metallic drone noted with a hint of glee.

A bubble of sour gas burped up into Kane's mouth. He winced at the empty heave's foul trespass. "I'd offer to put you in a sleeper hold then dangle you upside down, but I don't think you have a stomach to upset."

"Not all of us are composed of simple polymers, hydraulics and circuits, Kane," the thing said. "If you prick me, I will bleed."

Kane couldn't shake the feeling of familiarity in the enemy's voice. He just couldn't put his finger on it. "Great. A prick who bleeds. Would you like to demonstrate?"

"Oh, I wish, Kane. I would love nothing more, but you see, I'm not here to kill you. I don't even want to hurt you seriously, because my real contention is with the errant young Sam."

"He likes to call himself Enlil now," Kane corrected.

A metallic sigh hissed. "A rose by any other name still needs to be cut if it's the wrong color."

Kane struggled to focus his eyes, but a shove of a warm, human-feeling hand, left him swinging. "You want Enlil, so you do what…lure us out here to hang us up like beef?"

"The enemy of my enemy is…"

"Could you fucking stuff the stupid clichés and maybe keep me from swinging? Because I swear, I will aim for your boots the next time I spew," Kane growled.

"Sorry." Powerful fingers hooked Kane's belt, and his swaying halted. Thrush was too close for Kane to see anything but a powerfully muscled chest layered in the dark, synthetic fabric of a shadow suit.

"Oh, no," Kane groaned.

"What's wrong?" the familiar-sounding voice asked. "Oh, you're finally becoming aware of the situation."

"Let me see your damn face!" Kane growled.

"Touchy, touchy," Thrush-Kane replied. He stepped back, and finally, Kane's vision was clear enough for him to see that the metallic-toned voice had come from his own face. Hard, predator-sharp gray-blue eyes glinted to match the cruel smile on the doppelganger Kane's lips. It was identical to him, right down to the amount of scruffy beard growth on his jaw and the faint scar on his cheek.

Build-wise, it wasn't hard to imagine that the Thrush Continuum could easily replicate Kane's height and build. Kane had seen enough of both robotics and cloning to realize that his double was a hybrid of both technologies. It was also no wonder the voice sounded familiar, but so hard to place. Through the filter of Kane's own head, he only really had a chance to hear what he sounded like when listening to recordings of himself. The resonance of his eardrums and his skull had been enough of a filter to make instant recognition impossible.

"They're not going to fall for you if you sound like you're talking through a tin can," Kane snarled.

"That was just a show for your sake, Kane," the doppelganger replied, the metallic nature of his voice fading until he sounded perfectly human. "I wanted you to figure things out first."

"All right, then. Pin a medal on me, or put a bullet in my head," Kane snarled.

The duplicate shrugged. "Why would I want to do that? I'm just delaying you."

"For what?" Kane asked.

"Well, if I'm not able to use the resources of Cerberus to strike a fatal blow against Enlil, then I'll certainly need you around to avenge your slaughtered friends," the doppelganger said.

"I'll come for you first, Thrush," Kane growled.

"Somehow, I doubt that," Thrush-Kane replied. "After all, you wouldn't know how to program the mat-trans or the interphaser to reach the rest of me. Not unless you somehow beat the answer out of Enlil's relatives or our errant brother yourself."

Kane grimaced. "Either way, to get to your freakish robot brothers, I have to do the job you want."

Kane knew that he didn't have the cruelty in himself to duplicate his doppelganger's evil grin of glee. "By all means, now that you know how to come after us…"

Kane drew all the strength in his right arm and lashed out, swinging at the creature before him. Thrush-Kane simply stepped back out of the path of the punch.

"Now, if you don't mind, I really would be remiss if I didn't get to work hunting down that alligator-hided version of myself," Thrush-Kane said. He turned and released a wolf howl that cut through the forest.

Hollow, haunted cries echoed back.

"I'd say you have five minutes to get down off that tree before my cannibal friends show up," Thrush-Kane said. "If not, we might have to skip plan B to put Enlil out of our misery."

The doppelganger disappeared into the woods and Kane twisted, clawing at the bindings around his thighs and shins.

The wolf calls of the Appalachian cannibals resounded, drawing closer as Kane's fingers tore frantically at the ropes restraining him. He kept clawing, even as he heard the unmistakable whistle of a thrown hatchet slicing the air behind him.

Then gravity seized the lone Cerberus explorer, and he crashed to the forest floor, dazed but free. He scanned around for a weapon, anything that would give him an advantage against the deadly monstrosities stalking the valley.

Something crashed into his forehead, the impact threatening to send Kane tumbling into an endless descent into oblivion.

Chapter 9

It had been vital that Thrush-Kane capture the Cerberus explorer he was designed to duplicate. Though his skeletal structure and genetic makeup were absolutely identical to Kane's, thanks to the ex-Mag's prior encounters with other iterations of the transdimensional hive mind that had assembled a large contingent on the pancasement Orb, there would be certain factors that could not be duplicated without face-to-face contact.

The cloned muscle, skin and hair that wrapped around the flat-motor enhanced polymer skeleton would only take a simulation of the human so far, the cyborg realized. His brain, a semiorganic plasma matrix with superior processing ability, could only fake so much without actual conversation and in-depth observation. The programmed speech patterns developed from recordings of Kane's voice, taken from multiple sources, had held up to actual dialog with the captured human. The time span between the recordings and the current moment had allowed for some variation, but the plasma matrix brain adapted to the new patterns.

More importantly, Thrush-Kane was glad for the

chance to look into every detail of his counterpart's face. There were a few new bruises, not quite healed, that could be mimicked with pigment injectors provided for perfect duplication. A set of scissors had been the most vital, yet simplest implement of the disguise kit. The Thrush Continuum would not normally have taken such extreme measures for a simple subterfuge on such a backwater, technologically deficient world, but for the presence of one of Kane's most trusted allies, Brigid Baptiste. Her eidetic memory and highly acute senses would pick up the slightest of visual imperfections, rendering the doppelganger ruse a wasted, worthless effort.

Thrush-Kane would have to be acutely wary around Brigid. One mistake, one stray from established identity had the potential of turning an infiltration and rediversion mission into a bloody battle that he did not want to engage in. Brigid was not the only wild-card factor that Thrush-Kane had to worry about. There were the others of the Cerberus redoubt, including the brilliant Mohandas Lakesh Singh, and the ever-present and very capable Grant, the former Magistrate, mentor, friend and partner to Kane. Lakesh's razor-sharp intellect presented as much a challenge as Brigid's incredible analytical abilities and perfect memory, and the undeniable emotional and spiritual bond between Kane and Grant would provide unknown obstacles to overcome.

The level of familiarity of Kane's allies to the man that the cyborg was impersonating made his chances of success far slimmer, which meant that Thrush-Kane's ploy required far more than identical appearance. Though the ferrous content of his body was trimmed to the bare amount available in a normal human's makeup, his plasma matrix brain had sufficient wireless technology and image projection to render a very convincing addition to his ruse, He could project two distinct images in two types of medical examination machines. First was an X-ray machine override that would allow a highly convincing image of Kane's fractured skull. The second was an override that could allow interpretation by a magnetic resonance imaging device to view his brain as slightly traumatized, but not seriously injured. Enough injury to explain a variance in behavior, but not so much that Thrush-Kane would be under constant examination and confinement to a sick bed.

Thrush-Kane closed with the Fomorians, and the bestial men looked at him. He smelled the same to them, so they didn't immediately reach for the weapons he'd supplied them.

Calling them bestial was an understatement. Due to the ancient genetics that their leader had awakened within them, they were powerfully built, with rangy, apelike arms fully as long as their legs. Thick brows melted from sloped foreheads, only extending so far as necessary to protect the one or two eyes that they possessed. Some were truly cyclopean, with a centrally placed orb, while others had one side of their face seemingly fused over.

Those with two working eyes were hampered either

by one hand fused into a gnarled protuberance that could only be used as a club, or were missing an arm altogether. The one-armed Fomorians' loss of symmetry was made up for by a far thicker remaining limb, just as those with only one eye were gifted with a larger, engorged version of the optic organ.

Their skin was thick and leathery, though only good enough to protect against blunt trauma and lacerations caused by the smaller nails and teeth of less ferocious mountain predators. Against bears, modern blades or the primitive firearms of the Appalachian mountain folk, they were still mortal and vulnerable.

Only one among the Fomorians bore a resemblance to a normal human, and where the others were malformed and terrifying, Bres was tall, graceful and nearly angelic. Thrush-Kane knew this was due to the blend of genetic structures within his being. Bres the Beautiful either took his name from his mythological forebear, or was indeed the ancient Tuatha and Annunaki hybrid being reincarnated or kept young and vital by unknown means. Thrush was aware that Enlil had at least one daughter, a living goddess named Fand who at times assisted Kane and his fellow outlanders. Thrush-Kane wasn't certain of the mechanics of her existence, and refused to speculate, as he did with Bres.

The golden-haired, muscular Bres smiled broadly as Thrush-Kane approached.

"You have captured him?" Bres asked.

Thrush-Kane nodded, glancing over toward the

woman held within a primitive cage. "You've left their witch alive?"

Bres chuckled, following the cyborg's line of sight. "She's of the true blood, meaning that she will be as useful to my followers as the rifles you've brought us."

"To the Fomorians, or to you directly?" Thrush-Kane inquired.

"You're thinking that I would mix my perfect DNA with her diluted blood, creating something a little more powerful than my beloved warriors?" Bres countered.

"More powerful, or more capable of blending in with your prey," Thrush-Kane stated.

Bres's smile was bright and gleaming, though the malice behind his nearly golden eyes didn't match the warmth of the expression. "You have your task, false man. I have my future to forge here."

"Fair enough," Thrush-Kane said. "You need do only one more thing, and my business with you is complete."

Bres held out his hand, and one of his Fomorian warriors handed over a rifle to the master raider. Bres reversed the weapon and struck Thrush-Kane in the forehead hard. The ceramic-and-crystal reinforcement of the cyborg's skeletal structure was sorely tested by the powerful blow, backed up by the three-hundred-pound frame of the tall god among beasts. The impact hurled Thrush-Kane to the dirt as even his reinforced musculature and bones weren't enough to withstand the incredible strength of the golden-haired hybrid.

"Was that sufficient?" Bres asked.

Thrush-Kane reached up to the split flesh of his forehead, and his fingers came away, wet and slick with blood. He blinked in surprise, more than actual pain, as his plasma matrix brain had shut off pain sensations. The semiorganic mass under the nearly unbreakable skull ran through a rapid self-diagnostic check, and the infiltrator managed a sigh of genuine relief as he was still in perfect operating condition.

"More than enough," the cyborg informed Bres. "I'll take my leave."

"Haven't you forgotten something?" Bres asked.

Thrush-Kane's plasma matrix mind raced for a moment, then he regarded the weapon on his wrist. "Thank you."

"The weakest of my Fomorians must be tested to earn their place at our table," Bres said. "Their deaths will provide you with evidence of the battle that produced the head laceration."

Thrush-Kane regarded Bres's minions. Four of them stepped forward, armed with sample assault rifles that had been the impetus for the Appalachians to summon the Cerberus warriors to this mountain range. The four Fomorians were powerful-looking creatures. Two could wield an automatic rifle as if it was a pistol, a necessity formed by their off-limb being nothing more than a boney club. Those with both hands were one-eyed monstrosities, whose wide, visorlike single eyes twitched oddly, but could focus on the sights of their weapon with remarkable clarity.

Bres the Beautiful had awakened ancient blood within the Fomorians, but certain laws of thermodynamics had to be respected. The beings sacrificed limbs or eyes in order to gain superhuman physical strength. The ones who possessed cyclopean eyes had originally been unusually large and powerful humans, so when their bodies compressed, they retained all four of their limbs but their facial structures changed as the mark of their newfound identity. Those who had been normal sized lost the symmetry of their arms and a measure of mass from their off leg. This freed up muscle tissue and bone to bulk up the Fomorians to match the general size of their fellow mutants.

Thrush-Kane had also observed that the mutants were able to don and doff their enhanced appearance, though the effort was undoubtedly painful to go through as muscle and bone twisted and realigned. Bres could ease the agony of the change with a touch, and Bres had intimated that Balor, whom Thrush-Kane had never personally encountered, could do the same. Thrush-Kane wondered why such mercurial transformations were required, but he never asked. It had, however, made it useful to transform one of his followers into a duplicate of the water witch Granny Epona. Bres crafted a fused-skinned mutant into an attractive woman of indeterminate age, which indicated to Thrush-Kane that the Fomorians already had their own cache of incredible technology, but it was wielded only by a select few.

It became clear to the infiltrator that the matter of

man-eating among the Fomorians was not so much a form of cannibalism, but rather a means by which the monstrosities increased their size and power. They killed prey, and Bres transferred biomass from the corpse to the hunters. It was why the victims of the raiders had never been discovered. The cyborg, realizing that his skeleton was nonbiological, knew why he was not considered viable prey. His vat-grown flesh might contribute to their bodies, but his bones were wrought from plastic, nonferrous metals and other materials that could not be altered by whichever cellular manipulation Bres controlled.

"Weakest?" Thrush-Kane asked, not disguising the irony in his voice.

"They have failed the most often," Bres said. "They are hungry and eager, however, to prove themselves in combat with you. Do not take anything for granted in combat with them."

"How much of a head start do I have?" Thrush-Kane inquired.

"It is I who will be leaving," Bres informed him. "Then my warriors will count until fifty, and then proceed to remove as much flesh from your body as possible."

"And what if I don't care to wait?"

"Then you'll get at least one free kill with the element of surprise," Bres commented. "And you'll have three furious man-beasts attacking you with all of their might."

"Joy," Thrush-Kane said, approximating his human counterpart's sarcasm.

"Good luck," Bres said, striding off with the remainder of his cadre, back to the caves where Thrush-Kane had first encountered the godling and his monstrous progeny. "You'll need it."

Thrush-Kane looked at the quartet of man-beasts who were left behind to provide him with his alibi. They glared at him hungrily, but not with their usual lust for human flesh. His vat-grown skin and muscle didn't smell right; he wasn't an appetizing morsel to them.

How he enticed them was in the form of a human challenge. Clad in a shadow suit and armed with the powerful Magistrate side arm that he'd taken from the true Kane, the cybernetic doppelganger was a magnificent conquest. The Fomorians lived for conflict, and the more capable the opponent, the more glorious the victory.

Bres had not set up the creatures to fail. They had been promised the highest of honors among their tribe should they kill him, and given the brief time Thrush-Kane had observed these beings, he knew that they could damage even his artificial, high-tensile skeleton with their formidable strength.

It was a logical progression of events. Bres and Balor no longer required the gifts of Thrush-Kane, and thus they had no need to keep him alive and healthy. They had a baptism of fire with which to certify the worth of their disgraced allies, and if the

Fomorian warriors failed, then they were culled from the herd. If they succeeded, the Fomorians didn't burn any bridges with the transdimensional hive-mind entity.

Thrush-Kane looked over the quartet of creatures who chanted their count to fifty in low tones. They had gotten to nine, and the cyborg doppelganger whirled and raced up the slope.

A low chuckle escaped the throat of one of the Fomorians, the tempo of the count increasing.

The hunt was on, and Thrush-Kane was the prime target.

KANE ROLLED with the impact that split open his forehead, instinct taking over where conscious thought would have only slowed him. With an agility born of a lifetime of conflict, he tumbled down the slope, letting gravity haul him away from the menace that tried to rip his skull from his shoulders. Through the splash of blood that had gotten into his eyes, the Cerberus explorer realized that his attacker was a wounded black bear, a hatchet embedded in its shoulder.

Whoever had hunted the creature had done Kane a favor, because if the bear had retained the full strength of that limb, the swipe of its claws would have been too fast to dodge and too strong to resist. Still, the bear bellowed in rage, spinning. Kane rolled to a halt, digging in his heels in order to regain his footing. Rising into a three-point stance, his right arm free to deploy his Sin Eater, Kane cursed himself for forgetting that he had been disarmed by the half-human impostor.

A pair of slender-limbed hunters burst into the open, each of them wielding throwing hatchets and howling with joy. Upon seeing them, Kane could feel a moment of déjà vu. Somewhere deep within the corridors of time, memories bubbled to the surface of the same kind of creatures. Kane saw himself clad in furs and wearing blue paint upon his face, wielding a sword fully seven feet in length and engaging in mortal combat with such foes. The name for them shot to the front of his mind.

"Fomorians," Kane grumbled. He fought back the images of a besieged army of humans fending off the monstrous raiders, his massive claymore biting into their flesh, dealing out wounds that would have slain mortal men. Back then, it had taken an armed and armored ancestor with his army to deal with the creatures.

Now, all Kane had on his side was an angered, furious black bear and the hand axes that the Fomorian hunters had hurled.

"Meat for the fire!" one of the hunters cackled.

"Flesh for the limbs!" another sang in counterpoint.

The creatures were deceptively slender and single-eyed, obscenely distorted orbs planted haphazardly on their twisted faces. Judging by the height of the branch that he had been strapped to, Kane could tell that the two huntsmen were well over six feet tall. The black bear snarled in defiance against the cruel duo, its paw full of hooklike, razor-sharp claws slashing and gleaming as the Fomorians danced out of its reach.

"Who takes which, brother?" one asked, ducking away from the snapping jaws of the bear.

"Continue with your playmate," the other answered. "I'll deal with the human."

The first laughed hideously and lunged in, driving a clublike fist under the jaw of the bear, rocking it off balance. Kane was impressed by the power of the punch, as he estimated the black bear to be around six hundred pounds, in line with the largest member of that particular species. He remembered Brigid Baptiste informing him that this particular section of the Poconos holding several records for the largest bears hunted and killed in the twentieth century. The kind of strength to stun one with a single punch meant that the slender-limbed cyclopeans wouldn't need a hatchet to rip Kane limb from limb.

On the other hand, Kane had battled against menaces that possessed unearthly might before. He had gone hand-to-hand with Enlil himself, the seven-foot godlike king of the Annunaki. What Kane lacked in sheer physical might, he made up for with combat skill. Unarmed or not, there was no way that the lone Cerberus explorer was going to allow himself to surrender without a fight. With a howl of rage echoing the agony of the irate bear, Kane lowered his head and charged the Fomorian who had broken off to deal with him. Legs springing straight, Kane launched himself like a missile and speared the hunter in the belly. The impact drove the wind from the monstrosity's lungs, but it felt as if he had tackled an oak tree.

Their bodies crashed into the slope, and loose dirt and fallen pine needles served as a slippery surface. Kane and his opponent tumbled down the mountainside. The Fomorian tried to recover himself as he skidded on the ground, but Kane hammered his fists hard into his opponent's kidneys. Each punch felt as if Kane was striking a padded wall, jolts of pain shooting up his forearms, but the Fomorian grunted every time Kane connected. Whatever damage he was doing, it was enough to keep the creature distracted. The wild slide ended with a crash as the hunter slammed headfirst into a pine tree.

The sudden deceleration tossed Kane off the one-eyed monstrosity, but his limber limbs, quick reflexes and remarkable agility allowed him to somersault to cushion his landing. He got to his feet, seeing the Fomorian stagger slowly to his knees.

Kane couldn't let the hunter get to his full height. He scrambled up the slope and launched himself feetfirst at it. The flying drop kick caught the Fomorian dead on in the jaw and upper chest, all 180 pounds of Kane's lean weight giving his strike enough force to flatten the mutant. A deceptively strong hand clawed up, grabbing Kane by his belt. It took everything he had to maintain his footing as the Fomorian tried to wrestle him to the ground. Had the monster not been so incredibly strong, Kane could have lifted a foot to drive a crushing kick into his windpipe, but as it was, he needed to hang on for dear life, bracing against the Fomorian's grasp.

"You'll be a worthy addition to us," the Fomorian snarled.

Kane grimaced and twisted at the waist, driving his attacker's elbow into his knee. "Sorry. I'm not on the menu tonight."

The pivot should have dislocated his adversary's elbow, but all it did was rip Kane's pants and shirt, iron clawlike fingers shredding the fabric and freeing Kane from his grasp. It wasn't Kane's intended result, but he was now free, and he whipped his heel hard into the hunter's face. He'd been aiming for the windpipe, but the Fomorian was too quick. Rather than a raspy gurgle of strangulation from a collapsed trachea, Kane heard the sickening squelch of the Fomorian's giant eyeball bursting under the heel of his boot. The loss of the singe eye was accompanied by a desperate wail that keened through the trees, a high pitch that stabbed like an ice pick into Kane's brain.

"You bastard!" the Fomorian spit. "You fucking bastard!"

Kane stepped away from his blinded foe. With one hand clamped over the gory remnants in its socket, the Fomorian crawled to his knees, swinging his remaining limb around. Kane knew that he needed a weapon to deal with the blinded cyclops's brother, and that meant he had to take the Fomorian's remaining hatchet. Of course, even blind, the hunter had too much strength to simply knock out and disarm. Kane lunged, snaking one arm under the Fomorian's chin, the fingers of his other hand sinking into the monstrosity's scalp.

The Fomorian released his bloody eye socket, gore-stained fingers reaching for Kane as he tightened the headlock. The hunter was unable to gain a solid grasp on the Cerberus warrior, but the Fomorian's other hand locked around Kane's forearm. It was now or never, he thought, and he jammed both of his knees between the blinded creature's shoulder blades. Before the Fomorian could pry Kane's forearm from his throat, Kane threw all of his might into a savage twist. Tendons popped like gunshots, but Kane didn't relax the pressure on the hunter's neck. Now that the sinews of the creature's neck had burst, it was the turn of neck bone to grind, crunch and finally shift violently. Vertebrae scissored against each other, slicing through the Fomorian's spinal cord like a guillotine blade.

The six-and-a-half-foot corpse sagged in Kane's arms, and he released it. He was out of breath and feeling spent, and there was still another attacker up the slope, finishing its battle with the black bear, his knobby fists smeared dark crimson from beating a six-hundred-pound carnivore to death with his bare hands.

"Brother!" the Fomorian shrieked. "You killed him!"

Kane hurled himself at the corpse, drawing the hatchet from its belt.

At least now, Kane was no longer outnumbered and unarmed.

Not that it mattered to the screaming cyclops who flew down the slope, blood drenched fingers slicing the air like claws.

Chapter 10

Kane knew that the Fomorian pouncing upon him in a rage was over 250 pounds of predatory fury who had just beaten six hundred pounds of black bear to death. As worn down as he was from killing the other Fomorian, Kane knew that he couldn't rely on his reflexes to grant him the grace and speed to divert the path of the tackling beast. Standing up to take the hit would also be suicidal given the kind of strength and rage his enemy possessed. The only thing Kane could do was to fall flat on his back, six and a half feet of muscled monstrosity slicing through the air over his prone form. With a roll, Kane pushed himself to all fours, seeing the creature tumble out of control down the slope. Only his years of experience had been able to turn minutes of cool, collected analysis into a split second of decision on the cusp of a deadly attack.

Kane watched the Fomorian's out-of-control body skip down the mountainside, and he would have considered the situation comical if it hadn't been so deadly serious. The minute the Fomorian recovered his balance, he would come after Kane with blood in his eyes and murder in his heart. Kane had a hatchet, but his muscles were screaming for respite. While he wasn't helpless, he was still at a drastic disadvantage. Legs burning with the effort, he scrambled up to the bear, looking around in futile hope that he could locate any equipment that the first hunter might have dropped. A spear would be good, or any length of branch that would keep the Fomorian from closing to within grappling range. If those corded, muscular arms wrapped around Kane's torso, his spine and ribs would be crushed.

Gunfire crackled in the distance, and Kane paused momentarily.

Was it Grant and Brigid, defying the Appalachians' rules of engagement and coming to his rescue, or was it the false Kane, the thing sent by Thrush to infiltrate Cerberus? He cursed himself, realizing that each moment he wasted in battling the superhuman mutation on his heels was one step that Thrush's doppelganger closed with his friends back at the redoubt. And he knew full well why the cybernetic being was going to Cerberus—to locate and launch a deadly strike against Enlil. While Kane wouldn't mourn the loss of the lord of the Annunaki, he realized that such a conflict with the mad god and whatever resources he'd assembled would result in brutal losses on both sides. Thrush's lackey had no concern for Kane's partners, so any strategy formulated would be too brash, too vicious to entail anything other than grievous slaughter.

The attacking Fomorian popped up in Kane's peripheral vision, and with a savage twist, Kane hurled himself behind a tree trunk as a swinging fist sliced the air at him. The hunter was as swift as he was stealthy, and when the knobby knuckles of the man-beast struck the pine's trunk, Kane could hear the crack of wood. The tree groaned under its own weight, weakened by a blow that knocked the Fomorian's fingers out of alignment. The one-eyed mutation grimaced, clutching his pulverized fist.

Now, with a shred of advantage over the enemy, Kane launched himself, swinging the hand ax with all of his might. The wedge-shaped edge slashed down hard, aimed right at the bulbous, freakish orb in the center of the creature's face, but the Fomorian's wrist swung up. Steel bit into skin as tough as cured leather, then stopped as it struck the mutant's forearm bone. The creature let out a strangled gurgle of agony, wrenching his arm away from Kane. The hatchet's handle was ripped from Kane's grasp, but he wasn't going to waste energy fighting for control of the weapon. The broken-knuckled paw rose to seize Kane's tank top, but the Cerberus warrior pivoted, putting all of his weight into an elbow strike to the clawing mitt. Broken fingers released an ugly crunch as Kane connected, and reflexively, the Fomorian withdrew his hand, releasing a yowl of pain.

"Bastard!" the hunter snarled, swinging his arm, the ax still lodged in the bone, to smash the human that dared to defy him. Kane dropped to one knee and kicked his attacker's shin. The spear kick knocked the creature off balance, already dodgy thanks to the force of his swipe at Kane. The Fomorian toppled to the ground again, but this time, his momentum was lateral, not downhill. He wouldn't repeat the escapade of errors that had sent him sliding down the slope again.

Kane leaped, pouncing like a great cat, both hands latching around the ax handle jutting from the Fomorian's wrist. The leap and Kane's weight combined to pry loose the ax blade in the creature's bone. The Fomorian howled with pain. With one hand mangled and the other forearm sporting a savage laceration and a fractured ulnar bone, the Fomorian's single eye had gone red with rage. His maw opened, but instead of another cry of pain, a bellow of fury split the air. Rotted, malformed teeth formed raggedy, yellow picket fences in the Fomorian's mouth, and his breath stank of spoiled meat. The hunter lashed out with his mangled hand again, no longer conscious of any pain. Madness had taken control of the enemy man-beast, and Kane had only barely twisted out of the path of the falling blow. The impact sounded like a drum beat against the ground, and Kane knew that had he been a moment slower, his broken ribs would have speared through his chest muscles and he would be coughing up the gory remnants of his crushed lungs.

Kane chopped the ax toward the hunter's face, but the steel edge wasn't on target. Rather than pulverizing the Fomorian's face bones, the blade deflected off his cheek and merely carved off an ear, along with a ragged flap of flesh. The Fomorian reached for Kane's throat with his good hand, ignoring the banner of slashed flesh fluttering on the side of his skull. Long, powerful fingers clawed for Kane's windpipe, but he swung both of his legs into the mutant's chest and kicked out hard. The massive hunter seemed to resist being lifted off Kane for a moment, but the laws of physics and leverage were in Kane's favor. The Fomorian toppled backward as he was launched into the air, snarling in frustration at being thwarted yet again by his human prey.

"Damn you," the Fomorian spit, his livid eye locked on Kane. "Why won't you die?"

"Today's not good for me," Kane answered, crawling back to his feet, hefting his hatchet. "Can I pencil you in for next millennium?"

The Fomorian reached out, talonlike fingers wrapping around a rock the size of Kane's head. "No. It's now or never."

Kane braced himself as the monstrosity hefted the stone. He was going to have to rely on every ounce of his point man's instinct, the near supernatural edge of his razor-sharp perceptions. He'd need perfect timing to avoid the fifteen-pound missile that his opponent was preparing to throw. If he reacted too soon, he'd be off balance if the Fomorian changed his aim. An instant too late, and the rock would become a permanent part of his skull, evicting his brain with bone-shattering force. His eyes stung from where blood and sweat had dripped into them, but his bloodstream was so charged with adrenaline, he wasn't feeling that discomfort. His limbs felt wooden, however, genuine exhaustion threatening to overtake him once he survived this fight.

The Fomorian's chest and shoulder muscles flexed, alerting Kane that the throw was in process. The Cerberus warrior kept himself physically loose, not committing to any direction until he knew that the mutant hunter had committed himself to the attack. The one-eyed creature swung the stone around, putting all of his weight into the throw, and as Kane noted the shift of weight, he dived forward, slicing the air under the path of his opponent's toss. The rock flew like a bullet, its stony mass cracking against the thick trunk of a pine where Kane had been standing. In the meantime, Kane somersaulted, getting his feet beneath him again in order to launch his body at the Fomorian. He led the way with his hatchet, the wicked chopping edge catching his foe's abdominal muscles in a wicked, flesh-ripping swing.

At least it should have been a flesh-ripping swing. The dense muscle and skin of the beast did yield under the force of Kane's chop, but Fomorian flesh was not as elastic or pliant as human tissue. The hatchet stuck, and Kane felt as if he'd dislocated his shoulder with the sudden stop. A spray of blood gushed from the monstrosity's wound, dousing Kane's face and chest. It was a blinding splash of gore, and Kane backpedaled away from the Fomorian. Gangly fingers clawed at Kane, and only his keen reflexes saved him from his adversary getting a firm grasp on him. Nails dug into Kane's tank top and peeled the cloth off his body. The Fomorian snarled in frustration as he hurled away the rags.

The man-beast's other hand was now an insensate club, two fingers missing from when he had punched too hard into the earth trying to kill Kane. There was enough of a limb left, however, that it connected glancingly with Kane's head. Had Kane caught the forearm dead on, he was certain the impact would have shattered his neck, but this was a palm slap up the side of his head. Even the Fomorian's muscular wrist yielded, just enough flex to turn a fatal strike into a brain scrambling yet survivable punch. Kane let himself crash to the forest floor, further robbing the blow of its full power.

Going prone also gave Kane one advantage he'd work to end this fight immediately. He lashed out with both legs, scissoring the ankles of the Fomorian. With all his might, he twisted, driving the hapless mutant face-first into the ground and kept rolling until he'd bent the monstrosity's lower limbs double at the knees. With that kind of leverage, he had the Fomorian pinned and not knowing how to wrestle his way out of the grapple. It wouldn't last long, and as soon as the Fomorian pushed with all his upper-body strength into the ground, the creature would be free.

Before that could happen, though, Kane lunged, grabbing the waggling flap of flesh hanging off the mutant's head. It was a wild grab, but the creature's ear provided an excellent handle to the bloody banner of skin. With a firm hold on the sliced hunk of scalp and face, Kane straightened at the waist and pulled hard, fingers dug into the skin and ear of the man-beast. More flesh ripped in a hideous crackle, and the Fomorian let loose a wail of agony as the back of his head was stripped of skin. White skull and muscle tissue were exposed under the peeled dermis. Kane didn't want to take pleasure in the discomfort he caused, but there was a grim manner of satisfaction when he saw the Fomorian flailing around from the cruel tactic.

The Fomorian had at least seventy-five pounds and six inches of height on him, and his rope-cord arms made his reach much longer and deadlier than Kane's. Coupled with the ferocity to punch a bear into a bloody mash of crushed flesh and bone, the Fomorian hunter was not something that Kane wanted to treat fairly. With his opponent distracted by the gush of blood from the peeled scalp, Kane was able to bend at the waist again. He clamped both hands into one hammer fist and brought them down on the Fomorian's kidney. He hoped that the altered anatomy of his mutant foe was not that radically altered, and thankfully it wasn't. Driving both fists into a kidney-smashing chop, Kane put enough force into the blow to burst the organ in a normal human.

The Fomorian's cries of pain turned into a tight whine, his bulging cyclopean eye clenched shut against a fiery agony unlike anything he had ever felt. Though Kane wondered if his blow could penetrate the sheet of tough muscles bunched in the Fomorian's back, he was rewarded with the sudden limpness in his enemy's trapped legs. Untangling himself, Kane scurried to his feet. His back and shoulders burned from the Herculean effort of inflicting crippling pain against the man-beast, but Kane realized that he didn't have long to win this fight. He ripped the hatchet out of the Fomorian's wounded belly, and stomped one foot on the back of the monstrosity's partially defleshed skull, driving his face into the dirt.

One hand rose, wrapping Kane's ankle in a grip of iron. The few moments he'd managed to buy himself were nearly gone. Kane grimaced and brought the hatchet down on the exposed spot where the muscles connected to the base of the creature's skull. Bone caved in and flesh parted with the force of the brutal chop. The crushing fingers of the Fomorian loosened and slipped from around his ankle.

Kane staggered away, not bothering to dislodge the ax from where it had been stuck in the dead man-beast's neck. His only saving grace was that he had nothing left in his stomach to eject. Though he didn't keep a record of his victories in combat, Kane knew that this had to be one of the more gut-churning battles he'd ever engaged in. Completely drained by the exertion of the battle, he wanted to curl up under a blanket and sleep for a week.

No, Kane told himself. My body wants to recuperate, but right now, I've got to get back to Brigid and Grant before I have to fight any more of these things.

With a lurch, he pulled himself to his feet again, and

started his ascent when he heard the snarl of weapons. There was a gunfight going on only a hundred yards away, by the sound of things. Though it was hard to pinpoint, thanks to the echoes of gunshots bouncing off tree trunks, he could at least gauge the general direction and distance by the sheer mass of noise. The shooting had grown more intense.

Kane grimaced. He was unarmed, even if he could stomach ripping a bloody hatchet out of the corpse of the Fomorian. Bringing an ax to a gunfight was not on his list of things to do in life, and actually was on his short list of damn fool ways to commit suicide. He was tempted to just climb, and hope he could reach the tree line where the others would likely see him.

Kane paused and realized that climbing half-naked over the tree line would expose him to near freezing winds. Also, he had to deal with the blood loss from his clawed skull. He began going through his pockets, and realized that while these were cargo pants, they weren't the ones he'd worn on the mission. Those trousers had pockets loaded with useful items, including a thermal blanket that he could have fashioned into a parka, and a small packet of gauze and adhesive that could have formed a compression bandage. Just to satisfy his curiosity, he looked down the waistband of the cargo pants and saw that his doppelganger had taken all of his shadow suit, leaving behind only the tank top, boxers and socks.

Just enough clothing to protect him from the relatively temperate climate of the pine forest that clung to the side of the mountain. With a deep breath, he reached down and tore off the boxers from beneath his pants. Long strips of cloth came free, giving Kane at least something that he could bandage his bloody head with. It wasn't going to be the most glamorous field dressing ever applied, but at least he'd be shielding himself from infection and keeping his eyes clear. He had more than enough fabric from the underwear, so he stuffed the spare strips of cloth into one of the cargo pockets so that he could change his bandage later.

"Head wound dealt with," he muttered. He felt along his jawline and activated his Commtact. Kane cursed when he got no response from Cerberus. Whether his unit was damaged or there was a problem with the signal reaching Cerberus, Kane was on his own.

More gunfire now. This time, it was the unmistakable throaty roar of Grant's Barrett. Kane grimaced and yelled, but the range was at least three hundred yards. He scrambled, knowing that his partners would have blankets or the scouts would at least be able to provide a spare fur cloak for him. Three hundred yards, though, meant that the others might have mistaken the Thrush duplicate for Kane. Though his legs complained at the strain, he started pushing himself, fighting against the incline. He swung himself from tree trunk to tree trunk, using whatever handholds he could grasp to speed his ascent.

That wasn't helping the aches that were beginning to

awaken along his back and shoulders. Each extension of his muscles felt as if he were pulling himself apart.

"You get to the tree line, everything stops hurting," he said aloud, as if he could get his body to shut up about the damage he'd done to it. There were no deals to be made with his muscles. Every step was an exercise in will as much as strength, and his battle was now with a mountain, not the monsters that stalked its slopes.

He wrapped both arms around one pine trunk, the rough bark clawing at his skin as he used it as a support to rest himself. Sweat had drenched his upper body, and his hair was plastered to his head. Kane was glad for the bandage around his forehead as it absorbed the perspiration that would have been flowing into his eyes. They were already burning and stinging from the blood and grit that had gotten into them during his melee with the twin hunters, and he was fairly certain that he was beginning to suffer dehydration from his blood loss. The lack of tears to wash the offending debris on his eyes and the dryness of his mouth were good indicators.

Further confirmation came when he realized he'd lost a great deal of bodily fluid when he vomited earlier. He'd covered a hundred yards, though, since he'd picked up the pace to catch up with Grant. He could stand another two hundred before he could beg for a sip from Brigid's canteen.

Thunder pealed above him. Kane looked up, but he already knew that the skies above were blue and clear. One part of him hoped that it was perhaps the sonic boom of a Manta transorbital craft launched from Cerberus. The sensor equipment on the sleek, ultrasonic flyers would be able to peer through the trees and find him, latched on to a tree trunk, gasping for breath, fighting off chilling temperature drops and in desperate need of water. There were still a couple of people back at Cerberus who were qualified to fly the swift craft.

The thunder didn't fade, though, as it would have after the crack of a sonic boom. Instead, the rumbling sound increased in intensity, growing louder as it grew closer. Kane's fingers dug into the bark of the tree and he knew that there was only one reason for the sound.

Grant had started an avalanche. He'd probably been told that there was an army of the strange mutant man-eaters down the hill, and for all Kane knew, there probably were hundreds of them.

But one more thing was in the path of the thunderous landslide hurtling down the slope.

Kane. And right now, there was not a damn place for him to seek cover.

Chapter 11

It took Kane only a second to determine that the thunderclap above him was not storm related, nor was it a rescue ship from Cerberus. His keen senses and sharp mind worked together with their usual quickness to analyze the situation and make a decision. It was something that Brigid Baptiste had always grumbled about. Her intellect was undeniably greater, and her memories were stuffed with the knowledge of all the centuries of humankind, a storehouse of knowledge that was unsurpassed. But when it came to perceiving a danger and formulating a reaction to it, she awarded Kane with the sharper response. It wasn't officially a competition between the two, but there were benefits to both Brigid's incredible thought processes and Kane's instinctual adaptation to crisis.

The primitive urge in Kane's lower reptile brain was to run, and like many primitive reactions, it was a correct response. What his higher brain had to do was figure which was the most effective direction. The row of explosions that had started the rumble of the avalanche was on a higher elevation of the slope, meaning that heading downhill was suicide. The landslide would simply spread wider as more debris was knocked loose, scattering before the main mass that plummeted in gravity's greedy grasp. Uphill would take too much effort and be too slow and inefficient, and there was no guarantee that he'd slip past the widening arc of the avalanche's leading edge. He'd potentially plow right into a wall of rocks and uprooted trees roaring in the opposite direction at around 125 miles per hour.

Kane had to rely on his perceptions and cut through the prevailing drone of the accelerating landslide, locating the direction it was in relation to him. Making things worse was that relying on that kind of triangulation was eating up the vital few seconds that could mean the difference between survival and instant death.

The avalanche was off to his right. Move to the left. The two thoughts had taken place so quickly that by the time they could have been spoken aloud, the avalanche would be right on top of him. But to Kane, knowledge was action. His exhausted, leaden limbs surged at the command of his will, and he charged, each of his strides eating up ground.

He put everything into the mad dash for survival. He either emptied his tank of everything, or he died. Neither option seemed to leave him in a position where he'd be in good shape, but at least with the first choice, he'd still be breathing, and his sapped muscles wouldn't be crushed into a bloody pulp and smeared across a thousand feet of blasted slope.

The sound of trees snapping, their trunks bursting or their roots wrenching out of the dirt and rock that they'd clung to so savagely for years, signaled the damning approach of the landslide. Smaller rocks and pebbles whizzed through the air as if they were a rain of bullets, and Kane could feel them plucking at his heels and calves as he charged headlong away from the center of the avalanche. The peppering debris impacted his legs, informing him that the front of the turgid mass of collapsing mountainside had spread. The center had moved the swiftest, naturally, but the edge was working its hardest to catch up, and for as fast as Kane ran, he still was in the path of the expanding thrust.

He could only tell that the avalanche was closing in by touch and hearing. His eyes were focused on the path ahead of him. If he stumbled, tripped, was slowed one iota, his end would be certain. A pine tree cartwheeled behind him, its branches shattering as it tumbled. He could see its shadow as a brief slice of sun showed up through the cleared forest, but darkness blotted out the sky.

The core of the avalanche was now covered by a towering cloud that had blocked out the sun, and twigs and splinters stabbed into Kane's back. A rock the size of an apple bounced off his sore shoulder before it careened down hill, and a jolt of dread filled his gut. He was certain that he hadn't made it far enough, and by now, the landslide had expanded so that the big stuff was coming down on him. The impression of failure would have made anyone else lose a step, but Kane kept pushing on, even as he heard grinding and twisting trunks give off their final bellows behind him.

To stop running would be an act of surrender. Kane fought on, one step after another, his powerful legs hurling him two yards with each stride. A pine needle stabbed into his cheek, and wincing reflex almost inspired him to blink, but he knew that to close his eyes would be to make his steps uncertain. Kane ran with all of his might, not blinking, not allowing the acid seething in his thighs to slow him. The roar of the landslide reached a crescendo that made Kane feel as if his head were being crushed by the vengeful ghosts of the Fomorian hunters he had slain.

A branch spun and cracked him hard across the side. The impact slammed Kane to the ground and he rolled, arms clawing fruitlessly for a handhold. As he rotated, he saw that the sky was a smear of darkness that dominated everything around him. Kane stopped, his broad shoulders slamming into the roots of a pine tree that stood its ground as dust and pine needles seemed to bury him in a stifling cloud. Kane twisted, pushing his face against the trunk of the tree, using his body to block out the falling debris so that he could suck in a breath of life-giving air.

Kane ached, and he clutched the roots that had slowed him. The thunder of the landslide faded, but he couldn't tell if it was because the avalanche had passed him by or because he had been entombed beneath a wall of soil. All he knew was that darkness had engulfed him, and the only sensations he possessed were the firing of his nerves as muscles, skin and bone all protested their mistreatment. Just before he pulled up the urge to relax and sleep in the burial mound the Pocono mountain had constructed for him, he remembered the leering, cheerful face that Thrush had stolen from him, and how it would now be used to place Brigid, Grant and all his other friends back at Cerberus in grave peril.

The dirt was heavy across his shoulders, and his arms twitched as he fought to push above the blanket of debris. He grit his teeth, feeling his tomb crack and pour off his back. Finally his head burst above the soil that had engulfed him. He gasped down fresh air and pushed and writhed until he'd cleared enough dirt away so that he could breathe easily.

The air was still cloudy, but Kane could see a dim flare of sunlight through it. Soon enough, though, the cold air would drift down from the mountaintop. Already his cheeks could feel a chill.

Kane sighed. For now, at least, the tomb that had threatened to smother him was a shelter, blocking out the frigid air before it could rob even more life from his exhausted limbs.

"Rest a few moments," Kane muttered. "Let everything settle down, stay warm."

He wanted to blink, but he knew that if he slept, he'd lose daylight. Fighting his way to a warmer altitude while half naked and beset by mountain cold was going to be hard enough while he could see and be warmed by the sun's nurturing rays. In darkness, he'd be facing a cold he could never outrun.

Just until my arms and legs stop twitching, he promised himself, not even allowing himself to blink for fear that sleep would overtake him.

He had to stay awake in order to get back to Cerberus.

Kane didn't have any proof right now, but he knew in his heart of hearts that Thrush, the faker who had donned his skin and flaunted it before him, had inspired the avalanche.

Right now, the doppelganger was looking at the scar he'd carved into the mountain, and was wondering if the landslide had buried him, or if Kane still lived.

Kane clenched his fist beneath the dirt, then shrugged his arm free from the tomb. The pain had dulled from fire in his muscles to a constant throb. He pried himself out of the soil and stood, looking up the mountain, grimacing over the fact that he couldn't see through the airborne debris.

"I'm still alive, Thrush," Kane growled.

His legs wobbled, rubbery beneath him, and his mouth was dry and parched. Already his arms were tingling, bitten by the crisp mountain air. He'd need water, food, rest, medical attention.

But for now, anger at the false-faced usurper would be the fuel to keep him warm, to push his steps, first downhill then back to the parallax point.

Even if there were a hundred Fomorians between him and Cerberus, Kane had to get through them.

He started his trek into the half-buried valley.

FOR THE SPACE of a few moments, Bres the Beautiful was happy again. Most of his millennia-long lifespan had been spent in a state of numbness. It was why he was such a beautiful-faced and perfect-bodied being while his touch only mutated and deformed others to release their power. He had been given a gift, a power that had been buried deep within the core of his being. The joy of this present, handed to him by the Dragon King Enlil, was that he was immortal. No amount of force could slay him, and the spark of fire that motivated his body would never burn out.

There had been a curse to this gift, however. Nothing short of the kind of strength and brutality that could flay his everlasting flesh produced a sensation strong enough for him to feel. Brushing his hand through broken glass yielded the same numb feeling of lifeless fingers as it would running through the silken hair of a gorgeous lover. No pleasure would ever be great enough for him to be teased or tickled again, while it would take the strength of giants to cause him enough harm to savor the sting of parting flesh and snapping bone.

It was why he was so beloved of the Fomorians. Not only had Bres unleashed the might within their genetic code, the bestial force that had been constructed by the Annunaki to wage their war with the Tuatha de Danaan, but he also provided them with entertainment. The twisted freaks, the cyclopeans and their monolimbed counterparts, would engage in cruel games of competition to see who among them could garner the most response from their leader. Some took the opportunity to see how much damage they truly could do with their bare hands. Others devised wicked, skin-peeling tools of pain and cruelty to accomplish this goal.

And between each flaying, between each intense beating, the Fomorians cackled and howled with glee as Bres's body reconstructed itself, bones mending and flesh flowing like mud until he returned to his original shape. It was the only thing that kept Bres as sane as he was, those nights of torment and torture that broke the never-ending dullness and void of sensation that was his life.

The rumble of the avalanche was a mile off when Bres first noticed it, and for a moment, he glanced around, looking for clouds in the sky. Since it wasn't that, and there had been no aircraft for the past few centuries that would have produced such a sound, his vision turned toward an odd cloud that accelerated down the mountain slope.

"Avalanche!" Bres bellowed at the top of his lungs. The landslide was accompanied by a cloud of debris, and it spread quickly, tumbling toward the valley floor. "Balor!"

The greatest of Bres's children, the mighty giant with the baleful eye, torn from the lifeless face of Bres's father, leaped across the Fomorian compound. Balor had been propelled by legs that were easily as thick as tree trunks, layered with sheets of muscle that turned his seven-hundred-pound bulk into a swift, often graceful form as it moved. When he spoke, his voice was almost angelic, making his appearance even more of an abomination. "Father?"

"The prisoner—you must shield her," Bres whispered to his favored and most loved creation.

Balor's craggy maw twisted into a smile. His cyclopean head nodded, and with a leap, he soared twenty feet into the air, crossing the distance to Granny Epona's cage in a single bound. Seven hundred pounds of weight had been proportionally distributed across Balor's ninefoot frame, and he knelt over Epona's cage. Broad shoulders and a back rippling with muscle formed an impenetrable wall against whatever assault the mountain could drop on them.

This had taken only seconds, and the avalanche was still a quarter of the way up the mountain. Bres's perfect features darkened with anger, his lip curling in spite. The caverns where the Fomorian horde bivouacked honeycombed the slope up to a hundred feet off the valley floor, and the outdoor compound he had stood in was actually the ruins of an Appalachian outpost. Bres glared at the buildings where they had stored the rifles and vehicles granted to them by Thrush, and as he turned back toward the onrushing storm of stone, he knew that Thrush was once again a traitor.

Thrush had promised great things from their collaboration, but the moment that Bres had done one thing for the pandimensional mastermind, he ripped it all away in the most destructive and anger-filled way possible. He couldn't have just sabotaged the equipment that had been given to the Fomorians. No, he had to rip off the side of a mountain and hurl it down at them, a clear rebuke to Bres and his clan.

The world caved in on Bres as tons of mass moving at over a hundred miles per hour struck him. Wood and rock smashed against his perfect, normally unfeeling body. Flesh was torn from his bones in a manner that he had not felt since he was in Nagasaki. There, it had been the power unleashed by a nuclear explosion, concussive force and heat searing the flesh from his skeleton. Here, it was simply the power of gravity acting upon a loosened sheet of mountainside. Bones shattered and his eyeballs liquefied as they were driven from his face by the wave of devastating force that hammered on him.

The impact was over, and Bres was trapped in complete silence and darkness. Though he realized that it was simply that he was buried under tons of material, he allowed himself the fantasy that Enlil's grand gift had finally been spent, that he had been allowed to die.

His cheek twitched, and he realized that already the jeweled node that was at the core of his being had at least reconstructed part of his face. Vibrations shook the earth around him, their nearness causing his limbs to flinch in response.

There could be no doubt, even before thick fingers

pried a chunk of boulder away, revealing clear sky marred by the brown, fused features of his son Balor.

"Father?"

"I am well," Bres answered. "Our prisoner?"

"She is safe, though scared," Balor answered. "Who did this to us?"

"It was the one who passed himself off as our benefactor," Bres answered.

Balor reached into the dirt, his powerful hand wrapping around the trunk of Bres's body. The grasp splintered his ribs as he secured enough of a grip to pry himself out from under the avalanche's debris. Bres coughed up blood as the shattered bones lacerated blood vessels and internal organs, but they were already on their way to repairing themselves. For all the brutish power his son had demonstrated in clawing Bres out of the earth, that might was turned to gentle care as he was lowered to his feet.

"Bring the woman to me," Bres growled. "I have need of her gifts."

Balor nodded his massive, misshapen head. "Yes, Father."

The giant whirled and took off, running on his thick knuckles and the soles of his feet, the gait reminding Bres of a gorilla. Balor crossed the wreckage of the valley to a crater that had been torn open when Balor had dug himself out.

Bres frowned. He knew that Thrush had betrayed him. But he needed the granny witch's mystic power to give him more information.

Thrush had wanted to replace a man, someone of extraordinary ability and resources, which meant that the landslide could have been used to try to destroy him, as well. And right now, Bres had little time to waste finding him.

That meant using the psychic powers contained within Epona.

The human, Kane, would be the weapon that Bres could utilize to avenge himself upon the false man.

Chapter 12

Caked with thick dirt, Kane was glad that his perspiration had allowed for a protective shell. It was far less likely now that he'd lose body heat through his naked back and arms, though it wasn't the same as being clad in environmentally controlled smart polymers with heating and cooling elements. As it was, Kane stopped every so often, looking for muddy soil to smear on his body to replace the dried dirt knocked off by his trek down the side of the mountain. He'd considered using the freshly hewn corridor that had been carved out of the slope by the avalanche, but he wanted to have the element of cover and concealment. Right now, all he had was muddy camouflage, and concealment was pretty good for most of the foes he had who were limited to human perception.

Not knowing what kind of unholy supersenses the Fomorians possessed, he could have been walking through clearings with a gigantic neon sign carved into the air over his head, visible for miles. Thus, Kane kept to the trees, which handed him the added benefit of being thick and bulletproof.

Every so often, Kane would drop onto his butt and slide on the loose pine needles and mixed leaves of the forest floor. The wet, slippery surface was just about perfect for Kane to continue his trek with minimal wear and tear on his slowly recovering limbs. As of now, though, Kane was pleased that he could move his arms without severe discomfort. He still hurt, the ache wrapping him in a blanket that served to keep him awake and alert for enemies.

He had descended at least two thousand yards over the past fifteen minutes, and found an outcropping that looked as if it would give him a good view of the valley. Kane descended and crawled on his belly to the lip in order to minimize his profile. Peering over, he saw that hundreds of tree trunks stuck through the bulk of the landslide like shattered teeth through mashed lips.

Two craters had been torn out of the floor of the valley. They were massive depressions, going by the estimation of the size of the tree trunks poking from the soil. He frowned at the sight of a Fomorian who bounded around on all fours, his arms slightly longer than his legs as he galloped to this task and the next. Kane wondered if the scale he'd applied to the scene was correct when his gaze fell upon two figures, one a tall and magnificent humanoid with long, flowing golden hair, and a small, dark-haired woman. Both of their skins had a bronze tint to them, but Kane could tell that the woman's coloration came from sun and wind burning her face from life atop the mountains. As for the other, his hue was born of something unnatural. He gleamed oddly as the last rays of the day struck his skin. It was as if he truly were metallic-skinned, the glint of sunlight burning like fire on the highlights of his flesh.

"Bres," Kane whispered, sudden and ancient recognition settling in as he gazed upon the figure who had been torn from a jump dream, a glimpse of an ancient past recast whole. Kane's visual estimate of the man's height was dead on, because Bres truly was fully seven feet in height. The godling standing in the valley was virtually unchanged since an earlier warrior, fighting in the cause of Lugh, had seen the unholy prince of the Fomorians on the battlefields.

Kane's eyesight focused on the woman, and though he didn't have binoculars, nor the optical enhancements of his shadow suit, he recognized her, as well—Granny Epona, being exactly where she shouldn't have been, her wrists bound together by heavy rope, her shoulders stooped from the weight of the bindings. Jet-black hair fluttered in the breeze that turned Bres's golden hair into a living flame that flickered.

There was no way that the witch should have been down there, not when it had taken Kane this long to reach the bottom of the valley. The woman who had greeted them with the scouts had to have been someone, or something, different. A dread sickness filled his gut as he wondered if perhaps the scouts who had accompanied her were similar abominations, recrafted Fomorians cast into the skins of the Appalachians. If that was the circumstance, then he wondered if Grant and Brigid had been allowed to escape back to Cerberus.

"They're fine," he said aloud to reassure himself. "As fine as could be with an impostor posing as me in their ranks."

Kane slid back along the outcropping, moving slowly so as not to draw attention from the valley below. There were about ten Fomorians, not counting Bres and the apelike monster galloping around on his knuckles and feet. The Fomorians and their titanic kinfolk had applied their strength to hacking at a section of mountain while Bres watched over the captive woman. He was outnumbered twelve to one, and from the looks of things, the mutations were busy digging more of their brothers out of the mountainside. The odds could double or triple, and the only things that Kane had with him were his wits and skill. He'd been rendered almost crippled fighting two of those Fomorian hunters one at a time. The current odds, for want of a better term, sucked.

Kane pushed his worries aside. They would be a good guide to keep him aware of what would happen if he failed, but he had to move past envisioning failure and formulate a plan of action that didn't entail one-on-one combat with a twelve-foot, one-eyed gorilla. Of course, with everything buried beneath tons of rock and shattered tree trunks, Kane was not going to have any luck finding a rifle to even the odds.

He closed his eyes, wincing at the thought of having to go bare-handed against anything down there, especially with his limbs aching from fatigue. He ran his thoughts over the possibilities and focused on the idea of sharpening a branch with a flat rock, or perhaps splitting one end and tying a particularly sharpened simple spearhead in place. Stone would penetrate at least one Fomorian hide easily, but that meant leading at least a couple in pursuit. If he could pounce on one of the mutated hunters and take him down with a well-placed thrust, he'd get hold of a rifle and spare ammunition. Considering how the beasts had gone after a bear while wearing only a loincloth and carrying a simple hand ax each, the chances of getting more than a full magazine would be spotty.

Something mewled in the distance, making Kane open his eyes. Just what he needed while formulating his line of attack on Bres, an interruption by…what?

Kane squinted, and he caught a glimpse of movement. It sure as hell wasn't a Fomorian hunter stalking the woods for survivors. It was too small, too wiry and too quick.

Kane rarely saw feral cats in the wilderness, and those that he spotted were mostly blurs of motion, running away from him if they detected his human presence in their territory. Felines had long ago lost much of their trust and curiosity in regards to humankind. Sure, there were a few pets within villes or various other societies, but that was only due to an abundance of food and a surplus of time for their owners to pay attention to them. Elsewhere, the cats had reverted to their wild ways, being hunters of the small, and avoiding anything that was too big to get involved with.

So, in a day that had been filled with amazing sights and sensations, the approach of a brown, snaggle-toothed old warrior cat, staring at him with sharp, intelligent green eyes, proved to be most mystifying to Kane. The lean and spry creature advanced on Kane with an almost regal air. He was able to sense the ancient leonine majesty that was still prevalent in the feline's genes.

"Shoo," Kane whispered, waving at the thing. The cat ignored his warning dismissal, choosing instead to seat itself, staring at him. Kane grit his teeth at the little beast, but rather than be impressed, the cat released a bored snort.

Kane had the instinct to kick a clot of dirt at the wild creature, but those piercing emerald eyes peered deep into him, something tugging at his mind, stopping his kick. The cat's expression bespoke a familiar intellect, a friendly face. Epona sprang immediately to mind, and Kane couldn't help but notice the subtle rustle of thoughts echoing in the back of his subconscious mind, the sensations reminiscent of his telepathic rapport with Balam, the last Archon.

"Balam never required an intermediary to tell me what he thought," Kane said aloud to the cat, keeping his voice low so it wouldn't carry.

The cat's head tilted in response to the statement. Those almost human eyes never wavered from his own as the feline padded toward him, eventually making a gentle hop into Kane's lap. Instincts guided Kane's hand to the back of the cat's head, fingers scratching behind the animal's ears. "Makes sense. Not only have witches been known to communicate with their familiars, but Morrigan was able to see through the eyes of her raven messengers. That was also a gift shared by Apollo and Odin, two other gods whose chosen animal was the raven."

Kane winced as he felt the influence of Brigid Baptiste. Without her present, Kane had fallen into the role of lecturer as he wrapped his mind around the concept of intraspecies telepathic communication. All of this was known to him simply because he had gone back and done research on Morrigan, a familiar figure from one of Kane's jump dreams, a person whom he had met in an earlier life, according to Fand. As Kane researched the bits of that past existence as Cuchulainn, he was able to explore the myths of the Tuatha and other European gods. Given that the Annunaki lord Marduk had confirmed that he had been Zeus in Greece, then it was no surprise that the "powers" of many of the gods were repeated, such as the powers of remote viewing and communication through animal forms. Marduk had required a bit of Annunaki technology to broadcast his thoughts, utilizing cloned tissues as his transmitter. Epona's ability to do the same thing with simpler central nervous systems seemed as reasonable as the sun rising and setting. The weird thing was that Kane hadn't even remembered reading about this until Epona made contact with Kane through the feline.

Kane tenderly put a knuckle under the cat's chin. "I know *you* want me to continue scratching, old boy, but what does your granny witch want from me?"

A feint mew was Kane's undecipherable answer, but given how easily Epona had planted the idea of the cat being her representative in Kane's mind, her need for communication had faded for now. That, or she was being grilled by Bres, forced to search for him via her granny witch powers. Kane thought back to Bres, looming over the woman, and tried to decipher the order of events and the reasoning behind this particular contact. The cat could have been one of hundreds of animals that still survived on the mountainside in the wake of the avalanche, and Epona was legitimately searching for Kane in order to appease the irate Bres. It was unlikely that the animals were sent in search of trapped or injured Fomorians as Kane had seen the un-injured mutants digging at the slope, trying to penetrate into collapsed caves for their brethren.

That only left Bres looking for the Kane that the Thrush doppelganger had left behind on the mountain. It was logical that Bres wanted to catch up with Kane, most likely as a means of evening the score with whoever had unleashed the landslide on Bres's settlement of mutants. Whether that meant that Bres wanted to utilize Kane as an ally or pulverize the creature that Thrush wanted protected and out of the way was the question that weighed on Kane's mind. The answer to that would determine how roughly the Fomorian would

If offer card is missing write to: The Reader Service, P.O. Box 1867, Buffalo NY 14240-1867

NO POSTAGE
NECESSARY
IF MAILED
IN THE
UNITED STATES

BUSINESS REPLY MAIL

FIRST-CLASS MAIL   PERMIT NO. 717   BUFFALO, NY

POSTAGE WILL BE PAID BY ADDRESSEE

THE READER SERVICE
PO BOX 1867
BUFFALO NY 14240-9952

Get FREE BOOKS and a FREE GIFT when you play the...

LAS VEGAS
GAME

Just scratch off the gold box with a coin. Then check below to see the gifts you get!

YES! I have scratched off the gold box. Please send me my **2 FREE BOOKS** and **gift for which I qualify**. I understand that I am under no obligation to purchase any books as explained on the back of this card.

▲ DETACH AND MAIL CARD TODAY! ▲

366 ADL E4CE   166 ADL E4CE

FIRST NAME

LAST NAME

ADDRESS

APT #

CITY

STATE / PROV.

ZIP / POSTAL CODE

7	7	7	Worth TWO FREE BOOKS plus a BONUS Mystery Gift!
🍒	🍒	🍒	Worth TWO FREE BOOKS!
🔔	🔔	♣	TRY AGAIN!

Offer limited to one per household and not valid to current subscribers of Gold Eagle® books. All orders subject to approval. Please allow 4 to 6 weeks for delivery.

treat him, should Epona direct the hunters toward him via her psychic link with the animals of the forest. The cat didn't move, so it hadn't been summoned away by Epona, which didn't mean anything in itself. Still, the emotional bonding that had been projected through the animal informed Kane that Epona felt what her familiars experienced. If danger was en route to this spot, Epona would have dismissed the cat, rather than suffer its agonies at the claws of the savage mutations. As well, Kane's own perceptions were as sharp as ever, and he had no indication of danger looming, not even with his almost supernatural point man's sense. Rather, Kane was in a place of calm, the lounging cat exuding soothing, almost healing vibrations.

It was then that Kane's mind wandered for a moment, reexamining the moment that the bear had lurched into view. Though it had swatted him in the head, a single claw carving open his forehead, Kane now realized that the blow had not been intended to decapitate him as he originally thought. The limb that had been wounded had been harmed in the process of the bear lunging to protect Kane, not beforehand. The whole thing now stank of deus ex machina.

Kane looked into the cat's eyes and spoke clearly. "That was you with the bear, as well, wasn't it, Epona?"

A gentle paw reached out to rest on Kane's chin. There was a sudden, deep pang of regret in Kane's heart, a sadness that enveloped him as he caught the emotion in the cat's eyes. Epona was mourning over her ursine pawn. It could have been projection, but Kane also felt regret at the loss of the magnificent animal to the brutal fists of the Fomorians. At least Kane had managed to avenge his rescuer.

There was a brief flicker in the cat's eyes, and its raspy tongue brushed across Kane's bristly chin. The thanks of a witch for an act of justice against a murderer.

"So, is this a trap?" Kane asked the cat, feeling a slight bit silly. When the cat put its paw over his lips, the silliness disappeared. This was genuine conversation. It wasn't the mind-speech that he'd shared with Balam, though; it was more a transmission of ideas, sort of like classical music scores without accompanying operatic verses to make sense of things. Concepts were transmitted through nonverbal interpretation. For a moment, Kane felt the urge to bury himself under some foliage to hide from the Fomorians. It wasn't a precise exchange of thoughts, but the implication was clear. Epona wanted Kane to remain in hiding, and any efforts she made to assist Bres were only obfuscation.

Kane racked his mind to come up with a term for the process by which Epona had kept in touch with him through the cat's mind, and he went back to a term Brigid Baptiste had encountered in the *Fortean Times,* a journal of unusual phenomena that stretched from alien life to odd zoological specimens. Brigid was able to supply Kane with a lot of background information on creatures he'd encountered and odd places he'd been to.

The term that Kane cast about for finally came to mind: telempathy, long-distance emotional communication.

Epona's Tuatha lineage and skills made her brain quite powerful, but not on the scale that Balam's over-sized cranium allowed for. Kane doubted that humans had developed enough conscious complexity of thought to duplicate some of the extraordinary feats the First Folk had been capable of on so casual a basis. Epona probably looked as if she were pushing an invisible ten-ton weight from the effort expended to keep in touch with Kane. Her advantage was that Bres expected that kind of exertion when Epona sought out Kane on the mountainside.

Kane still had to admire Epona's ability, however. She'd shown the capacity to manipulate animals and use them as intermediaries for long-distance communication. The cat, as if sensing Kane's appreciation, licked his cheek again. The warm and gentle rasp of the feline's tongue had an emotional substitute, not the adulation of an animal but the chaste touch of Epona's lips conveying a silent thanks.

"Trouble is," Kane spoke up softly, "I have to get back home. How the hell is a cat going to help me against an army of Fomorians?"

The cat's eyes flashed, and it swung its gaze down the mountainside. Kane followed the direction of those sharp, humanlike orbs to a spurt of activity among Bres's mutants. Most of the Fomorians were still busy digging their brethren out of the caves, but a few of them had broken off from the group and were directed to a small group of crates that had been torn out of the dirt by the gigantic, gorrillalike monstrosity. Kane squinted, concentrating on the creatures as they took long black objects from the crates.

"A hunting party, for me," Kane muttered.

A repeat of the urge to hide was transmitted by the cat, but this time Kane knew it wasn't his own instincts being spurred. It was simply a message. He glanced toward Epona, and saw Bres wrap his hand around her chin.

That wasn't an act of affection. It was menace, pure and simple. From the gore spattered all over Bres's clothing, he had to have suffered serious wounds, and yet his body looked hale and healthy at this distance. Given that he could remold the Fomorians into strong, inhuman beasts, Kane didn't doubt that Bres had the ability to craft flesh with a whim, including rebuilding his own when subjected to horrendous injury. It would be a tough fight, if and when Kane got to it.

Kane returned his attention to the Fomorian hunters as they armed themselves. They seemed adept with the weaponry, even the single-handed creatures. He couldn't distinguish the make of the rifles from this distance, but they couldn't have been the big booming rifles like Grant and the Appalachian mountain scouts had required. Kane didn't think that they'd need that kind of punch against mere humans, on reflection, but rapid fire put them in a league past the hapless mountaineers who were limited to bolt-action designs.

Would Thrush have given these beings weapons they could use to harm each other?

A dull note of dread struck Kane in the stomach as he knew that no agent of Thrush, no matter how willing to serve the collective, would be harmed by a weapon it had given out freely. Kane took a deep breath as he realized that small arms were not going to carry the fight against the doppelganger who had taken his place.

"One thing at a time," he told himself, his mood grim. As the sun disappeared behind the western mountaintops, Kane knew that he had to get some more clothing, as well as a means to even the odds against the deformed creatures who had assembled a hunting party for him.

He watched as the shadow of a peak loomed across Epona and her captor.

Kane had two lives to protect now.

"Come on, cat," Kane whispered. "Let's go rescue your granny."

A faint mew was his answer, and the pair stalked off like panthers on the hunt.

Chapter 13

The touch of Bres's fingertips on her chin made Epona's skin tingle. Whatever power resided in this near-immortal golden being, a mere caress transferred the depth of the power she was dealing with. It was no surprise to the granny witch. He laid hands upon outcasts and rebuilt them as he saw fit, pulling horrors from the depths of their being and placing them on the surface. Bres lowered his hand from her face, and Epona's head swum as if she'd just been unplugged.

"Don't disappoint me, witch," Bres said, his voice icy. "I will make hell seem like a release if you do."

Epona shook her head. "I'm searching for Kane."

Which was a lie, of course. She'd locked on to him almost immediately, familiar with his emotional signature. It took her a few moments to find a mammal or a bird in the vicinity that hadn't been frightened off to the high hills by the avalanche and make contact with him, but finding him had been easy. Bres didn't need to know that, however. The strain that brought out the wrinkles in her forehead could as easily be scouring the mountainside as the exertion needed to send through messages to the lone Cerberus explorer.

Still, Epona knew that she was playing a dangerous game. She'd watched Bres take one of the Fomorian womenfolk and recarve her into an exact duplicate of Epona. That, plus the tingle of his touch on her unmutated skin, added up to the simple fact that she had to look as if she was making progress.

Epona didn't want to know how far her bones could be stretched and her flesh melted until she considered death a pleasure rather than a punishment. As if Bres could read the fear in her features, he smiled.

Had it not been Bres, the expression would have been warming. He was a beautiful creature, and such emotion on his face seized her heart with romantic headiness that she hadn't experienced since she was a young girl. Her every instinct was to mate with this perfect, finely crafted example of masculinity and power.

But there was the knowledge of Bres's true nature.

His outsides were immaculate, irresistible. His thoughts, his lusts, his deeds, however, which lurked beneath the skin, were a litany of horror and torment toward humanity across the millennia. Bres was pure, living evil, cast in solid gold and polished to the point of gleaming brightness.

Bres granted power and sought only cruelty. His "children" lived to inflict pain. They didn't hunt for food; they hunted for sport, for fun. There was no reason for them to track down prey and brutalize it. The Fomorians weren't stupid and could craft spears or bows and arrows with which to take meat with human swiftness, but no. Epona had felt firsthand the horrors of what various animals had experienced. This wasn't hunting; it was torture.

She could hear the laughter coming from the mutants as they took their time ripping living flesh off their victims. Epona hadn't been scanning for the activity; it was pure horror that shot like lightning to any mind that was attuned to the simple beasts of the mountains. Even when a deer was shot with one of the mountaineers' .50-caliber rifles, the buck didn't generate a feeling of horror. Quick death was something all animals expected.

The Fomorians were monsters, all the way down to their rotten souls. They sought out Bres as much as he sought out them. The anger and hatred for the outside world stained their spirits, which was all Bres needed to see.

It gave Epona a moment's pause, but if Bres could read minds, he would have known instantly what she'd been up to. Shielding her thoughts was not a gift that Epona had been taught by her grandmother. No, if Bres had detected the duplicity of Epona's plan to aid Kane in escaping the Fomorians and returning to Cerberus, he would have been twisting her body like taffy, subjecting her to unending pain and madness.

Or did Bres intend to lure Kane in, using her as an unwitting pawn?

Epona swallowed hard.

"Something wrong, Epona?" Bres asked.

"What if I can't find Kane?" she inquired.

"Then my hunters will. And I will peel all that is useful from his carcass," Bres said. "I will drink his mind, and then I shall forge his flesh to my children, increasing their strength."

Epona frowned.

"Yes, dear. I can imbibe the brains of my enemies, and when I do, I learn their every secret, things they weren't even aware that they knew," Bres stated. He caressed her cheek. His touch was like the heat of a campfire, warming, strengthening. "Just as I learned from other witches before you. Your gifts are not unique, my dear."

Epona bit her lower lip.

"No, I didn't know what you informed him of," Bres continued. "But I knew you'd look for a way out of this prison. I would have. Remember, Epona, I've walked this Earth since humankind was young. I am the scion of gods, and the sire of monsters. History trembled at my passing, when I made myself known. You do not spend centuries among a people and not learn how to play them like a flute."

Epona felt her stomach twist in horrified regret. Bres rested his hand on her shoulder and the warmth passed through her body. Calmness filled her, not the body-wrenching agony she'd expected from him.

"You've done well, child," Bres said. "I shan't be drinking your mind this night. But if I'm lucky, I'll have a whole mountain full of brilliance and ability to work with."

"Oh, no," Epona muttered breathlessly.

Bres grinned. "And when my master sees what I have done to the enemies who have plagued him so viciously, I shall be given whatever I want."

"And what do you want?" Epona asked nervously. She tried to concentrate, but Bres's grasp on her prevented her from focusing. His touch was interfering with the connection she had with the rest of the world through her gifts.

"I want to be free of this life," Bres said. His grin was empty, cold. "And if I do not get my wish, then I will make certain that you will join me in torment."

Epona fought back a sob.

KANE CROUCHED in the bushes, knowing that he had to be careful. The cat had gone silent, no longer motivated by an outside source, which had Kane kicking himself. He'd trusted the water witch and her ancient secret powers, but the sudden lack of impressions threw his instincts into overdrive. His stealthy approach to the Fomorian camp had required too much attention on his part to make him aware that his line of communication to the Appalachian psychic had faded, so subtle was the connection they had developed. Now that he was in the midst of enemies who were easily strong enough to tear his body in two with their bare hands, the rustle of her mind against his was gone.

So much for having a sliver of an advantage over the Fomorians, but Kane didn't blame the witch woman. The Appalachian had been feeding him a string of impressions that had coupled with Kane's own experiences, the hidden memories of his former lives that had been stirred to the surface thanks to jump dreams, the machinations of Fand and encounters with the Tuatha de Danaan. Bres was as familiar to Kane as Enlil and Sindri. Since the memories of ancient warriors were far removed from current conditions, Kane realized that Bres was more than just some freak.

The being he faced was immortal, and immortal beings were dangerous because they brought experience to the table. Kane didn't doubt that the godlike golden child of the Fomorians could plan and connive with the best in the world. Epona would have been manipulated by Bres with deft skill, and Kane himself would be facing a foe who had likely conquered a million enemies across his extremely long life.

Long odds were stacked against Kane, and there wasn't a firearm that was going to even them. The cat alongside Kane looked at him, as if sensing the tension in the human. He nodded to the animal, who bounded away, somehow combining grace and silence with full-out retreat.

Alone again, Kane scanned the area for the presence of any Fomorians who might have been hanging back in order to guard the cache of arms that the big beast had dug up. Kane spotted the big thing, and unbidden, another memory surfaced—Balor of the Baleful Eye.

Like the other two hunters he'd battled, this creature was a cyclops, but this one resembled more fully the more traditional illustration of the great Titans. The others had oversized orbs, but they had been off balance, placed either to one side or the other of the face. This creature's solitary eye was smack in the middle of a heavy brow, perched right above a nose that looked as if it had been mashed flat, its nostrils then slashed and torn to tatters that fell over a twisted pair of lips. Balor was a nightmare, and was molded in the form of the great Fomorians who had dared to wage war on Lugh, the god of light who sought to free the land of the Fomorian hordes.

Kane rubbed his throbbing forehead. This kind of memory dump had to have been facilitated by more than just the telepathic communication. He always attributed his points man instinct to an unusually centered spirit, allowing him to pay attention to subliminal cues, processed ordinarily by his subconscious mind. That level of awareness was something that had been developed, as well as instinctually felt. However, Kane had been exposed to multiple varieties of psychic phenomena over the years since he rejected the rule of the barons.

Balam's telepathic machinations had certainly opened Kane to sensations far beyond normal human understanding. This had left him more sensitive to information that he normally wouldn't have known, although to a more logical explanation, Balor and Bres were central, vital figures in the world of Cuchulainn and the Celtic gods who had become known as the Tuatha de Danaan. His research into the life that Fand claimed he possessed had given him inroads to the lore that should have been alien.

That still didn't explain how he recognized Bres without a flicker of doubt.

Kane maintained his position in the bushes, hiding from the workers who had gathered around Balor. The mutants hammered and clawed at the dirt, and Kane could see that some of the creatures possessed only one arm. These particular Fomorians had both eyes, and Kane wondered at the odd alteration of their bodies, no longer symmetrical in their mutated forms. Epona had informed the Cerberus explorers that they had been molded in this way by the hand of Bres himself, and for a moment Kane didn't know the purpose behind it. The loss of a limb hadn't seemed to impair the strength of the single-limbed Fomorians any more than the loss of an eye affected the perception and capability of their cyclopean counterparts. There was even one of the beasts with only one arm and one eye, and yet it maneuvered and dug with all the strength of the others.

Rather than each of the beings having symmetry, Kane realized that they had sacrificed one arm or one eye to increase the potential of the other. With a limb at double the mass, and an eye with presumably proportional optic capability, the mutations had removed a weaker part of their body to enhance a stronger part. Kane thought about hand and eye dominance, and made the correlation of the changes Bres had made in these beings.

Bres.

Kane hadn't seen the golden godling in a while, and he cursed his inattention. Bres knew that Epona had been assisting Kane, which meant that the search party would be a feint, something to make Kane commit himself to a penetration to seek out supplies and gear. Would Bres come after Kane on his own? The godling was seven feet tall and perfectly proportioned with muscles stretched across his frame in enviable sheets that simply added to the sheer impression of power for the being.

A millennia-old creature would be consummately skilled in combat, allegedly, but fighting was a perishable skill. He and Grant sparred constantly, and kept their gun hands trained by shooting every week. A break in that regimen would mean that they each would lose a step. Bres, being immortal, was not guaranteed to have a perfect memory of all of his moves, and even then, he showed no sign of scar tissue, meaning that pain would not be a motivational factor. Bres would be the kind who got by on brute force and clumsy power, so combat finesse would not be a part of his repertoire, if after all this time Bres actually remained hands-on.

Kane grimaced, and he focused on what he needed to do—get a weapon, and get clothing to protect him from the encroaching night cold. And to live long enough to do that and make it a worthwhile effort, he had to avoid whatever traps Bres had laid.

Kane had armed himself with a sharp bit of rock, and he'd further chipped and honed its edge. Around the base of the primitive stone knife, he'd wrapped a length of his shredded underwear that he'd torn for bandages. It wasn't the best of equipment, but at least it was more deterrence than a harsh word. Would it be enough of an advantage over a Fomorian's superior size and strength? Kane didn't have any delusions.

Once there were no Fomorians in view of the crates, Kane skulked toward them. He had reached some of the sealed boxes and crouched beside them for cover, his eyes, his ears, his nose all tuned finely in search of opposition. No one seemed to be skulking behind him, and if they were, they produced less noise than a breeze.

Kane took a moment to scan the crates, hoping for some form of survival clothing provided, but the Fomorians walked around half-naked, even Bres, so the man resigned himself to the fact that they didn't require coats. What he did spot was a canvas tarpaulin, olive-green in color. It wouldn't be the best of camouflage, but the tarp could be fashioned into something protective. He wrapped the tarp around him like a cloak, tying the corners around his neck and waist in order to take the whole of the rough cloth. Already, his back and shoulders welcomed the respite from the chill of sunset. A length of cord gathered up much of the material so he'd minimize snags in case he had to break and run through the woods.

Clothed and provided with a modicum of shelter and

concealment if necessary, Kane looked at the crates. From his time in the remnants of the Soviet Union, he recognized the unmistakable profile of the Avtomat Kalashnikov Model of 1947. No wonder the Fomorians had little trouble operating the rifles—the AK-47 was one of the most simple and soldier-proof firearms ever developed by twentieth-century man. Kane took one of the rifles, a model with a folding steel stock, and located another crate that had dozens of loaded magazines. He grabbed five and tucked them into a fold of his tarp cloak, the way he'd tied it off allowing it to perform as a backpack.

Armed and clothed, he was almost ready to leave when he spotted an AK bayonet. The knife was a crude, almost indestructible little tool. It wasn't the sharpest of combat knives, but it had plenty of utility items in its handle, and even its handguard could be utilized as a screwdriver or can opener. Kane grabbed the tool, tucking it beside his caveman stone knife. It couldn't hurt to have a backup knife.

Now it was time to leave, because Bres hadn't wasted time ripping out water or food supplies.

Kane debated finding Epona, but Bres wouldn't harm her yet. She was still worthy bait, and no trap had been sprung for him so far. Retreat and reorganization were all that Kane could hope for now, and he knifed through the growing shadows, reaching the tree line without a cry of alarm.

So far, so good, but there was no guarantee that Kane

wasn't still working according to an ancient demon's plan. All he could hope for was to stay alive long enough to think of something, all the while keeping his eyes and ears peeled for skulking shadows filled with mutated monsters thirsting for his blood.

KANE HAD TWELVE FEET of cord and a ten-foot-by-ten-foot square of tarpaulin in addition to the bayonet he'd stolen and the stone knife he had on hand. First Kane laid down on the extended canvas and measured himself against the fabric, arms extended. Using the sharper chipped and honed edge of the stone knife, he cut a square specifically to produce a simple parka. He cut a hole in the center for his head, and slipped the whole thing over himself, laying it across his shoulders with the points running down on his front and back center-lines. The other two corners hung over his arms, giving him plenty of warmth, as well as freedom of movement.

Since he wasn't going to be getting anywhere resembling shelter anytime soon, he cut three-foot lengths of cloth and tied them around his upper arms and wrists in order to provide him with sleeves. He took another three-foot strip and wound it around his chest, tucking it in as a secure wrap. Simple, crude clothing, but it kept him warm, and the tough canvas would protect him from scratches and bruises. Kane also fashioned a hood to contain the warmth that would escape through his head.

"Fashioned," Kane muttered. "This isn't fashion. This is survival."

Sure, the shadow suits offered all manner of extras that could allow him to walk in Antarctic blizzards without discomfort, but with this, Kane felt *dressed,* not naked or clad as some kind of ersatz superhero. There was a reason why he pulled on cargo pants and jackets over the shadow suit when he could. Right now, Kane resembled some form of ragman, a vagabond from some medieval fairy tale, but he didn't have to worry about self-conscious body issues while prancing around in body-hugging fabrics.

Kane took a section of the remaining tarp and the cord and constructed a knapsack that he could put over his shoulder. He left it mostly empty except for samples of roots and acorns. The roots he'd bite into and suck out the moisture and minerals. The acorns were food. Not the most ideal of meals, but it was something. If Kane managed to snag some meat, he'd wrap it in some of the remaining canvas to keep a spare supply on hand. A second, smaller bag hung at waist level, dedicated solely to the spare ammunition for his confiscated rifle. The AK he slung under the parka so that a glint of metal in moon or starlight wouldn't betray his position. He'd also created a canvas sash where he hung the ammunition bag and into which he tucked his two knives.

Kane even retrieved his bandage material, replacing it with a section of tarp around the handle of the length of sharpened stone.

That was another benefit of the hood. It kept his head bandage safe from a direct assault by the elements.

As he quickly assembled his canvas survival armor, he had found a length of branch with one end split. He took another strip and tightened it around the split end. If necessary, Kane would be able to make a spear with his stone knife stuck in the split end, but the bindings would prevent the broken end from splintering beforehand. As it was, the branch made a fine cane and cudgel, far more usable for navigating through the woods up and downslope than if he'd assembled it into a spear right away.

"I dub thee cane of Kane," he muttered softly. A smirk crossed his lips as he hefted the shank of wood.

Not much, indeed, since he was relying on a three-hundred-year-old rifle design as his most modern piece of equipment, while everything but the bayonet was pure Stone Age. The thing that inspired the most confidence was a windfall length of wood.

No, Kane wasn't ready to surrender to the elements, nor to whatever trap Bres had in mind. He might have manipulated Epona into drawing him in, but Kane had struck and faded into the night so swiftly, the Fomorian hadn't realized that he'd been there.

There was movement in the distance, the heavy footfalls of the mutants as they searched for him. The hunters were good, spread out in a line to make the most of their numbers, but the man they sought was a veteran of hundreds of hunts, as both predator and prey.

By the time they reached this clearing, Kane would be long gone, staying two steps ahead in this game of cat and mouse.

Chapter 14

Balor was a conglomeration of unusual parts. His massive, brutish body belied some form of primitive gigantic ape, something from the dawn of history best suited to punching out one-ton carnosaurs. His voice was that of a young boy, no older than ten, or a nasally pitched adult woman, soft, lilting at times and sharp and shrill at others. His mind was sharp, though. While it was trapped in a form that looked monstrous and unintelligent, Balor was hardly dim. He had been educated by Bres, whose millennia of experience led to nights of the beautiful godling reciting the best of thousands of years of literature to Balor. He had been with Bres for forty years, constantly learning new things with every passing day. Though his head was tiny in comparison to the rest of his awesome body, he was not a victim of microcephalopathy. Bres had just simply added layers upon layers of muscle and bone onto him, turning Balor into a titan.

And then there was his "baleful" eye. It glowed a sickly radioactive green, and was the size of a fist. When Balor looked at his reflection on the surfaces of puddles, the emerald shimmer seemed alien to him—he never saw it, never felt it, even when he opened up the depths of the baleful eye's true power. It was just like a normal eye. He even possessed normal depth of field, just as when he had two eyes. The glow, however, was something he'd never noticed in normal everyday life. The power of the orb in his skull was on multiple levels, and when Bres had given it to him, the godling claimed that it had belonged to Bres's own father, kept safe for thousands of years.

He remembered when he was reborn as Balor. He was just a young boy, his voice still high, not having dropped with the onset of adolescence due to hormonal imbalance. Bres had dug the eye out, and there, surrounded by dozens of murdered Appalachians, those who had tormented Balor before his defection to the side of the Fomorians, he unveiled the eye.

The front half looked normal, a regular eye, but the back was a bowl of metal and electronics with a cord of pink polymer that resembled an engorged, wormlike optic nerve. Balor only remembered the fire and the pain of transformation; he didn't want the calming caress that would have numbed his nerves. The agony he was twisted through as bodies were fed onto him, adding layers of biomass to his frame, was the cleansing process that helped him sever his link to when he was a human.

Now, he was truly the son of Bres, Balor the Second, mighty beyond all, stitched together from a dozen carcasses and a strange, ancient device that gave Balor powers beyond all normality.

It was one of these powers that picked up the presence of warm footprints in the ground, pools of heat where hands had touched the ground or crates. Bres had explained the process as thermal imaging, but to Balor, it was his rainbow sight, capable of peering through foliage or tracking a person by his passage. Balor's flat, ragged nose twitched in irritation, and he loped toward Bres, who stood, watching over the witch.

"Kane was here. He took supplies and left," Balor explained.

"He left?" Bres asked.

"He moved in when I wasn't watching. That's the only way he could have snuck past," Balor grumbled.

Bres cursed under his breath. "I'll get in touch with the hunting party via radio."

"I want to snatch him up," Balor begged. "Let me go after him."

"No, son," Bres whispered softly. "There will come a time when you may face this human, but now is not it."

"He cannot harm me, and I will be gentle," Balor pleaded.

"I said no," Bres growled, the angry authority in his voice snapping on Balor like the crack of a whip.

Balor lowered his head at his father's command.

"You have brothers to free from imprisonment in the side of the mountain," Bres cooed, stroking the huge lantern jaw of his titanic offspring. "We cannot afford the loss of my army."

"Yes, sir," Balor whispered, thoroughly admonished.

With that, he sprung back toward the cliffs and applied his might to tearing away slabs of rock and clots of soil with renewed ferocity, shovellike fingernails clawing through material as if it were soft sand, not compacted earth and stone. Shoulder muscles shifted like icebergs crashing in an arctic ocean, each movement precise, yet bearing the power of a bulldozer. He had been tempted to use the full fire of the baleful eye, but the lambent radiation would only cut holes in the dirt, and perhaps penetrate into a tunnel and sicken his brother Fomorians. Even they could not stand in the harsh emerald glow of his dread stare. No, this was a matter of brutish strength alone.

Such was his task until his father deemed it the appropriate time for him to set out in search of the man Kane, descendant of Cuchulainn.

When they met, it would be the meeting of the sons of the gods. Balor's twisted lips turned up in a grim smile. The battle would be glorious, a challenge that Balor had sought all of his existence.

WITH THE AID of his walking stick, and shielded from the elements by his impromptu canvas outfit, Kane was able to ascend the mountainside much more quickly than before. The leverage of his cane helped him use all of his strength, not just his legs, to haul himself up the steep slope. Behind him, there were four of the Fomorian hunters, put on his trail because they noticed that he'd stolen by them. Kane wondered if perhaps one of the Fomorians had a form of enhanced senses to have detected his passing.

The hunters were skilled, Kane had to admit. He had done much of his traveling by walking toe-heel, minimizing his stride and footprints. Still, when it came to ascending loose soil and the detritus of the forest floor, he couldn't help but make some mess. That they could follow his spoor in the darkness of night was a credit to their skill.

Perhaps they wanted him alive, because not one of them had unslung his rifle, but Kane wasn't going to gamble too much on that presumption. Bres wanted Kane for something, and given the stories of cannibalism among the Fomorians, it was likely that whatever means Bres had to gain information would not be pleasant for Kane.

It was time to make things a little more difficult for the Fomorians, so Kane stopped climbing and scurried laterally on the mountainside. Traveling on a more level incline allowed him to make the most of his escape and evasion skills. His tread grew lighter, and very little was disturbed as he passed. It was about a three-hundred-stride detour, and Kane paused to crouch behind the cover of some boulders. Hunger and thirst rumbled in his gut again, and Kane pulled out a clump of grass to chew on the roots. Moisture exploded in his mouth and refreshed him. He made certain not to leave any sign that he'd paused among the rocks, scanning by touch for any fallen blades that would have been visibly out of place here.

Swallowing the last of the juices from a second serving of roots, Kane put the pulp under a flat piece of stone to hide it. In daylight, it might have been noticeable if the Fomorians had wandered this far, but right now, he had the impression of frustration emanating from the hunting party. He kept low behind the boulder, unmoving, his canvas hood and parka helping him to blend in with the shadows around him. As he watched, he saw a lone Fomorian pacing. The creature had withdrawn his rifle, hard eyes scanning for signs of his prey.

Kane held his ground, remaining silent, his breathing slowed until it was inaudible to the one-armed hunter sweeping the mountainside. While killing one of the creatures might have given him the opportunity to steal more supplies and even the odds, the group of hunters were operating in coordination. One move, a flurry of violence, would produce enough noise to alert the other three who were on the stalk, keeping their eyes and ears open for anything out of the ordinary. Rather than risk a confrontation and putting himself in the sights of a trio of the strong, determined mutants, Kane opted to remain stealthy, using his own senses to keep track of the threats hunting for him.

The one-armed Fomorian held his AK-47 like a handgun. The thickness of his forearm and the bulge of his biceps informed Kane that no amount of recoil would throw off the creature's aim, and his binocular vision meant that his marksmanship would be unimpeded by any mutations. A sharp whistle cut the air and the Fomorian halted.

Kane didn't move, remaining still as the stones he hid among, only his eyes sweeping for the origin of the piercing signal. Due to the echoing properties of the trees on the mountain slope, Kane wasn't able to triangulate the origin of the whistle. It was possible that his enemy had surrounded him, but to turn his head to look further would only betray his position.

If the hunters were certain that they knew where he was, the whistle would have been followed by more verbal means of communication. Kane returned his gaze to the Fomorian that he could see without moving, and saw that the hunter was in the middle of stuffing the barrel of his AK through his belt. The hunter's face was twisted in obvious reluctance to give up the chase; perhaps he smelled something, or his acute ears had picked up Kane's heartbeat. Whatever, the Fomorian had sensed that he wasn't far from his prey.

The Fomorians were to regroup, Kane interpreted as the mutant turned and headed back toward his brethren. As soon as the creature was out of sight, Kane rose slowly. He glanced at the source of the shrieking whistle from before, and while it was an upper-level outcrop, it was empty for now.

Was this really a game of cat and mouse? How much

did the hunters know? What kind of special senses or assistance would these creatures have had?

Three good questions, but Kane would concentrate
on these later on. Right now, he padded off silently,
moving another hundred yards before he stopped against
the trunk of a pine tree with an exposed tangle of roots
that offered cover. Tucked in the soil beneath the tree's
trunk, Kane watched his back trail. He'd used his
walking stick to disturb some ground he'd passed
through, well within his line of sight, more as a test for
how good his stalkers had been. The line of the staff
prints had been a turnoff about twenty-five yards from
his current hiding position, and Kane had climbed fifty
feet before tucking the stick under his armpit and skit-
tering with a minimum of disturbance back toward this
hiding spot.

If they possessed superior senses of smell or a means
of reading his body heat from his footsteps, then the feint
wouldn't have worked due to the backtrack. Two Fomorians grunted softly as they spotted Kane's false trail.
The sharp whistle broke the night silence once more, and
the other two arrived, not in a rush and maintaining
noise discipline. If Kane hadn't been versed in how Sky
Dog's tribespeople were able to imitate local birds
around the Bitterroot Mountain Range where the
Cerberus redoubt was based, he could have been fooled
into thinking that it was some form of local screech owl.

Kane scanned the area from his peripheral vision to
make certain that the four in the open weren't a distrac-

tion to keep him occupied while other hunters sneaked up behind him. No, he was in the clear for now. The four mutants started slowly up the mountainside, watching the trail that Kane had started. They hadn't seen his other movements inscribed in the dirt, and when they reached the top of the fifty-foot climb, they looked all around.

The leader of the group grunted in frustration, then waved for the others to spread out. They did so, watching the slope. They had counted on him moving laterally once more, which meant that their senses weren't superhumanly keen.

That was a relief to Kane, who slithered out of the shadows and started back down the hill. He now knew that his enemy had only one or two members of their group who had preternatural senses, but he was also aware that his foes were strong and clever. Their sense of discipline in small-unit tactics and skill at tracking made them formidable opponents. The addition of automatic weapons was only a minor advantage to their already impressive list of abilities. Kane needed to get his own advantages, and that meant a few things had to be done.

The primary course of action was determining how to liberate Epona from Bres's clutches. Stealth was going to be his best course, as he didn't relish fighting a creature who made the average Fomorian look spindly and puny. Right now, Kane needed her ancient Tuatha powers to complement his own skills, but if immediate rescue proved to be too difficult, then Kane would fall back to a second option, which was reaching the top of the mountain.

The Fomorians were currently running a wild-goose chase, and they might get a clue again and try searching farther afield. The hunters wouldn't waste their time returning to camp, even if they thought he might try something. Bres and Balor were back there, adding to the numbers of Fomorian tribesmen ready to hunt and fight. Kane could skirt the compound, figure out how to rescue Epona and then either with her in tow, or on his own, head to where the Cerberus explorers had left the communication equipment linking them to the Appalachians. The false Kane wouldn't have had the time or energy to sabotage the radio, and when Kane got in contact with Cerberus redoubt, he'd be able to warn them of the real danger. His Commtact still wasn't working, though Kane wasn't sure whether the problem was with his comm unit or back at the redoubt.

Slicing through the night like a panther, Kane moved silently, leaving little trace as he closed in on the Fomorian compound. If there was going to be a fight, at least this time he was prepared. Kane figured the amount of time since the avalanche, and he was closing on perhaps an hour and twenty minutes by his reckoning. He wondered about the turnaround time for Cerberus to send teams back to this area in order to help the Appalachians against the now decidedly dire threat of Bres and the Fomorians. Would his partners be paranoid enough to be concerned about his being replaced, and if so, would Thrush's doppelganger play into that paranoia, slowing them?

Kane figured for at least an hour and a half of medical tests, perhaps closer to two. He thought about his current course, back toward the Fomorian base, and then turning and heading to the top of the mountain. Add in the necessity to have Grant refit his equipment and head out with CAT Beta while Brigid stayed behind with the false entity...

It would take Kane an hour and forty minutes to get Epona and return to the mountaintop. He figured that would be about the amount of time it would take for Cerberus to feel as if they had successfully contained a possible impostor and sent Grant and Domi to deal with the ancient race of mutants. Given Grant's and Edwards's size and Magistrate training, both men would be loaded for far more than bear, with grenade launchers and heavy antitank rifles in their gear. Ideally, to deal with the Fomorians, Kane would have opted for something like the mobile armor suits utilized in New Olympus, but Lakesh and Brewster Philboyd were working on modifications of the basic gear skeleton layout. As much as the New Olympian pilots were skilled at the use of the high-tech battle armor, they had sacrificed much to be able to utilize the suits. The original cockpits had been designed for smaller than human servitor races, like the Transadapts, so a human had to be an amputee to handle the current cockpit layouts.

Increasing the size of the suits and the control chairs had been one idea, but the accompanying extra mass took up room that the war armor had originally been re-designed for sensor and weapons systems. While there were suggestions of forearm mounts replacing the shoulder weapon pintels, akin to the Magistrates' Sin Eaters, there was controversy whether the arm mounts reduced the effectiveness of the gear skeletons. Part of the success of the Olympian fighting armor was that they could do chores and act as heavy-lifting equipment. The shoulder guns had been out of the way, letting them be fighters in addition to being superhuman laborers.

Thus, Philboyd had been studying the designs in order to make smaller versions of the big combat suits.

Here, on a mountainside, wrapped in canvas, Kane wondered what it would be like to be plugged into such a thing. He had worn other types of uniforms—Magistrate armor, battle dress uniforms, the high-tech shadow suits. He couldn't imagine donning an articulated exoskeleton.

Time enough to make such speculations later, he reminded himself sternly

Check on Epona, and then try to reach the parallax point before Grant and the others come back to clean up the Fomorians left over from the landslide.

Kane fitted his stone knife into the notch at the end of his cane. Even on a stealth run, the use of its flesh-piercing point would mean the difference between dis-covery and evasion.

It was time to see if he could rescue a witch.

Chapter 15

Cerberus

Daryl Morganstern was in the middle of laughing at Wynan's joke when Thrush-Kane approached him. Where Morganstern was a bit shorter than Brigid, Wynan was a mere five foot seven with black curly hair contrasting with a pale, rusty brown coloring. For a moment, the infiltration cyborg was reminded of the antithesis of Kane and Grant, with Morganstern's "Grant" being small, scrawny and big eared. A smile flitted across his lips at the concept that Brigid Baptiste had found her own means of getting together with a different take on her *anam-chara*, this time opting for a variant who was more brain than brawn. Thrush-Kane didn't know whether Wynan was the scientist's first or last name, since he wasn't called anything else.

"Hi, Daryl?" The android made his halting introductory statement, removing as much of the bass, and by extension the menace, from his voice.

"Oh, uh, Mr. Kane," Morganstern replied. He hastily reached up and pulled off his glasses, folding them to put them in the pocket of his shirt.

"Don't worry about your glasses," Thrush-Kane said.

Morganstern looked down at his breast pocket, then chuckled nervously. "Oh, I wasn't afraid that you'd hit me. I just didn't need them right now."

Wynan raised his hand meekly. "He uses them for magnification purposes. Reading small print, working with tiny devices…"

Thrush-Kane tilted his head, stooping so as to meet Morganstern eye to eye. "Daryl, this isn't high school, and I'm not some kind of jock here to push you around."

"Forgive me if my nerd senses were left tingling, okay?" Morganstern said.

Thrush-Kane sighed and rested a calming hand on his shoulder. "We're going to talk. Man to man, friendly, and here in the middle of the mess hall. I'm not going to haul you off to some secret corridor and punch you bloody."

"But don't worry about implying that all I'm interested is in carnal relations with Brigid?" Morganstern asked hastily, a tremor shooting through his body.

"What?" Thrush-Kane tried to process that sudden exclamation, and realized that for all the intellect the young man had, he still had been ostracized. It took a few cycles of mental calculations to realize that Morganstern was indignant over the earlier remark about "how many moves until mate." The android brain directed his clone body into a sigh. "I'm sorry about that joke. It was mean, and it was crude, and it was just locker-room talk."

"From talking with the Magistrates, they sounded just like football players, except with guns, not balls," Wynan spoke up. When this drew Thrush-Kane's gaze, he inched back out of the conversation.

"All right. So this seems exceedingly like your old high school—"

"And college," Morganstern spoke up.

"Like all your school days," Thrush-Kane amended. "You want to stop interrupting me?"

Morganstern nodded so fast, Thrush-Kane wondered if he'd begun to have a seizure.

"Relax, both of you," Thrush-Kane told them. "I'm here on Brigid's behalf. She's my friend, and I'm just interested in who she's interested in."

"Our fields of common ground are very small," Wynan spoke up. "I could demonstrate via a Venn diagram—"

"Is she dating you, Wynan?" Thrush-Kane inquired.

Wynan held his bare wrist up under his face and looked at it as if he was examining a watch face on it. "Whoa, is that the time?"

"I'm not chasing you off," Thrush-Kane told him with a sigh.

"Yes, sir," Wynan answered.

Humans, the infiltrator thought, putting his face into the palms of his hands. It was a wonder that they had evolved as far and survived long enough to have built his original iterations, what with their surfeit of neurotic tendencies and insecurities. "I'm not a sir, Wynan. I work. Lakesh might make you call him sir—"

"But, Kane, we *respect* you," Morganstern said. "Why can't you let us show you some honor?"

Thrush-Kane raised an eyebrow, surprised. "Honor? Respect..."

"Don't you think you deserve respect?" Wynan asked.

Thrush-Kane searched, looking for the man's sense of humility. The thing was, Kane existed in a world where he'd fought to escape an artificial caste system, where honor was bestowed because of genetic purity. Kane himself had been specifically bred by Lakesh, and for a while, at least according to the female Kane of an alternate casement, had resented the idea of such manipulation.

"Everyone deserves respect. I'm just not a 'sir' type of person," the doppelganger finally answered. All of this was way off the normal path that the infiltrator had intended to follow. He'd come here looking for something that would give him an insight into the mathematician Morganstern's thought processes that would have assisted in the creation of an encryption algorithm. Without a means of deciphering the equation that Morganstern had utilized to secure Cerberus redoubt's computer security, Thrush-Kane's plasma matrix computer brain couldn't hack into it. He was counting down to the moment when the mat-trans was going to send Grant, Domi and CAT Beta back to the Appalachians.

If the explorers got there, then there was a likelihood that the real Kane would hook up with them. With the discovery of his replacement, access to computer records would be shut down. When that happened, any chance of uncovering clues as to the location of Enlil would disappear. The effort to plant him in the redoubt would have been all for naught.

Spending time coddling the feelings of a couple of nerds new to the Cerberus operation was something Thrush-Kane didn't have time for. He had eight minutes, and even at his remarkable intellectual computational speeds, he'd have trouble reprogramming the mat-trans with a blind jump destination. It was just a stroke of luck that the Thrush Continuum, through its knowledge of Annunaki technology and studies of Lakesh's prior quantum physics theories, that the android already knew the proper coding necessary to operate the mat-trans.

Morganstern tilted his head at the expression of humility presented by Kane. "I'm sorry. What would you like to be called?"

"By my name. Kane's good enough," the false man answered.

"All right. So what do you want to talk to me about?" Morganstern asked. He pushed a napkin toward Wynan, and Thrush-Kane caught a glimpse of it. One look was all that was necessary to burn the image of the napkin into his mind, and already a subroutine was flipping the napkin upside down and deciphering the mathematician's handwriting.

"About Brigid. I just wanted to make some assurances that you don't have to worry about any jealousy," Thrush-Kane said. "I want her to be happy, and you seem to have something in common with her that I really can't give her."

"I'd just assumed…" Morganstern began.

Thrush-Kane had already started working the equation on a subprocessor. Operating at two million calculations a second, the plasma matrix brain hurtled along in an attempt to translate the kind of thought processes that went into the purpose of the scribblings he'd seen. Deciphering the napkin was difficult, to the point that the doppelganger's brow furrowed in concentration.

"You'd assumed that the two Spandex-clad superheroes of the redoubt had something going, right?" Thrush-Kane asked.

"Wynan mentioned that you were more of a roguish space captain than a man of steel," Morganstern admitted. "However, it's hard not to think of you and her as anything but a couple."

The mention of science fiction brought up correlations in the plasma matrix memory of the android. The napkin's equations were a means by which wormholes in space time could be theoretically located and operated, but in a manner totally different from the means by which Lakesh's own calculations had opened the doors to matter transfer.

Morganstern's equations explored hyperspatial existence, which had not been a discipline that had been followed in many dimensions. Thrush was aware of a particular casement that was hyperspatial in nature, but the mathematics required to maneuver in such an environment assumed logical leaps that still needed justification.

"Brigid and I care about each other, that much is true," Thrush-Kane said, his struggles growing easier now that he realized that Morganstern was working to apply a valid but understudied theory and applied equations to the special cases of physics necessary to operate in a different environment.

It was the tiny sliver of information that gave the android everything he needed to penetrate the algorithm that had protected Cerberus's encryption. Now, having made that correlation, he was able to return to the task that Kane himself would have taken, which was assuaging the concerns of a man who was interested in Brigid.

Morganstern's face grew ashen in response to Thrush-Kane's statement about how much Kane and Brigid cared about each other. The infiltrator suddenly felt a pang of regret, and immediately worked to clarify it. "We're friends. And that's all we are. *Anam-chara,* if you understand Celtic lore."

"Soul friends, that's what she said," Morganstern answered. "But going by what she's said you've told her, you've known each other across multiple lifetimes."

"Yes," Thrush-Kane responded. The impostor suddenly seemed lost. Why in the flying blue hell did he give a damn about what this mathematician felt?

Because that's what Kane would do, came an answer.

It was straight from the memory core dedicated to behavior parameters and information to continue his impersonation of the real Kane. The man we are supposed to be is not greedy. If anything, he's selfless, capable of sacrificing himself if it means others will survive. His role in the world is to risk everything to make sure humankind survives, be it recovering ancient technology or warding off conquerors from other universes.

"We've known each other, but there's only been one reality we've found where we've been anything close to romantically involved," Thrush-Kane continued. "That was an alternate future that we have avoided."

"The laws of causality state simply that your choice merely caused a branching in the scheme of things," Morganstern said. "That time line still exists, though we are currently not involved in it anymore."

"And right now it's irrelevant," Thrush-Kane continued. The impersonation memory banks were in full control of his mind now. All the other functions of his plasma matrix not devoted to the ruse or the operation of his body were directed toward crunching the equations necessary to delve into the Cerberus command system. As it was, the android brain began to overheat. Morganstern's equations were good, but the infiltrator was working against more than just one mathematician. Bry's mastery of computer security, bolstered by the efforts of the lunar base programmers, was something that was taxing his computational capabilities. The infiltrator realized that this much effort was overclocking the semiorganic blob residing in his reinforced skull, and it was beginning to have an effect on him.

"Kane?" Morganstern asked.

Thrush-Kane rested his forehead against his palm. "Sorry. Didn't think my head was hit that hard."

"Wynan…" The mathematician spoke up.

The little scientist was already at the trans-comm unit. "We need a team to the mess hall, stat. Kane is suffering delayed effects of head trauma."

Morganstern tilted Thrush-Kane's head backward and pressed a napkin beneath his nose. "Tell her we've got a nosebleed!"

"Nosebleed?" Thrush-Kane asked, pushing Morganstern away for a moment. He tried to access his self-diagnostics, but none of the command structures of his own brain were working. The effort necessary to wirelessly hack into the redoubt's computer mainframe had seized up every non-essential process.

Thrush-Kane looked at his hand as it came away from his nose. His palm was drenched in red, and he knew that his prior self-diagnostic assessment had been off. When Bres had struck him in the head, it was with an amount of force that had somehow transmitted through his nigh-unbreakable skull.

"Head back," Morganstern grunted. "I used to get these all the time. But then, I hadn't been smacked in the head by a mutant."

Thrush-Kane allowed his body to be manipulated by the scientist.

"Brigid was right. You've got a damn hard skull," Morganstern mentioned. "But whatever hit you weakened you."

That's because Bres was as calculating a bastard as I am, Thrush-Kane thought. He kept silent, minimizing the need for his plasma matrix to do anything but ensure his survival. A nosebleed was a minor emergency, and had he been truly human, it would have been an indication of a subcranial hemorrhage. For the clone body wrapped around a semiorganic skeleton, however, it was simply an instance of blood vessels draining. Without his internal self-diagnostic routine, there was no way to know the cause of the organic damage. A touch to his brow, just above his nose, revealed an intense point of heat. Luckily, everyone present was too concerned about the blood pouring out of his face to take note that their "Kane" was now running a fever of 130 degrees Fahrenheit.

Simple logic informed the infiltrator robot that Bres's blow had damaged the cooling processes of his semiorganic brain. When the heat overwhelmed blood vessels in the sinus cavities, the tissues had dried out, crumbled and blood vessels flooded his sinuses.

If DeFore and the medical staff investigated him too closely, they'd see the kind of overheating damage released by an out-of-control android brain. No human's skull could overheat that much without outright killing its owner. Thrush-Kane had to do something to shut things down. The dominant personality called upon the subbrains, looking for a response.

We have successfully penetrated redoubt command code, came the answer. Emergency diagnostic process running to minimize and return plasma matrix to normal operating procedures.

"Too late for that now," Thrush-Kane slurred. "Turn out the lights…."

"Kane?" Morganstern asked, holding a napkin up to his nose. The bleeding had slowed now that the android's brain was aware of the overclocking problem. "Turn out what lights?"

The mess hall suddenly went pitch-black. Screams filled the room with the sudden plunge into darkness, and since the redoubt was built into the side of a mountain, there were no windows to admit natural light. Emergency lights came up within a few moments, but for the expanse of the mess hall, there were a half dozen twin-bulb units that offered a reddish-orange glow. It wasn't the most ideal of illumination, but at least the oppressive weight of absolute darkness no longer crushed in on the Cerberus residents.

"The trans-comm's out," Wynan said, coming back. "Daryl…"

"I'll be right there," Morganstern answered. "Kane, can you hold the napkin in place and stay still?"

"I'll try," Thrush-Kane responded numbly. His plasma matrix was shutting down everything it could inside its own system in order to lower the stresses against the body wrapped around it. As such, physically the infiltrator seemed drunk or impaired by blood loss and concussion. While that had fit in with the results of DeFore's prior testing, thanks to wireless projection producing those results especially for her equipment, Thrush-Kane felt intensely ill. He looked at Morganstern out of the corner of his eye and noticed that whatever sympathy he felt for the young man had evaporated.

Kane impersonation subroutine disengaged. That part of his brain was rendered silent, so the emotions of the hero he was attempting to duplicate disappeared. Unfortunately, the core personality, no longer hindered by the spark of compassion built into that subroutine, now felt something completely different. It was lucky for Morganstern that Thrush-Kane felt physically weak and didn't want to jeopardize his impersonation; otherwise he would have sat up and begun throttling the mathematician right then and there.

Right now, Cerberus was in a state of turmoil because of the altered command parameters of the environmental systems. The nonlethal set of changes mostly dealt with lighting and room access. There was pounding at the mess hall doors as trapped Cerberus personnel tried to enter.

Thrush-Kane sat up, having recovered much of his strength after a near breakdown of his inorganic computer. If he was alone in the dining room, he would have been able to open the doors with a whim. However, if he demonstrated such capability now, it would become clear that he was the architect of the emergency power-down.

His Commtact remained silent, which was another of the results of his invasion of the central core. With doors locked down and the communications systems knocked out, he had thrown the redoubt into complete disarray.

Thrush-Kane grimaced in regret that he hadn't been able to directly force a confrontation between the forces of Cerberus and Enlil. Had he been the kind to lay curses against those whom he despised, he would have called down a pox upon Bres for the way he had altered the playing field. The Fomorians could have enjoyed themselves with Kane, testing their worth against that particular champion of humanity. Instead, with the wild hunt called down onto the android impersonator, Thrush-Kane was stuck waiting for the Cerberus heroes to finish their conflict with the Fomorian raiders who tormented the Appalachians.

Of course, that would allow Grant and his allies to discover the real Kane, who had been left behind. The Thrush Continuum had specifically wanted a means by which to back up its efforts against the renegade Enlil, and so he had been left alive, if hampered by the presence of the Fomorians. Thrush-Kane was now left with a base with a disabled mat-trans unit. If the jump chamber was functional, he risked exposing his ruse. He doubted that the avalanche had done as much to the immortal Bres, a being who claimed to have been alive millennia ago. Why Bres would have engaged in such sabotage of his assault was hard to decipher, unless…

Thrush-Kane went to check on Brigid Baptiste's

report regarding the entities they'd encountered. The archivist was always good for a thorough chronicle of the
events of their jumps, no matter which reality she was
from. The infiltrator fought off a wave of desire rising
through him.

Just because the real Kane is too stupid to think of
her as his perfect mate doesn't mean I have to indulge
in such idiocy, the impostor thought.

"Kane?" Morganstern spoke up, interrupting his
internal debate. "Kane, you should lie down."

"The bleeding's stopped," the impostor growled. "I
feel better. Besides…"

Morganstern dared to put a hand on his arm. Somewhere in the depths of his mind, a voice called out. It
was the nobility of the original Kane templates they had
used, the impersonation personality that was the cover
against discovery.

Don't hurt him, even if it's only to maintain our cover,
the Kane impersonation pleaded.

Thrush-Kane's right fist flexed, tendons popping, but
he fought off the urge to put his fist through the mathematician's face. "I'm fine. My balance is good. I'm not
dizzy."

Morganstern stepped back, noticing the clenched fist.
"No offense intended, Kane."

The impostor nodded, looking down at his white
knuckles. "Sorry. Stressed over the sudden blackout.
Have you tried calling anyone over the trans-comm? My
Commtact isn't working."

"We're in the dark, lights and communication," Morganstern replied. "Wynan already has the access panel off, but the wiring itself is in pristine working order."

Thrush-Kane frowned. "You think this could be Enlil making a move against us?"

Thrush-Kane's brain suddenly resonated with the voice of Brigid Baptiste as she recorded her log of the Appalachian mission, and had tagged a section regarding her speculations about the Fomorians. Bres is traditionally known as the son of Balor, and the gods, as well as the Fomorians, are their descendants, in a parallel of the mythology of Greece. Whereas Zeus was the son of the Titan Chronus, Lugh, powerful king among the Tuatha de Danaan pantheon, was the grandson of Balor, through Balor's daughter Ethniu, who from my studies bears a remarkable resemblance to Fand. After comparative studies among mythology and known history as related by Balam, it is quite possible that the Annunaki were the creators of the Fomorians in their battle with the Tuatha de Danaan, and Lugh himself may have been a crossbreed, such as Enlil's daughter Fand, combining the genetic—

Lugh was the grandson of Balor. And Bres boasted that he himself was the son of Balor. Bres's resemblance to the Tuatha's remarkable physiological superiority and his considerable strength could have made him one of many of Enlil's children. Fand was a daughter of the same Dragon King.

Thrush-Kane reeled. Why would Bres help, then

sabotage, an effort to infiltrate Cerberus and lead an assault on the most powerful of the Annunaki? Because Bres wanted to return to his ancestor's favor. The betrayal of the Fomorians was a calculated, cold plan set in motion to protect the king of the overlords, made up on the spot when Thrush-Kane had been overheard bragging to the captive Kane.

"Kane! Wake the hell up!" Wynan shouted. "You're zoning out!"

"Bres and Enlil were linked. Bres is the grandson of Enlil," Thrush-Kane said out loud.

Morganstern tilted his head. "Kane, we need you to focus on the problems we have right now."

Thrush-Kane's lips tightened into a bloodless line. He had to sell this next bit of information hard and fast. "You don't get it, do you? Something else got into Cerberus along with us. That's why I was really captured. I'm some form of Trojan horse."

Morganstern and Wynan looked at each other. Thrush-Kane could see the thought processes going between the pair.

"We'd have noticed a biological entity," Wynan declared.

"But we'd also have noticed if there were microscopic constructs, akin to nanotechnology, that were brought in via the transporter," Morganstern mused. He looked at Thrush-Kane, then reached out toward the false man's face. "What if it was something that we wouldn't expect?"

Thrush-Kane pushed aside Morganstern's hand. "What are you talking about?"

"You were unconscious, correct?" Morganstern asked. "Given what we know about the kind of technology the Annunaki have, they have specific signals that can alter DNA radically in a manner that defies the conservation of energy."

"Right, mass doesn't just spring out of nowhere," Thrush-Kane said.

"So what if we're dealing with some form of mathematical theorem, but one that could be housed in the most innocent of devices, such as your Commtact insert. Not the plate, but the implant on your jawbone," Morganstern replied. "Once we'd gone over you with a fine-tooth comb and found absolutely everything we expected to find, especially the Commtact implants—"

"They stored a computer virus in my Commtact implant, and once I was hooked back up with the full plate system, I became a carrier who infected the Cerberus mainframe," Thrush-Kane answered.

Morganstern nodded. "Insidious. But highly likely."

"So how do we jump-start the mainframe again?" Thrush-Kane asked. "Especially if we can't communicate."

Wynan had something pulled apart on the table next to the intercom. Thrush-Kane recognized it as some manner of keyboard-faced watch. "Daryl, get a fork, some diet soda and unscrew a nut from under the table. We'll need some kind of battery power to get the door mechanism unlocked enough for Kane to pry the doors open."

"Will that be enough power?" Morganstern asked.

"Only if you use a thirty-two-ounce cup," Wynan replied snottily. "Move it, math boy!"

Thrush-Kane had dodged a bullet so far. Cerberus was in a state where Grant couldn't possibly be sent to find the real Kane, and with the help of the two lunar scientists, he'd constructed a plausible alibi for how the redoubt had been crippled.

Maybe he'd get a chance at Enlil after all.

If Thrush-Kane hadn't been so relieved at the excuse that could clear him to continue his hunt for Enlil, perhaps he would have noticed Daryl Morganstern talking with cafeteria worker Clem Bryant, or the grim worry etched into the mathematician's face as he spoke with one of the most capable minds in Cerberus.

Chapter 16

The Appalachians

Kane had approached to within earshot of a Fomorian guard who had a radio unit on hand. The mutant was paying attention to the progress of the hunting party that had been sent after Kane, and right now, they were backtracking and searching thoroughly for whatever path Kane might have taken to elude them. Little did the hideous pursuers realize that Kane was a mile away from them, crouched in shadows and foliage, effectively invisible.

"No sign of the human's return to the compound," the guard said. "Perimeter patrols are still on alert now that we've got the manpower."

"This monkey is a tricky bastard. He's a legend among men for a reason," came the crackling anger over the radio. "Balor's keeping his Eye out, too, right?"

"No, we just assumed that the Eye of Balor is too useful, and we should challenge ourselves," the guard grumbled, sarcasm dripping like venom off his words. "Big as he is, and cool as his damn eye is, Balor's just

one man. Mutant. There's just one Balor. And he can't
see everywhere at once!"

"Bres's balls!" the hunting party on the other end exclaimed. "We're sorry we hurt your feelings. Tell you
what—next time you're getting your vagina cleaned,
we'll spring for a badger to be thrown up it."

Kane could see the anger screwing up on the guard's
face. "You're all bastards."

The guard pivoted angrily, resisting the urge to grind
the field radio into splinters in his massive fist. This
creature was one of the single-armed monstrosities, and
his sharp eyes searched for any movement. Only by
avoiding the Fomorian's peripheral vision was Kane
able to move more than a few inches, even in the
darkness and foliage camouflaging his presence.

Kane made a short dash and knelt in loose soil that
had been thrown up in the digging efforts to rescue other
Fomorians trapped in caves under the avalanche. One of
the benefits of his canvas parka on top of the body wraps
he'd fashioned for himself was that the rough tarp was
relatively moisture resistant, but it still picked up wet
mud as he slid through it. The mud not only gave Kane
another layer of lifesaving insulation, but it provided
him with further visual camouflage, both to regular
eyesight and any enhanced optics he'd encounter. That
Balor—the largest of the Fomorians—hadn't called out
an alert meant that Kane's visual signature was minimal.

Oblivious to the ghostly passage of Kane, the
Fomorian guard pivoted again and looked for more signs

of intrusion. It wasn't the fastest Kane had ever gone, but he left no footprints, made no sound and, most importantly, hadn't made any sudden movements that would be visible as a shadow in the corner of some mutant's eye. While he was armed and well rested now, he was still outnumbered, and each of Bres's mutant horde was more than a physical match for him. Caution was the order of the day, and true stealth was required.

The flurry of activity that would be required to knife an unsuspecting sentry would betray him immediately. The sight of his motion, the sound of the attack and the scent of fresh blood spilled would point the Fomorians toward the intruder within their ranks. Once it had gotten to that, there was no way that Kane could endure their attention.

How he'd survive if he saw an opportunity to snatch Epona and flee was something he hadn't quite worked out yet, but advance strategy wasn't Kane's forte. Adaptability and resourcefulness were more his game.

"Father," a young, almost feminine-sounding voice spoke up.

Kane slithered closer to the sound and spotted Balor and Bres, seated around a fire. Over the glow of the flames, he could see a frightened face. Epona was seated with them, her arms clutched to her shoulders as she gathered her cloak around her as a shield more from fear than from cold.

"Balor?" Bres asked. The voice issued again, incongruously from the huge, apelike being seated at the fire.

"If Kane does not return for the woman, how will we be able to get after Thrush?" Balor inquired.

"We will have visitors soon," Bres answered. "You do not know the stories of the outlanders, do you?"

"I have heard them, but why would those humans risk their lives just to help a group of obstinate hermits scattered across a mountain range?" Balor asked.

"Because these humans are not as the rest. They are survivors, like the outcasts who refused to bow to the barons in their villes, but they are not self-centered. They are warriors, but they have deluded themselves that they possess a cause," Bres explained.

Balor shook his cyclopean head. "They must be afraid of Enlil taking roost. That's how the witch explained it. It's the only thing that really makes sense."

"You have to learn, my son, that there were once great herds of these humans who strode across the land. Many of them were either sheep or disgruntled loners who hid out from the world. But there were many who were not ruled by base design," Bres said. The beautiful godling stood up, scanning into the night sky. "They dreamed of a better world."

"What could be better than our life?" Balor asked.

"They would see us as low beasts, living hedonistically off the pain and suffering of our prey," Bres said.

Balor shrugged. "So? Even in their literature, their vanity and greed is apparent. What they call love is simply animalistic rutting dressed up with pretty language. There is an inherent dishonesty in their way of life, a denial that to live, you simply must kill. Crops were grown to be cut down. Animals raised to be slaughtered for meat. Lower classes forced to breed to provide labor and cannon fodder for their wars. We take no slaves. We fit in with the cycle of life, and don't imprison our food in a no-win lifestyle that ultimately ends in death on a dinner plate, or as refuse to be ground up and fed to their kin."

Bres smiled at the beast's statement. Kane's stomach turned at the fact that the monsters before him had a philosophy that had its own powerful logic. It was why Kane often felt best when he was living among Sky Dog's tribe. There was a freedom of the hunter-gatherer lifestyle that allowed for an almost placid worldview.

The trouble was, Kane couldn't afford to live that way all the time. He was a man who was driven by duty to fight against oppression and cruelty. There were cultures around the world that had risen further than the perfect equilibrium of the Native Americans around the Cerberus redoubt. They sought civilization, not the false iterations that had sprung up between the time of skydark and the reunification programs of the hybrid barons. It was why Kane so readily had fallen into his duties as a Magistrate, before he realized the corruption in the system.

Another pang of nausea hit Kane as he realized that Balor, despite his size and brutish appearance, was far more than a mindless slab of muscle with superhuman strength. The unholy glow of Balor's single eye hinted at technological advances that at the very least would make it impossible to hide from the monstrosity. Couple that with agility, speed and intelligence necessary for the barbaric hunting the Fomorians had mastered, and Kane was facing a truly formidable opponent.

Kane slithered silently, remaining low to the ground, his ears peeled.

"We do have a life without lies and without pretense," Bres answered. "We take what we need, and we do not take more than we have to."

The body-racking spite Kane felt for Bres tingled all through his skin. Though he resembled his kinsman, the Mad Maccan, Kane's familiarity with the being was on a more instinctual level. The beautiful shimmer of the godling's skin, the perfection of his limbs and features, were a blatant lie, hiding the rot and fury within a moldering soul. Bres's first armies had lain siege to the Tuatha de Danaan at Enlil's beck and call, and the bloodshed of that conflict went beyond mere soldiers slaying one another. Towns of innocents had been sacked, noncombatants tortured and cannibalized in wild orgies of violence and cruelty that made strong men vomit when they came upon the aftermath.

Bres, for some purpose, had remained silent and out of the way for a while. Perhaps the reunification program had been an inspiration to grow the might of the Fomorians back to the days when the Annunaki and the Tuatha de Danaan still warred incessantly.

Kane refocused his attention on his immediate situation. He had to ensure Epona's safety and survival. The terrified witch was withdrawn and looked as if she'd need to be carried out of the Fomorian compound. Kane knew that logically, he should leave her behind and come back when he had more assistance from his allies back at Cerberus. However, the woman's ashen, catatonic state was not something to which he could abandon her. Not with cruel predators like Bres and Balor responsible for her care. Rescue was not going to be easy, but turning his back on someone in need was something that Kane refused to do.

As he closed with her, he felt the familiar rustle of a transmitting mind. He had to have been five feet behind her, slithering on the ground soundlessly when he was close enough to "hear" her thoughts. Since no animals were coming close to the compound to speak to him, and her concentration was so deep, he wondered if she was scouring the mountain slope in order to locate him.

Kane closed his eyes and sent himself into a state of centered calm. It was a way that he had been able to put aside the conscious fears and subconscious instincts of horror and revulsion he'd felt toward the alien-like Balam. That semimeditative state was how he'd become more comfortable with Balam's telepathic communication, and Kane wondered if that state of mind would make it easier for Epona to reach him.

Epona, I'm right behind you, Kane thought.

A jolt of surprise crawled back along the mental projection, and Kane braced himself against a reflexive

wince. Moments later, the unbridled joy of a telempathic embrace engulfed him, waves of relief and joy
flooding.

Easy, Kane thought. What are you trying to do?

He wondered exactly how Epona was reading what
he communicated telepathically. However, she made
herself perfectly clear in terms of emotional imagery and
stimulation. She understood him, especially his questions, and now she was transmitting the sight of Grant
arriving, bringing all the Tigers of Heaven, the citizen
soldiers of Aten and the robots and footmen of New
Olympus.

Cavalry, Kane interpreted. But is it the one I envisioned?

There was a tinge of disappointment, and Kane had
his answer. Epona was in concentration, disguised as
fearful torment, utilizing her granny witch powers in
order to bring in enough of a distraction to allow her to
escape. Kane's return to retrieve her was merely icing
on the cake, and Kane was given the distinct impression
that she was ready to run as long and as fast as she
possibly could.

Give me a countdown—I'll add to the distraction,
Kane projected. Bres had drifted into reciting poetry for
his brute-bodied son. Balor was in rapt attention, following his father as he paced and performed.

A sentry in the compound gave a cry. "The hunting
party has reported a contact!"

Bres paused, looking toward the sentry. Neither of the

two mutant leaders seemed disappointed at the interruption. "Watch her, son. This could merely be a feint."

Balor turned his baleful eye toward Epona. Even now, Kane could tell that there was some manner of weaponry within the fist-sized cybernetic orb in his face. Its sickly green glow bespoke lethal doses of radiation. Again, Kane remembered his prior life, how Lugh had utilized a mirrored shield to repel the deadly gaze of Bres's father in order to get close enough to slay him. Kane didn't have a shield, and he doubted the canvas and mud of his camouflage would do much more than add a tenth of a second to his resistance to whichever death ray spewed from the glowing green eye.

But it was an eye, and it blinked, a massive lid flopping down over the iris and cornea like a bouncing window shade. Balor blinked, so he still retained the basic mental instinct put into humanity across its millennia of existence. Kane's fingers clawed up a ball of mud, forming it and packing it. He'd need perfect timing in order to pull this off.

Kane kept watch in his peripheral vision, alert for the sounds of the Fomorians as they gathered by Bres at the base of the mountain, keeping watch on the hunting party. They couldn't see, but Kane heard the distant, tinny rattle of a radio.

Epona sent Kane the image of a deer leading the hunters on a game of cat and mouse, letting them get close just enough so that they still thought that there was something still worth hunting, but staying just beyond

their range of vision. Kane smiled at Epona's resourcefulness. He also envisioned thousands of eyes peering
down upon them from the remaining trees on the mountainside. There was a horde, waiting on the witch's summoning. Whatever the creatures were, they were
invisible in the night, and yet had enough numbers to be
considered a distraction. Thousands of eyes, the mental
image repeated.

Not a horde. A great flock.

Epona straightened. "Kane…"

Balor turned his eye toward her. "Where?"

"Here!" Kane shouted.

The green, glowing eye swiveled toward the Cerberus
warrior, who rose and hurled his ball of mud with all of
his strength. His throw was on target, smacking Balor
in the face over his eye. Reflex forced the great brute to
throw up both of his hands to claw away at whatever had
smacked him and left a mushy smear all over his vision.
Kane charged in that moment of distraction. On the
mountainside, the explosive fluttering of thousands of
bird wings went off at once, sounding for all the world
like a thunderstorm of gunfire.

At the base of the hill, Bres and his minions would
be scrambling for cover as the clear, starlit sky suddenly
turned black and the screeches of owls, nightingales
and ravens split the air. Birds of all manner had taken
wing, their throats belting forth the war cries of their
species. The night shook with the combined cacophony
of wing strokes and birdsong, and the great flock

dropped out of the sky, zooming and dive-bombing the Fomorians in a wild aerial dance that kept the mutants off balance. Those with flesh-tearing beaks and meat-rending talons struck when they could, causing further distraction with their scratchings.

In the meantime, Kane brought up both feet and pistoned them into Balor's broad chest, knocking the huge Fomorian off balance and onto his back. Blinded by mud and caught by surprise, the giant was momentarily easy prey. Kane sought to further stun the bestial titan by jumping again, driving his heels into the flat slabs of muscle over Balor's ribs. The Fomorian grunted as breath exploded from his lungs, but a massive paw rose from his splattered face to grab at Kane. The Cerberus warrior lashed out with a decisive kick that jarred the brute's forearm bones. It felt like kicking a tree trunk, but the blow stopped the clawing grasp from catching anything but empty air. Kane wanted to avoid gunfire, knowing that even through the flock's valiant distraction, the chatter of an automatic weapon would still be noticeable.

Balor sat up, but Kane had already leaped off the titan's torso. Kane grabbed Epona's hand, and the two of them ran with all of their might into the woods.

"He can see infrared," Epona panted as they raced in the darkness.

"We've still got a few seconds before he can clean the glop I threw at his eye," Kane answered. "We need distance now."

"The right," Epona urged. "There's a running stream about four hundred yards away."

The icy waters would make the trail they left with their body heat hard to follow. It was a good idea and Kane took it. Behind them, all manner of rodents and small fauna scurried about to confuse their back trail. For a brief moment, Kane had a mental image of a jungle lord who had summoned all the beasts of his land to his aid with a single piercing howl. Epona had called out to every living animal for dozens of miles, and they had descended en masse in a desperate bid to confuse and distract the Fomorian raiders. Already, Kane heard Balor cry out in his soft, lilting wail that Kane and Epona had escaped.

"Flee," Epona gasped as they continued to run toward the stream.

"We are," Kane answered.

"No, the birds, lest they feel the horrors of Balor's eye," Epona responded.

Kane didn't blame the witch woman. If Balor's eye was anything as dangerous as the Silver Hand of Nadhua, then its destructive capabilities were remarkable. The hand had been utilized by Maccan, the mad Tuatha de Danaan, and it had the power to crush flesh and bone at a distance with waves of invisible force, as well as produce a solid globe of energy capable of repelling sheets of automatic-weapons fire. Only Grant's phenomenal strength had proved sufficient to wrestle Maccan into redirecting the hand's blast into the ceiling of the Mars pyramid, shattering it and causing the great relic of the Tuatha de Danaan to collapse around them.

As the Silver Hand of Nadhua was from the same era, a weapon in the war between the Annunaki and the Tuatha de Danaan, it stood to reason that Balor's eye could carve huge swathes of destruction through the great flock that Epona had summoned. A searing crackle of air hissed behind them, and Kane glanced back to see that several pine branches had been charred by some beam.

"He's not interested in the birds right now," Kane grumbled.

"If we stop," Epona gasped, pausing to cough from the effort of their desperate escape, "if we stop, we are lost!"

Kane fisted his folded rifle and stopped to line up the AK's sights on a glimmer of green bobbing through the trees. As soon as he had a clear sight, he triggered a stream of autofire that chopped through the air. Balor's childlike voice wailed in stunned surprise, accompanied by the spark of metal on metal. Kane had managed to hit Balor in his massive eye, but the bionic nature of the organ had prevented it from being a deadly impact. Still, the green, glowing iris disappeared in the woods, and Kane turned to catch up with Epona, his legs pumping quickly.

"He will not be harmed," Epona said with frustrated disgust.

Kane grunted. "He's slowed down, isn't he? I'm not looking for anything other than escape."

They reached the stream, and Epona ran in until she

was knee deep in the icy water. Kane was on her heels and the two people stopped.

"Which way?" Kane asked.

"Upstream will be difficult, but it will bring us closer to the radio you left for us," Epona answered. "That is your plan, correct?"

"Call for help, and hope they bring all the guns and armor the Fomorians can eat," Kane replied.

Epona smirked. "It won't be a pleasant feast for them."

"I hope not," Kane said. He took Epona's hand and they splashed upstream, grateful for their cloaks as the chilling waters soaked their feet and calves.

Cold feet were far superior to the icy stillness of the grave.

Chapter 17

Cerberus

Clem Bryant rubbed the dark brush of his goatee as he listened to Daryl Morganstern's hurried but hushed dissertation of a conundrum. Bryant, even though he currently worked in the cafeteria of the Cerberus redoubt, was a gifted oceanographer before he was placed in cryogenic stasis in the Manitius moon base. With the bold new world he had been awakened to, Bryant's knowledge of deep-sea conditions, marine biology and other fields was mostly academic in nature. The closest he got to work with marine biology was when he baked fish sticks on Fridays.

Still, that hadn't stopped Bryant from seeking mental stimulation elsewhere. The man had one of the finest minds among the Manitius staff, which normally made for a cunning chess opponent for the young mathematician Morganstern. Indeed, Bryant was a particularly frustrating opponent since his mind wasn't constrained by the limits of mathematical proof, enabling him to utilize more organic and chaotic approaches to dealing with things. Now, in a cafeteria illuminated only by the harsh orange glow of emergency lights, Bryant had been given a problem that Morganstern was worried about.

Bryant had listed the brief facts that Morganstern had related.

Point one—doubt that Kane was who he was.

Point two—medical tests inconclusive and without anomaly.

Point three—interest in Morganstern in midst of crisis.

Point four—sudden nosebleed coinciding with the crash of Cerberus environmental controls.

Point five—too readily agreed to a plausible sounding solution imagined off the cuff.

Point six—potential involvement with a transdimensional being, Colonel Thrush.

To Bryant, the puzzle defied the available scientific evidence. Genetically and chemically, this Kane was identical to the one who had gone out to the Appalachians. That could be inferred from conversations with Brigid Baptiste, and this particular being had been given a leave of duty due to the head trauma he'd suffered before arrival. According to DeFore, he'd only suffered a concussion, as well as a large laceration.

From Brigid's prior appearance, even Bryant had noticed that she was in a distracted state. How would that influence her assessment of Kane? Bryant wondered.

"Kane's working with Wynan to get the doors open,"

Morganstern said. "But right now, I don't think it's wise to let him out of here."

"Is Wynan aware of your suspicions?" Bryant asked.

"A semisentient mathematical construct inserted in a communications device was one of Wynan's first science-fiction stories," Morganstern said. "I'd been rather merciless in that Wynan didn't realize that an equation just can't be conscious."

"In this dimension," Bryant corrected. "Remember, Colonel Thrush is an artificial intelligence that has sought out alternate-universe counterparts of himself."

Morganstern took a deep breath. "So there could be a renegade math problem on the loose in Cerberus?"

"Doubtful, but if you see a train leaving Cleveland at 110 miles per hour, head for the surface—"

"Clem!"

Bryant smirked. "Sorry."

"What do we do?" Morganstern asked. "Am I just grasping at straws because Kane is at a loss for a logical explanation? Or is he fake?"

"How was Kane's demeanor once you offered him a logical explanation for the sudden breakdown in the environmental controls?" Bryant asked. "We have several possibilities for how Kane could be a counterfeit, since we're dealing with clones, androids, cyborgs and multiple dimensions. Add in the fact that Kane returned with a concussion, which makes any missteps in behavior readily excusable, and we have strong probability that we're dealing with a perfect duplicate."

"But no proof, since they ran him through the wringer medically and forensically," Morganstern replied. "I'd been working on some figures on a napkin earlier when Kane came to talk to me."

"What figures?" Bryant asked.

"Well, Lakesh is always looking to improve the capabilities of the interphaser. We were working on hyperspatial potential for the Mantas, utilizing a variation of interphaser technology," Morganstern answered.

"What other projects had you worked on for Lakesh recently?" Bryant asked.

"Remember back when you helped Lakesh decipher the location of an old Soviet antialien weapon?" Morganstern asked.

Bryant nodded. "We had been spied upon by another party, hackers who had penetrated our mainframe via the old ARPA network that was the groundwork of the Internet."

"I developed an encryption algorithm to make such penetration difficult, if not impossible," Morganstern said.

"Kane saw the napkin?" Bryant asked.

Morganstern nodded. "Could another dimensional version of the man understand that kind of math, and extrapolate my thought processes in designing equations?"

"You're assuming that this is just Kane," Bryant said.

"They checked every part of him," Morganstern countered.

Bryant frowned. "Not every part that would have not

been visible except through electronic means, such as an MRI or X-ray."

"A computer brain? The weight variation would have been noticeable," Morganstern said.

"You're assuming human brain and human computer technology," Bryant said. "The octopus has a brain fully as complex as a human's, capable of full emotional range and problem solving. However, it's of a different type than a human brain, so we automatically assume it's inferior in intellect and capacity, despite the often artistic talents these creatures show. That's just a variation of intelligence in our own dimension, on our own planet."

"A computer that doesn't utilize our own technology, and would be indecipherable from a normal brain on an X-ray and could alter the imagery of an MRI, despite being subjected to an intense magnetic field," Morganstern said.

Bryant nodded. "So we're dealing with an organic or semiorganic brain, capable of transmitting and receiving signals enough to engage in wireless hacking of our system. Kane suffered a nosebleed?"

"After he'd taken a look at the equations on my napkin," Morganstern mused.

The two scientists spoke at the same time. "He overclocked his brain processes in order to crunch the numbers of the algorithm."

"So he's fake?" Morganstern asked. "Because we haven't developed anything other than theoretical proof that he's anything but Kane."

"Circumstantial evidence is all we have," Bryant explained. "But I'd bring this up to Brigid. She's distracted and worried. Perhaps this will make her doubts all the more founded. With the confirmation we've developed, she'll be the one capable of dealing with the impostor."

"And that means we have to open the cafeteria," Morganstern replied.

Bryant shrugged. "I'd like to be back online for the midnight snack rush."

"Save me some Swiss rolls," Morganstern said.

"If you want to live to taste them, you'd better figure out a way to tell Brigid without letting the Kane impostor know what you're saying," Bryant warned.

Morganstern thought for a few moments, then a smile crossed his face.

"Remember that last game you played with me?"

Bryant chuckled. "Where I spelled out 'touché' in chess moves?"

"You're my hero," Morganstern said, clapping the oceanographer on the shoulder.

Bryant shrugged as Morganstern went off to assist Wynan and the false Kane.

BRIGID BAPTISTE HAD pretended to leave Kane alone with Daryl Morganstern, but she had stayed just outside the cafeteria doors in order to keep an eye on him. She had been hoping to continue her observations while the man was no longer under the pressure of scrutiny. Brigid knew that her eidetic memory had made her the most

difficult of problems for an impersonator, as she would
be able to detect the smallest of differences. As she had
hung back, listening to Kane and Morganstern talk, she
still had not heard anything that would be a proved break
of personality from the man she knew.

That didn't particularly mean anything, though, as
Colonel Thrush not only had access to technology that
could build an identical being, down to the clothing and
scar tissue, but also be able to gather information from
other universe's counterparts in order to model behavior
and background data. It was a frustrating deal, made all
the more difficult by a line she remembered regarding
conspiracies: "The lack of proof of a conspiracy is, in
itself, proof of the effectiveness of a conspiracy."

She knew that the line referred to how delusional
theorists could rationalize outlandish acts of covert mind
control and other menaces without a shred of proof. It
had been mathematically impossible to prove a negative,
in her experience, and she doubted that Morganstern
would have found much more luck in terms of a
solution.

Then the blackout hit, and the cafeteria doors slid
shut, protective baffles jammed into place. Brigid had
keyed her Commtact, but there was no signal. The
central communications hub that carried the frequency
that the Commtact operated on had been locked down,
as well. If she could have seen in the pitch darkness, she
would have stumbled toward a trans-comm, but she
already suspected that there was nothing happening on

the wall panels. She heard disconcerted whimpers and cries as the absolute blackness engulfed everyone.

Brigid keyed the glow dial on her wrist chron and had something to see by. To her amazement, several other Cerberus staff had their own forms of illumination in their pockets. Veterans of the Manitius base would have had the sense to prepare for a power failure, or have a light handy to conserve energy reserves. The blue-green glow of her watch gave others a means to see her, which made her feel a little better.

Finally, after a few moments, the emergency lights kicked in. Brigid turned and saw that the blast shutters had lowered over the automatic sliding doors.

"That's all wrong," Brigid muttered. She checked her watch again and realized that in only a few minutes, Grant and CAT Beta would have been transmitted back to the Appalachians on their errand of ending the Fomorian menace. The timing of the shutdown was far too suspicious to disregard, even though she still only had circumstantial evidence.

Brigid paced outside of the cafeteria, running through the time line of events, trying to place the reason why someone would want to grind Cerberus operations to a halt. The only logical reason was that there was something back in the Appalachians that would be discovered on a renewed sortie. Even if power was restored quickly, the sudden shutdown would require extensive investigation, especially in the field of computer security. A simple power glitch would not have dropped blast doors, segregating the sections of the redoubt. The recent hacking of the system had inspired a new round of security protocols, and Brigid frowned as she realized that the mathematician, Morganstern, was one of the brains behind the encryption that shielded their mainframe.

She reviewed the series of events that had preceded the sudden shutdown, filtering out the very convincing conversation between Kane and Morganstern and concentrating on nonverbal cues of what was going on. There was movement on the table. It was Morganstern passing off a much-scribbled napkin to Wynan. She knew that the two young men were working together in an effort to replicate the process by which the mat-trans had been reprogrammed to engage in interplanetary teleportation. While wormhole-based transmission of matter across vast distances was feasible, especially with the discovery of parallax points, redoubt staff was exploring the technology to make space travel easier.

Brigid rewound her mental image again. Kane saw the napkin being moved. It was upside down, and slid so quickly you'd need a photographic memory to recall what had been written on it. But Kane watched the napkin for a moment, anyway. She focused on his eyes, and he was paying close attention to the little scrap of tissue paper passed between the scientists.

As if Kane was able to read what was written on the napkin, and read it so quickly that he somehow comprehended it. Brigid had the leisure of her intellect to freeze the memory, invert it and delve into the equations that had been scrawled on the napkin. Kane would have needed a supercomputer in his brain to do the same thing, which wasn't possible. Electronics would have shown up in an X-ray of the man's skull.

"Electronics aren't the only means of computation," Brigid said to herself. "I'm so used to the prevalent digital technology we use that I've disregarded other forms."

"Excuse me?" someone asked, shining a flashlight toward her. It was Brewster Philboyd, the blond, middle-aged astrophysicist from Manitius.

"I was talking to myself, trying to deal with a problem," Brigid confessed. "Sorry."

"I talk to myself all the time. Only way to get some decent conversation sometimes," Philboyd answered. "Well, what kind of technology are you thinking about?"

Brigid frowned. "For one thing, the most efficient information-processing device we have to date is the human brain, properly trained. It can decipher equations, translate languages and store massive amounts of data. Not an ounce of electronics is involved in that, simply biochemically produced electricity."

"Though input and subsequent programming is still merely on-off, binary programming on a sublime level," Philboyd replied. "Some theories of artificial intelligence have been able to determine that with sufficient stimulus, a computer would be able to develop its own emotional responses independent of actual programming, the same way a human being does by having six senses. Still, how would that kind of a computer be able to hook up with a computer wirelessly?"

"I've encountered cloned central nervous system material that had been utilized to telepathically hijack the original user. Indeed, there is evidence that all human minds have the ability to transmit information over long distances—it simply needs the proper 'switches' flipped," Brigid said.

"All right," Philboyd said, looking at the shuttered door. His brow wrinkled as he looked it over. "I assume we're talking about someone here who might have been replaced by an artificial life-form, correct?"

"We think that Colonel Thrush might have infiltrated Cerberus utilizing a manufactured life-form," Brigid confessed.

Philboyd nodded. "I've always wanted to take a look at that guy. According to Grant, he seemed like a barrel of laughs."

"If by laughs you mean near total genocide of the human race," Brigid countered.

Philboyd shrugged. "That kind of attitude makes me less squeamish about disassembling them to find out how they work."

Brigid smiled at Philboyd. "Trust me, we wouldn't mind that. He would, and considering that he escaped from a singularity—"

"Yeah. Problematic," Philboyd responded. "So your major problem is that you're trying to figure out if you could fit an artificial brain inside a human head, while still maintaining enough processing power to hack the Cerberus mainframe."

Brigid nodded.

"And how would it know the proper encryption for our mainframe?" Philboyd asked.

Brigid sighed. "It managed to get a sample of the kind of mathematical theorems that could be developed by the person who designed the encryption."

"So we're looking at a few dozen tetrahertz of processing power," Philboyd speculated. "The whole brain would have to be artificial, but not necessarily inorganic. And it would have to take up more space than the usual brain, which actually only utilizes half the available room inside of the human skull. The human brain only utilizes a fraction of its cognitive ability, so if we were to allow for a minimum of human equivalency, we're looking at an organ twice the diameter of the standard brain, and that extra diameter goes purely toward higher functions."

"It could work?" Brigid asked.

"Walking, moving, breathing, eating, all of that's handled by the reptile brain, which is a core of neural tissue at the base of the skull, with fingers extending through the core. The upper lobes have all the stuff necessary for personality," Philboyd said. "The exact nature of the design is beyond me, but we're looking at the square cube law. For every time an object's size is doubled, its mass is cubed. We take that cubed level of mass and make it an efficient form of computer, based off the template of the human brain..."

Brigid winced. "All right, I know what happened."

Philboyd frowned. "But you're not sure that Thrush would have access to that kind of technology."

"He and a thousand of his alternate bodies are living in a globe a quarter the size of the moon that flitters between dimensions effortlessly," Brigid countered.

Philboyd nodded. "Okay. He might have access to that kind of technology."

Brigid leaned against the armored shutter over the cafeteria door. All the tension left her and she sighed, suddenly released from a crushing grip of doubt. Her shoulders had been clenched so tightly, looking for some signs, some form of proof. Now that she had it, she felt right again, and the strangling grip of her suspicions relaxed.

Philboyd rapped his flashlight against the shutter. He got an answer on the other side. "Who's the robot brain?"

Brigid looked at the door. "Kane."

Philboyd froze before he could tap something out in code. "What?"

The astrophysicist looked at the door and took a step away from it. "He wouldn't happen to be in there, would he?"

"I was keeping an eye on him from the door when the power outage struck," Brigid said.

Philboyd took a deep breath. "So that door opens up, we're pretty much screwed because we've got a fake Kane running around."

Brigid nodded. Something flashed in the corner of her eye and saw that it was a door intercom control. The digital readout flashed a line of random seeming numbers after all the LEDs came to life on it. Brigid looked at the screen, memorizing the numbers on sheer reflex.

"Who's there?" came the image.

"Brigid," she typed into the keypad.

"Good," was the response. The numbers passed by again. She consciously noticed that they were mixed with regular numbers, followed by the ASCII image of a horse head on a base. Suddenly patterns began forming, unbidden in her mind. The fast string of numbers formed a code that she managed to recognize instantly. Chess moves on a board. "Trying to make sure this stays online. Working off an improvised battery."

"Everyone okay in there?" Brigid typed into the keypad.

"Yes. Kane's helping us with the door," the response came. From the chess moves, she recognized that it had to be Morganstern sending the text messages on the intercom. At first she thought that Morganstern had been attempting to give her his moves in their ongoing game, but there were far more than seven piece movements. Eight boards had been indicated by the alphanumeric code, and already, she was moving pieces in her mind.

The chess strategy was utterly random, not having anything to do with previous games, but then she repeated the chess maneuvers, all of them working at once, laying down lines in their wake.

They weren't game moves. They were instead forming letters on the chess board in block letters.

"Kane fake," the quick string had said. Had Morganstern actually input that information in the actual terminal, there would be a good chance that the fake she was aware of would have torn his head off and used it to batter open the blast panels. Coding the message in the form of chess moves gave Baptiste the warning, while resembling random program testing and glitches.

"Thanks, Daryl," Brigid typed back.

"Door released," Morganstern entered.

Brigid stood back from the door, drawing her TP-9 from its holster. Philboyd walked behind her, fingers plugged into his ears. Brigid tucked the weapon behind her hip as the door lurched. Fingers clawed around the jamb and the man she had assumed was Kane was attempting to open the door. She could see his muscles stand out on cable taut arms. There was no mistaking the lean, powerful musculature of the man, and finally the door had been pried open.

She could see the familiar gray-blue eyes staring at her.

"Brigid, what happened? You get stuck in the hall?" he asked.

Brigid Baptiste didn't answer. She shot the man in the forehead with her pistol.

THRUSH-KANE WAS growing tired of people using his forehead for target practice. First the idiot Bres had done minor damage to his internal cooling system, and now the Baptiste woman had planted a bullet just above his brow. He lowered his head, sneering in derision at Brigid, the brass button of a flattened bullet snagged in the folds of his forehead bandage. The high-tensile polymers of his artificial skeleton were sufficient to resist the might of Bres's powerful arms; the few hundred foot pounds of pressure released by a small-caliber handgun weren't going to cause much damage.

"Baptiste," Thrush-Kane said with a sigh.

"Well, if my speculations weren't enough, a bullet-proof skull is the surest evidence of your illegitimacy," Brigid said, still holding the pistol at eye level.

"Kane's a damn idiot for thinking he can do better than you, Baptiste."

Brigid shrugged and fired again, this time aiming for a different part of the man's face. Thrush-Kane shifted ever so slightly in the brief moment it took to translate the flexion of her finger muscles into a dropped hammer. The 9 mm slug chewed off a chunk of cheek flesh, but the bone held. Another movement and Thrush-Kane reached for her wrist, driving the handgun to aim toward the ceiling.

"Why are you trying to kill me? I want to help you eliminate Enlil," Thrush-Kane inquired, his bloodied face close to Brigid's.

The archivist brought her knee up between the doppelganger's thighs, an impact that should have distracted even Kane at his best. She felt his testicles mash against his pubic bone, but Thrush-Kane's face didn't register any pain. What Brigid felt was an unholy amount of pain on her wrist bones, loosening the grasp on her pistol.

"A kick to the nuts, Baptiste?" Thrush-Kane inquired. "I would have thought Kane was a better instructor than—"

Wynan and Morganstern both jumped onto Thrush-Kane's shoulders, their scrawny arms wrapping around his in an effort to pry him off Brigid. The scientists' combined weight should have unbalanced the real Kane, but Brigid knew all too well that they were dealing with some form of enhanced being. A part of her mind speculated that Thrush-Kane had augmenting flat motors installed along or within his artificial skeleton.

"Let her go!" Wynan spit, writhing as he yanked on the infiltrator's left shoulder. Morganstern sank his teeth into Thrush-Kane's right biceps, drawing blood but not inducing any more pain than a bullet to the face or a knee to the genitals.

Thrush-Kane sighed and shrugged off the two men, then glared at them. "As you wish."

With a flick of his arm, Brigid was deposited into the scientists' laps. The bogus Kane had her pistol, and he twirled it like some form of Old West gunslinger before stuffing it into his waistband. Thrush-Kane looked at Philboyd, who stood in the hall in front of him. "Are you going to try to get in my way, little man?"

"Naw, man, we're cool," Philboyd said, stepping aside.

Thrush-Kane sneered and took off down the darkened hallway.

Philboyd immediately rushed to Brigid, who was already working her way to her feet. "You all right?"

"A little bruised," Brigid answered. "Daryl? Wynan?"

Morganstern waved his hand, wincing in embarrassment.

Wynan was blinking. "I think I felt her butt…"

Morganstern glared at his friend. "We're going to have words later. Go stop that fake…"

Brigid pulled Morganstern close and planted a passionate kiss on the mathematician's lips. "Thanks."

Morganstern blushed. "You probably came to a similar conclusion—"

Brigid cupped his cheek. "Every good mathematician needs someone to check their numbers."

"Be careful," Morganstern said softly.

Brigid nodded, knowing that being unarmed, she was going to need a lot of luck to deal with a cybernetic opponent that felt no pain.

Chapter 18

The Appalachians

As Kane looked over the scene, he didn't know which was more of a punch to the gut, the lifeless mountain man scout, his face twisted in horror as his body was pulled and stretched like a piece of taffy, or the pile of electronic garbage that had been left behind in the place of the radio that Cerberus had left for the Appalachian mountain folk. He silently mourned for the murdered young man, catching the pained regret on Epona's face.

"They didn't have to do this to him," Epona whispered.

Kane rested a hand on her shoulder. "Right now, we've got work to do."

She nodded, looking numbed. "I didn't feel his loss, and he's been dead since before the avalanche, given the condition of his body. Why wouldn't I have felt it?"

"Doesn't matter right now," Kane said. "We have to hide, because this is the first place they will look."

"The Fomorians did this?" Epona asked.

"It wasn't my duplicate. He wasn't drenched in fresh

blood," Kane answered. "Plus, I don't have the arm span to pull a man apart like I was unkinking a spring."

Epona stumbled along, helped by Kane. The cold water and their wet footwear made things uncomfortable for quick walking, but it was better than being fully immersed. They had taken a minute to wring out their leggings after leaving the frigid stream. Despite toughened feet on both of the veterans of the wilderness, damp boots and socks caused chafing. Going far was out of the question, but getting out of sight was vital. Kane found a small wash that was overgrown with roots and bushes.

He stuffed Epona inside and perched at the entrance, muddy canvas wraps making him imperceptible in the darkness. That was good news for the next several hours of night, but come the sunrise, Kane was going to need more than that for sufficient camouflage. He grimaced in frustration over the murder of the scout, and idly wondered where the man's weapons had gone.

Adding a .50-caliber rifle to his arsenal would have made things a little easier in case he had to fight with Balor or the Fomorians again before dawn. Then again, judging from how the creature merely cried out in pain when shot in the eye by an AK-47, Kane didn't harbor any illusions that Balor would be anything less than a full-blown, unstoppable menace that could only be dealt with by another god.

The radio's utter destruction might have been a stratagem of Thrush's to prevent Kane from calling for help once he had escaped this far up the mountain, but Bres's minions had completed the task with brutal aplomb. Of course the two madmen would have been in agreement about keeping the Cerberus teams from returning to this stretch of the Poconos. For Bres, the intrusion of Grant and other combatants from the redoubt would mean that the slim advantage they held over the Appalachian nomads would be gone. For Thrush, it would mean that they'd discover the ruse, although given the brainpower back at Cerberus, Kane didn't think that there would be much of a chance to fool them. Sure, they looked identical, and after a few moments, sounded identical, but there would always be some flaw that would keep the disguise from being fully effective. When that happened, Kane could count on his allies to act without hesitation.

Kane frowned. Just because they would act didn't mean anything. The doppelganger was stealthy enough to sneak up on him, and swift enough to knock him unconscious without a fight.

"Kane, there's nothing we can do for them right now," Epona said.

"Was I making too much emotional noise for you?" Kane asked.

The witch woman smiled, then cupped his nape, the touch of her fingertips intoxicating. "I wasn't 'listening.' I could see it carved into your face."

Kane snorted. "Sorry."

"Don't be," Epona said. There was a brief, awkward moment, but Kane slipped his arms around the woman, embracing her tightly. He wasn't certain how much intimate contact she wanted, but for now, all she welcomed was being held. That was fine with Kane.

It wasn't a lack of sexual attraction that kept him from being more affectionate toward the witch woman. Sure, she had the title of Granny, but her age was not apparent in her features, and her body was lithe and strong. The gorgeous green of her eyes was intoxicating. It was simple logic that held him back. Giving in to his attraction for her would not only be a fatal distraction while they were being hunted, but it would also be wrong. The woman was tired, distraught, emotionally brittle. To take advantage of her would be like looting corpses, grisly and ghoulish.

Epona was in pain, and she was as concerned for her people as he was for his friends back at Cerberus. Kane stroked her jet-black hair as she rested her head on his shoulder.

"You said that you spoke with me when you first got here, but I'd been their prisoner for a few days," Epona said.

"Bres can mold these monsters, but apparently he can make something as pretty as you are," Kane said.

"I was afraid of that," Epona replied. She closed her eyes, and Kane felt the psychic rustle as she picked through humanoid thoughts in the vicinity. "Bres held off on an attack, though he had been preparing for it. One good thing that your duplicate did was to throw off his timetable."

"Right now, though, he's got all of his troops out and on the hunt. If there are more scouts in these parts, they'll run into each other," Kane said.

"Yes. I'm looking for them, though you already feel that," Epona said.

"Now you're probing me," Kane muttered.

Epona managed a weak smile at the sarcasm. "I can feel my scouts nearby."

"How close?" Kane asked. "And can you contact them?"

"Not without making the duplicate suspicious," Epona admitted. "And if I do that, there's no telling what that bitch is capable of."

"Your choice. Rest here, or we head for your scouts' camp and I'll deal with the counterfeit," Kane offered.

The witch woman chewed her lower lip. She took a moment to wring out her damp footwear once more. Kane could see the livid flesh from where the contracting leather of her boots and the bunched fabric of her stockings had worn her feet raw. "Damn it. Usually people complain about my hooves, and now they don't turn out to be the indestructible calluses I was proud of."

Kane took the stockings and dug a small pit for them at the bottom of the wash. He buried them and packed the soil tightly. He sniffed the air and was pleased to note that the scent of the socks was greatly diminished. Pulling the strips he had torn for bandages, he returned and wrapped the woman's raw, aching feet.

"What about changing your head dressing?" Epona asked. "It looks soaked through."

Kane grimaced. "I'm not going to be walking on my head."

Kane turned to one of his pouches where he still had several feet of torn canvas and cord. He set about making impromptu foot wrappings for the woman, tying them off at the ankles so that she wouldn't be stepping on the wound rope when she walked. They were securely tucked, like mummy bandages from an old video he'd seen. Her calves had cord securing the canvas wrappings higher up. Epona flexed her feet and smiled.

"Not the prettiest, but they're comfortable," she pronounced.

"Good," Kane said. He reached into a supplementary pouch and pulled out a tuber for her to munch on. "Eat and regain your strength."

"According to my scan, the Fomorians are still a half hour behind us," Epona said.

"That may be true, but I'd like to keep that lead," Kane told her. "If not, depending on how much time it takes to bring down your impostor, we'll have Bres and his boys breathing right down our necks the minute we put her down. Especially if I have to use my rifle."

Epona frowned, then nodded in agreement.

"So is there some special code that you can shout to instantly convince your tribesmen that we're not psychopaths or phonies?" Kane asked. "Because if you don't have that, things are going to get pretty awkward for a moment."

"Sorry. We're secretive and paranoid of outlanders, but we're not that well prepared," Epona answered. "Awkward is an understatement. A dozen men with high-powered rifles…"

Kane sighed. "I'll think of something."

Epona rubbed her forehead, wincing at some internal embarrassment. "Hang on."

"You didn't think of using your 'familiars' with your own people?" Kane asked.

Epona shrugged. "I'm exhausted, hurting, and this root tastes like a petrified turd. Your concentration would be off, too. Besides, you were a shot in the dark. I tried because it's been said that you have a sight beyond normal sight. I figured it was some manner of psychic sensitivity."

"So it wouldn't work with someone who hasn't been exposed to telepathy?" Kane asked.

Epona took a deep breath. "I don't know. What I do know is that you, thanks to repeated encounters with mental projections, have a trained ear for it."

Kane nodded. "I've been told that before. Even had a vision at an oracle temple once."

Epona raised an eyebrow. "No kidding."

Kane held his hand over his heart. "I'm not the lying type."

"You're going to have to come back to the mountains and tell me more about that instance."

"It took only a few seconds," Kane said with a shrug.

Epona rolled her beautiful green eyes. "So perceptive, and yet thick as a brick."

Kane put his hand over his mouth to stifle an embarrassed laugh. "Oh. Come back later."

Epona winked. "Come on, Oracle. I've got magic to work, and you've got a Fomorian to beat the hell out of."

Kane checked the stone spear point lodged into the end of his cane. It was still strong and solid. He knew that he was going to need it.

CILAIN HAD TAKEN to the role of Epona easily, thanks to the fact that she had also received lessons alongside the granny witch. Where Epona had been driven by her sense of duty, Cilain saw the benefits of the powers gained through the old ways. When Bres had whispered into her ear one dark evening, Cilain allowed herself to be swept up by his beauty and power. Let Epona trade in her strength in slavery to a tribe of mountain nomads; Cilain wasn't going to let her powers make her a servant.

Cilain was meant to be obeyed. Bres also promised her youth and strength beyond her sister in faith. If she had to wear Epona's skin for a while, then it was worth it.

Bres had layered muscle onto her, and her flesh and bone were three times as dense as a normal person's. Cilain remained as lithe, as smooth, as perfectly formed as when Bres found her. Instead of haphazardly molding flesh and marrow onto her as he had done at the pleading of the Fomorians, Bres crafted a bride for himself, like the great Fomorian mothers of old, the voluptuous beings who were bedded by immortal Tuatha de Danaan.

"Granny." Erik, one of Epona's scouts summoned her. "It appears as if the men of Cerberus do not return. Sooner or later, the Fomorians will come to us."

Cilain matched Epona's frown of concern, even though she welcomed the slaughtering horde that would sweep down and cleanse the mountains of this small group of vermin. It hadn't taken Cilain long to locate the back trail to the mountain folk's new home. Only a few brief words of small talk were needed to cement the knowledge. She wanted to smile, to revel in the joy that would come when she walked among the primitive, superstitious thugs who had felt that a leader was meant to stoop the lowest, rather than demand that her minions stretch to the heights of greatness.

They had chosen Epona because the deluded crone-in-training claimed a love for her people.

"We must wait, Erik," Cilain answered. "Grant promised us that he would return, and he would bring the force necessary to drive the Fomorians from the valley."

Erik's brow furrowed as something fluttered in the night. Cilain tried to see what it was, and caught only a flash of wings that barely broke the darkness. Erik seemed as if he was suffering a headache, and Cilain took a step back from him. "What the hell?"

Cilain scanned, expanding her consciousness, and she

picked up the thing that had intruded. It was an owl that had sliced through the night, leaving only a hushed breeze in its wake. She reached for the nocturnal predator, but was rejected as the owl was already being used.

"Something's wrong," Cilain said out loud. "It has to be Epona at work…."

Erik squinted, his hand dropping to the knife in his belt. "Her? But why? What do you mean?"

"She is Bres's queen, and she has the power to influence your thoughts," Cilain said. She wished that she'd thought to have familiars on hand in the camp to provide her with a means to ward off any attempts by an escaped Epona to influence the scouts.

It was too late to be concerned with measures that should have been taken. Obviously the scouts had no clue as to the true limits of a granny witch's power. She had to fill Erik with fear, and the only way to do that was to lie and play upon his ignorance.

The owl flashed closer again, and Cilain reached out to grab it, physically this time. A game of wills would be too slow and costly, when the death of the meddling bird would cut Erik off from Epona just as readily. As her fingertips brushed the owl's soft down in a flash of speed she summoned from the depths of her being, something else loomed in her peripheral vision.

"Get away from her!" Kane bellowed, charging at Cilain with his spear.

The stone point stabbed at the witch's side. While the razor-sharp rock carved through her furs easily and even drew blood by slicing Cilain's skin, her six hundred pounds of muscle and sinew served to be as spear-proof as a log. Kane grunted as he stopped cold, pinioned on the haft of his own weapon as Cilain growled angrily.

"Kane shows his true colors." Cilain continued to lie. She grasped the shaft of the spear and twirled it away from her. Kane, jammed against the other end of the weapon and still clutching it from his battle charge, was lifted like a doll and flew along with the improvised lance.

Erik looked at Cilain, slack-jawed. "Epona was never that strong."

Cilain sighed. "Stupid little boy…"

The owl flashed by her again, a flurry of wings and talons exploding in her face. Cilain swatted the bird aside, irritated by all of the interruptions. If the Fomorians were going to drag their feet so that Kane and Epona could reach the mountain folk first, then the bride of Bres had to take matters into her own hands. She grabbed Erik by the upper arm, her fingers closing down like the jaws of a bear. Bone snapped under enormous pressure and the scout screamed in agony.

Kane's walking stick crashed across Cilain's face, and it broke into splinters and chunks of useless wood. Still, it had jarred the Fomorian woman enough that she released her victim.

Cilain shook shattered wood out of her hair, then glowered at Kane. "Trying again?"

"I don't like bullies, witch," Kane returned.

Cilain reached for Kane, but this time the Cerberus

warrior was ready for her strength and speed. Her fingers clutched only empty air, and Kane powered a kick into her midsection. Both Kane and Cilain were surprised that the blow actually lifted her off her feet, Cilain because she was aware of her five-hundred-plus pounds of weight and Kane because it felt as if he'd kicked an armored blast door. The Fomorian woman toppled to the dirt and cursed loudly as she rolled into the campfire.

Other scouts had come, alerted by the sound of battle, but Erik, his arm dangling uselessly, threw himself between the Appalachians and the battling pair.

"It's not Epona!" Erik called out.

"Protect me!" Cilain shouted. "This madman—"

Kane knew that he needed more concrete proof that Cilain was not what she appeared to be. That meant he had to go as savage as possible. He hurled himself at the Fomorian impostor feetfirst, both of his boots crashing into her face. The effect was threefold. First, it shut Cilain's mouth. Second, it made Kane feel as if he'd taken a hammer to his own knees. And third, when almost two hundred pounds of man drop-kicked a woman who looked to be half his size in the head, and he bounced off as if he'd struck a wall, the mountain scouts shouted in dismay, drawing their rifles.

"She's Fomorian!" Kincaid, a second scout, spit in dismay.

Cilain rose to her feet, glaring at Kane. "You miserable little monkey."

"Shoot her!" Erik shouted.

"No!" Epona shouted from the edge of the forest.

Kincaid lowered the muzzle of his scout rifle, looking at the real Epona in confusion. "But—"

"No shooting," Epona hissed.

Cilain chuckled. "The Fomorians are tracking you, and if you start a gunfight, they'll home in on us."

Distracted by Epona's arrival, Cilain was unprepared for Kane's next attack. If guns were out of the question, and she'd taken his best kicks and still could walk, it was time to return to a more primitive assault weapon. Kane jammed his AK bayonet hard into Cilain's throat, putting every ounce of his weight into the stab. The tough steel blade tore the Fomorian woman's skin, creating a three-inch cut, but the force of the blow bent the knife. Coughing, Cilain backhanded Kane, hurling him to the ground.

"When's it going to be my turn to have my density increased?" Kane grumbled.

"How about I just crumple you into a ball the size of an orange, Kane?" Cilain asked, walking toward him.

Kane speared his feet between the Fomorian impostor's shins and rolled, using leverage to knock her off balance. She crashed into the dirt and Kane continued his twist, untangling his legs from hers and jamming the heel of his boot into her right eye. The blunt, hard sole provided more of a cushion, and since the impact was farther from her neck and shoulders than the previous drop kick, it actually snapped her head back. Skin tore and Cilain screamed as she felt her eyeball burst under the pressure of the impact.

Kane tried to withdraw his foot, but fingers like iron talons wrapped around his calf. It would only be a moment before the Fomorian witch would brace his foot and proceed to snap his leg like a twig. Kane folded and shoved the barrel of the AK deep between Cilain's breasts, the spoon-shaped muzzle spearing into her skin. Kane hoped that Cilain's body would absorb most of the noise from the rifle's muzzle-blast as he pulled the trigger. The weapon wanted to jump under recoil, but snagged in superdense flesh, it was pinned solidly. There was no flash of light, no crack of thunder, only a gurgling growl as thirty steel-cored bullets punched through a chest wall of solid muscle and reinforced bone. It took the first third of the magazine to shatter enough of Cilain's toughly armored flesh and sinew to get into her internal organs.

It was then that Cilain's spiteful growl turned into a torrent of bright red blood pouring from battered lips. Her grasp on his lower leg loosened and she slumped in the dirt.

Kane dragged himself away from the Fomorian woman, his calf throbbing from the pain of the enormous pressure of her fingers. He had to test his toes and ankle to be certain that she hadn't fractured his shin with only the strength of one hand.

Taking a deep breath, he tried to stand up, and despite a searing ache in his calf muscles, his leg didn't fold beneath him.

"Did it make a noise?" Kane asked.

Epona looked, shocked, at her slain doppelganger.

"Did the rifle make a sound?" Kane demanded.

"No, it was muffled by her body," Kincaid said. "It was hardly a rustle."

Kane nodded, sighing in relief. "Epona…"

The Appalachian witch knelt by Cilain's body. "Sleep well. Your torment is done, sweet sister."

Kane grimaced, not in the pain inflicted by Cilain's fists, but in regret over Epona's loss. Somewhere in the past, the two women were friends, family. He'd taken away any chance of reconciliation, and he could feel that his victory and survival had taken on a dark, hollow shame.

"Do not blame yourself," Epona said, her voice rough with sadness. In the firelight, he could see her cheeks glistening with tears. "Cilain brought this on herself. She danced with the devil, then slept in his bed."

Kane frowned. It was with sick reluctance that he had to break the silence. "We have to get ready for the Fomorians. They still are a half an hour behind us, and Balor is with them."

Kincaid and Erik looked at each other in horror. Kincaid spoke up. "We could try to run, but Balor is faster than any horse, even over this terrain."

"And to fight…how many are there?" Erik asked, his words raspy with pain.

Kane tore his gaze away from the mournful Epona. He wondered how he could minimize the impact of his words, but he couldn't. He only had the truth. "All of them."

Erik clenched his eyes shut. "We can't fight that."

Kane strode over to Erik's rifle and picked it up. "Then I'll slow them down so you can get away."

Kincaid shook his head. "That's suicide."

Kane worked the bolt on the rifle, checking to see if it was loaded. Satisfied that the weapon was ready for war, he leaned it over his shoulder and regarded the Appalachian men before him. "No. That's saving your lives. I don't intend to die. I intend to stop Bres."

Chapter 19

Cerberus

With the redoubt blacked out, operating only on emergency lighting and its communications systems completely disabled, Brigid Baptiste knew that she was running a fool's errand as she pursued Thrush-Kane through the hallways. Cerberus staff was either working to open locked doorways, or wandering in confusion. No one had been shot, though Thrush-Kane had no qualms about inflicting injury on people who interfered with him.

Brigid wished that she had time to run to the armory, but those doors were probably locked, as well. Still, given that the doppelganger showed no discomfort even after injuries that would have left even the strongest man hobbled over in agony, Brigid had no idea what kind of weapon could rob the false man of his ability to do harm. A bullet to the forehead only produced annoyance, and not even from discomfort.

A soft squelch vibrated up Brigid's jaw and she paused, touching her Commtact plate.

"Brigid, are you there?" Bry asked.

"You've got the radios up!" Brigid exclaimed with relief. She broke into a jog again, following a trail of bewildered Cerberus staff, and pried open doors. For now, it appeared that Thrush-Kane had been taking a random path through the redoubt, more to lose Brigid than approach someplace directly. "Bry, tell Grant and the others that we have confirmation that Thrush placed an infiltrator in the redoubt."

Bry sighed on the other end. "What gave you that hint? The communication blackout, the power-down or the blast doors isolating entire sections of the base?"

"Any of that could have been done from the outside," Brigid replied.

"So how did you confirm it?" Bry asked.

"Bitch shot me in the forehead," Thrush-Kane interrupted. "Yammering biological trash!"

Brigid couldn't resist a smile at the frustration evident in the impostor's voice. "Party line, Bry. Can you cut him out of the loop?"

"We're not doing this through central communication," Bry said. "Just booster antennas."

"Like you think you can stop me?" Thrush-Kane asked.

Brigid slid to a halt at a corner and saw the tall silhouette of the infiltrator standing in the shadows. She held her tongue, knowing that the false Kane not only was at least as strong as the original, but was armed with a handgun. Brigid hadn't even picked up a butter knife from the cafeteria.

"Just counting all the invasions we've had here at Cerberus," Bry chided. "An Annunaki armada. A Tuatha de Danaan utilizing an ancient weapon glove. Energy beings. We're still here, Tinkertoy."

"But why would you want to stop me?" Thrush-Kane asked. "I'm here to go after Enlil. You've got my vast intellect and obvious physical superiority to lead you once and for all in a campaign of extermination that will rid the Earth of the Annunaki threat."

"Extermination," a deep voice boomed over the Commtact web. It was Grant. "Yeah, I'm a fucking idiot for thinking you could be the real Kane."

Thrush-Kane sighed. "Grant, welcome to the conversation. Now shut up and let the people with brains do the talking."

Brigid sneered at the cyborg's dismissal of her partner. Unfortunately, she didn't have the means to wipe the arrogance off Thrush-Kane's face. Grant snorted in derision, and Brigid whirled to see him moving stealthily up the hall.

"Right," Grant answered the cocky impostor. "I'm the dumb one. You couldn't even hold on to your disguise for an hour after we physically cleared you."

Grant reached into his gear bag and handed Brigid her .45 pistol and holster. Brigid nodded in thanks for the weapon and slid it into the shoulder harness. The big ex-Magistrate handed her a Copperhead submachine gun, as well, and the archivist took the compact weapon. No need to assume it was unloaded—Grant was a professional, and responding to a crisis in the depths of Cerberus. All Brigid had to do was work the safety switch on the side of the Copperhead, and that was a silent click.

"What else could I do?" Thrush-Kane asked. "You were going to jump out to the Appalachians and find the real Kane. But that's the joy of this plan. I've broken up your perfect trinity. He's fighting for his life against Bres and sixty rampaging mutants, and you're trapped in this redoubt with me."

"We're trapped with you?" Grant asked. He was sub-vocalizing as he bantered with Thrush-Kane, so his voice wouldn't carry around the corner. The big man had his Sin Eater out, ready to launch a torrent of thunder-bolts against the cyborg. Brigid shook her head, then pointed to her forehead. Grant raised an eyebrow as Brigid made a gun with her fingers, pantomimed a shot and tapped her forehead hard.

Grant nodded, understanding her. "Thrush, you're outnumbered, outgunned and surrounded."

Thrush-Kane threw back his head in raucous laughter. "Come out from behind the corner, you pre-tentious ape! You think I'm so stupid that I couldn't notice you and Baptiste skulking there?"

Grant stepped around the corner, but instead of getting into a face-off, he leveled his Sin-Eater at Thrush-Kane and opened fire. A 6-round burst ripped out of the machine pistol, heavy-core 9 mm slugs chopping into the impostor's chest. Divots of skin and muscle exploded beneath the fake's T-shirt, spattering it with more blood, but Thrush-Kane's only reaction was to stagger back a couple of steps. The false man's shoulders jerked in a spasm of repressed laughter as he looked down at his gore-smeared shirt.

Grant tilted his head, then took aim at Thrush-Kane's forehead. The doppelganger jerked forward in a blur of motion that caught the ex-Magistrate off guard. His rounds missed the impostor's head, and the powerful construct slammed a palm strike into Grant's own broad chest. His 250-pound frame was lifted off his feet and he sailed several feet down the hall.

Brigid triggered the Copperhead submachine gun at contact distance from Thrush-Kane. A blazing fire of 4.85 mm rifle rounds chopped viciously, carving up the false man's centerline before the last cartridges in the magazine discharged into the cyborg's bloody face. The submachine gun ran empty after its 40-round payload, and for a moment, Brigid thought she'd actually inflicted harm on the infiltrator.

Thrush-Kane lurched, turning back toward Brigid, half of his face hanging off a shimmering pink skull in tatters. "Baptiste, Baptiste, Baptiste."

"Oh, this is going to suck," Brigid growled as she swung the rifle hard at him. Thrush-Kane blocked the stroke with his forearm, and Brigid grunted as the impact of the Copperhead's frame sent vibrations rattling up her slender but well-muscled arms.

Thrush-Kane straightened his arm, fingers wrapping

around the receiver of the gun. With a squeeze, he compressed the metal box containing the firing mechanism
of the Copperhead into a crumpled mess of mangled
steel. Brigid let go of the rifle before the cyborg could
toss the weapon aside. "Yes, this is going to suck. You
killed the flesh shell wrapping around my skeleton with
your antics."

Grant rose to his feet, glaring at Thrush-Kane from
down the hall. "But you still manage to talk and talk.
Whatever happened to the good old days when you put
a bullet into an asshole and they shut up and died?"

"Welcome to a whole new world, Grant," Thrush-
Kane responded. "My skeleton may not look like the
other Thrush androids or cyborg constructs, but it's
every bit as effective and powerful."

Grant growled and charged at the bullet-riddled
impostor. Thrush-Kane braced himself for the charge,
fully aware of the incredible strength of the largest of
the Cerberus prime team. What the infiltrator hadn't
been anticipating was that all of that physical power
was guided by a savvy mind and years of experience.
Knowing that he was going up against a superior foe,
Grant didn't tackle the Thrush cyborg head-on, but
crashed into his adversary across its thighs and knees.
Thrown off balance by the impact, Thrush-Kane
howled in surprise as he slammed face-first into the
floor, leaving behind a smear of blood and chunks of
torn face.

Grant shoulder rolled to a stop and crouched on one

knee, looking at his foe. Thrush-Kane raised himself off the ground and glanced at the ex-Magistrate.

"Our files don't do you justice, Grant. You are strong, yes, but no stronger than any other man your size," Thrush-Kane said. "But it's how you use that body that makes you truly dangerous."

"You disregard my brains, and it turns out it's the strongest muscle in my body," Grant responded. "All that robot hydraulic power you've got in your skeleton might give you the strength to bend steel with your bare hands, but you don't have a tenth of the talent necessary to make it really dangerous."

Thrush-Kane chuckled and sank his fingers into the floor, prying out a concrete chunk. "I just haven't been thinking big enough."

Grant's shoulders sagged as the cyborg wrenched a fifty-pound slab of stone over his head as if it were a pillow. With a surge, he hurled the concrete block toward Grant, forcing the ex-Magistrate to dive out of the way. The stone dented the wall behind him, the collision raising a cloud of powdered concrete.

Thrush-Kane's act of tearing up the floor had peeled the flesh from his fingers, and Grant could see the pink-white artificial bone, semitranslucent in the orange glow of the emergency lights. The ends of the fingers were pointed like claws, and Grant had no doubt that if they lashed out, they'd rend his flesh as if they were the talons of a raptor.

Brigid reentered the conflict, blazing away at the

cyborg with her .45. "Grant! Fall back and get some more help!"

Thrush-Kane flinched as 230-grain slugs sparked off the naked part of his skull. "Foolish little bitch. What makes you think you can damage this skeleton?"

"Kane wouldn't give up, so neither do we," Brigid growled in defiance. "Grant…"

Thrush-Kane looked back toward the ex-Magistrate, who had gotten back to his feet. "Keep wasting ammunition, Baptiste. I have to pull your annoying friend's arms and legs off his torso."

"Bring it," Grant taunted.

Thrush-Kane took one step, then another, starting to close the distance between himself and the brawny Grant. "It'll be a shame. You actually are a worthy opponent for an—"

A thunderclap resounded in the hallway, cutting off the cyborg's lamentation. Brigid thought her brains were going to leak out of her ears from the force of overpressure ripping through the hall. However, she saw that the cyborg was knocked off his feet, writhing on the floor.

Edwards stepped out of the gloom, holding his Barrett rifle. "Everyone okay?"

"Next time, slowpoke, you provide the distraction for the superstrong cyborg," Grant complained.

"Oh, I saw you. You were having the most fun you could with your pants on," Edwards replied.

Domi and Sinclair had their Copperheads trained on

the fallen cyborg as his limbs twisted and flailed un-
controllably.

"Sorry we were late. We had more trouble with the
locked-down doors than we thought we would," Domi
told Brigid. "Is he supposed to still move after a hit in
the head from a Fifty?"

Brigid looked down at the cyborg. His arms and
legs still writhed, but they had no strength to them,
and coordination was reminiscent of a newborn in a
crib. Half of Kane's face looked up at her, lips attempting to mouth words with only a portion of their
length remaining. It was a pathetic-looking example
of a being that had seemed so cocky and full of confidence earlier. A crushed stump of jacketed lead was
lodged in naked skull, cracks emanating from its
center.

"It doesn't look as if the brain was destroyed," Brigid
admitted. "Though the impact of that bullet certainly
produced massive trauma."

"Thank God for head wounds," Sinclair said, flicking
the safety of her Copperhead as Thrush-Kane's movements stilled. "Looks like a Terminator."

"Well, he's not going to be back," Grant said. "I don't
care if any of the scientists want to break this thing
down to examine its guts, we're stuffing it into a mat-
trans and dumping it at the bottom of the ocean,
provided we have a parallax point that sits there."

"Even if it's at the surface, it'll probably just sink,"
Domi answered. She watched the downed cyborg

warily, her ruby-red eyes taking on a darker, angrier glint in the emergency lighting of the base.

"That's all good, but the infiltrator shut down the computer system. We can't just dump him somewhere until we get the redoubt back online," Brigid said.

Grant loomed over the fallen Thrush construct. "Edwards, hand me your rifle, then go find something that can restrain this son of a bitch. Chains, steel cable, something."

"Got you," Edwards answered, tossing the Barrett to Grant.

"You're not going to move from this spot until you're sure he can't move under his own power," Sinclair said. "Good idea. The moment the heroes let their guard down, these crazies always sit up and commence to slaughter all over again."

Grant smirked as he aimed the Barrett at the downed cyborg's damaged skull. "You got that damn straight. Funny how life imitates art, if you can call old slasher vids art."

"One thing that confuses me," Brigid said as she reloaded her .45 pistol and kept it in hand, staring down at the inert foe, as if expecting it to explode back to life. "He hacked into the computer system, and yet did nothing to restore power to the doors in his path. He just peeled the blast panels aside."

"Maybe hacking the power back in order would just take too much time," Sinclair offered. "Yanking doors open is quicker."

"But where the hell was he going?" Brigid asked, frustrated with the lack of logical motivation for Thrush's chosen path through Cerberus. "You'd think for all his braying about how he wanted to take out Enlil, he would do something like head to the hangar and steal a Manta or a Deathbird and fly off to hunt down Enlil."

"Maybe he wasn't done looking in the computer for Enlil?" Domi asked.

Brigid felt a wave of nausea pass through her as she looked down at the shredded corpse on the floor. "He could wirelessly connect to our mainframe. He was an artificial intelligence. And that means he could inject himself into our computer systems, leaving his body behind…"

Edwards returned with an armload of chains. "Wait, you guys are saying I popped the cyborg in the head with a Fifty, and all I did was give him an excuse to evacuate his body?"

Grant grimaced. "Edwards, help me tie this thing up solidly. Brigid, Domi, get to the command center and see what the situation is with the mainframe. Sela, head to the cafeteria and bring back Philboyd and whoever the hell else knows about computer programming. We're going to need our best brains on this."

The lights came on throughout the redoubt, but that didn't stop the Cerberus Away Team members from setting about their tasks with grim, desperate urgency.

Colonel Thrush had just gone from disguised cyborg

juggernaut to a ghost in the machine. And this ghost had a known history of brutal, deadly murder.

THRUSH-KANE HAD to give credit to the feral albino woman and the soldier jocks of Cerberus. They had enough imagination to realize that the still weapon before them was a time bomb waiting to go off. He had shut down his skeleton's control apparatus in order to conserve the resources of his plasma matrix, realizing that he had to work quickly if he was going to have a chance to launch an assault on Enlil. And he hadn't completely uploaded his consciousness into the mainframe as they had assumed, but he still was operating within the cyberspace landscape of the powerful system.

He had accessed dozens of hard drives within the base, pulling information off them with skill. Thrush-Kane needed to gather whatever data was relevant to the hunt for Enlil and the surviving Annunaki. It wouldn't be enough just to kill the wayward Thrush entity. Enlil had usurped the pandimensional android's identity, using the body and mind for his own purposes while Enlil's true form remained as a mummified corpse, kept on ghoulish display in the Manitius lunar base. The irony of usurped identity was not lost on the infiltrator as it realized that he had not only taken over Kane's place, but had also taken command of the redoubt that was his hated pawn's home.

The mammals who meddled in Thrush's affairs were only a secondary source of irritation, however. The true goal of this penetration was to locate Enlil and do his best to unleash vengeance.

Thankfully, Lakesh and Bry had done much to restore the satellite network of surveillance that hung in orbit around the devastated Earth. With those powerful eyes in the sky peering down on a nuke-blasted world, the humans of Cerberus had a means of searching the globe for anomalies that were indicative of threats like the Annunaki and other menaces. Thrush-Kane ran over the records of the base and discovered a few instances of Annunaki drop-ship sightings, faint streaks of light as the high-tech, silvery disks slashed through the atmosphere at high speed. While Bry and other computer operators were working on code to bring such stratospheric, ultrasonic disturbances to the humans' attention, Thrush-Kane had no such limitations in regards to worldwide surveillance. Now that he had plugged into the mainframe, he was able to see the whole of the Earth's troposphere all at once.

It was good to have a brain that had exponentially more perceptive ability than even a group of humans. With millions of square miles of the Earth's surface visible at once, and a reference for what the passage of an Annunaki ship looked like, Thrush-Kane was able to scour the globe with ease. Minutiae that would have been missed by the human eye or a wandering attention span didn't escape the notice of the powerful plasma matrix brain as it piggybacked the Cerberus mainframe.

The Earth spun beneath his eyes, and in a manner of

minutes, he picked up a streak of silver slash in the blue sky, heading toward the Poconos.

Thrush-Kane would have doubled over with laughter if he was still using his body. All this effort to scour the planet, and Enlil had a scout ship hurtling toward Bres and the Fomorians in the mountains of Pennsylvania.

"Ah, Kane, it looks as if we won't need to use you as our backup plan for revenge on the Dragon King," Thrush-Kane said. "The bastard is coming right to you."

The infiltrator scanned through the Cerberus computer system, looking for weaponry that could be accessed from the mainframe. He found nothing in the redoubt itself. Its armory was meant for equipment utilized by humans, not over the AARPA net. Thrush-Kane grimaced in disgust that Lakesh hadn't bothered to directly hack into an old Air Force silo to keep a nuclear missile or two in reserve. That kind of firepower would have been sufficient to purge Enlil and his reptilian kin from the Earth.

So what if a little more radiation and fallout was released into the atmosphere? Entire tracts of the world had been wasted by a convulsion of atomic violence, and humanity and other life-forms had returned and recovered from such environmental atrocity.

A couple more nuclear explosions wouldn't affect the landscape.

"Fair enough," Thrush-Kane grumbled. He looked for external links to other redoubts across the country. Surely one of them would be connected to a nuclear weapons stockpile. There were hundreds of sites to go through, and for a normal man to get involved, it would have taken hours. The plasma matrix, in conjunction with the Cerberus mainframe, found what it needed within a minute.

It was a silo complex with six Intercontinental Ballistic Missiles, each of them carrying seven submunition warheads. Those warheads each carried a 2.5 megaton yield, and could bring annihilation to multiple cities with one launch or carve a crater out of the Earth's crust with a focused salvo of detonations. Poring through the system, Thrush-Kane discovered that only three of them were in working order, avoiding fuel leaks over the two centuries of inactivity, or their electronics systems remaining intact.

Twenty-one warheads, capable of unleashing the equivalent of 150,000 tons of TNT, were now at Thrush-Kane's disposal. He reached out to the ICBMs, already calculating the trajectory that would deposit them right on top of Enlil, Kane and Bres.

"Fifty megatons per irritant is a sufficient bit of scratching, no?" Thrush-Kane asked himself.

The ICBMs didn't respond to him. Thrush-Kane reached out again, but a wall of black ice slid into place between him and the control module.

"Let me guess… Bry and Lakesh managed to jumpstart the mainframe?" Thrush-Kane mused aloud.

"This has gone far enough." Kane's voice cut through the void of cyberspace.

If Thrush still had a face, it would have been twisted in confusion. "You're an impersonation protocol. A tool. A puppet at my command."

"Kane is never going to be anyone's puppet," the memory construct said as it floated in front of the infiltrator. "You want to go after Enlil, wake our body up, snap the chains binding us and steal a Manta to go after him."

Thrush chuckled. "This is easier."

"It's sloppier. It'll pump thousands of tons of fallout into the atmosphere, and anyone not killed by the initial blast will be poisoned. Pennsylvania will become a dead zone," Kane warned.

Thrush grabbed at the Kane construct, attempting to seize the artificial intelligence model. Kane, on the other hand, grabbed at the figurative wrists of the Thrush cyber-entity, holding it at bay.

"This is insane. We came here to destroy Enlil at any cost!" Thrush demanded.

Kane shook his head. "You made me too perfectly in his image. I might just be a shadow, but I still know what's right and what's wrong."

"Damn you!" Thrush cursed, struggling with the digital counterpart of Kane.

On the edge of cyberspace, just outside of the command console for 150 megatons of nuclear death, two electronic entities battled with all of their power.

Chapter 20

The Appalachians

It had taken considerable effort to wrench the AK-47 from the chest of Cilain, the Fomorian stand-in for Granny Epona. Kane made certain that the barrel was unobstructed and checked his supply of ammunition for the weapon. He had three and a half 30-round magazines, which wouldn't be much of a deterrent with a few dozen Fomorian hunters similarly armed.

Epona watched the Cerberus warrior as he made his preparations for the coming combat, her eyes raw from the tears she shed for a lost sister. The hardest part for the granny witch was that Cilain had been lost to her even before Bres whispered sweet promises of eternal youth and limitless power into her ear. Cilain had learned the parlor tricks of the ancient Tuatha de Danaan magicks, but she had ignored the true lessons of responsibility for that power. Her greed had been in place before the seduction by a golden-skinned, perfect-bodied devil.

Kane looked up from his preparations. "You should

have gone off with the rest of the scouts. This is going to be a nasty fight, and I can't slow down to watch over you."

Epona summoned up the strength for a smile. "I will need no such protection, Kane."

The Cerberus warrior frowned. "You're getting all majestic on me now. I suppose comparing oracular powers is off?"

Epona strode to him and caressed his cheek, her piercing emerald eyes meeting his. "Don't even think about backing out of that. No. I'm summoning all my reserves of strength. You won't be battling the Fomorians alone. You will have the mountain, scarred and wounded as it is, fighting alongside you."

Kane took a deep breath. "I don't think flocks of birds and swarms of rodents are going to make much of a dent in a full-on Fomorian assault force."

In the distance, thunder rumbled in the sky. Kane knew that this was a clear night, and out of the corner of his eye he saw a streak like a shooting star.

"You've got to be kidding me," Kane muttered.

"Enlil has arrived, finally summoned by his faithful servant Bres," Epona announced.

Kane nodded. "Things just became a lot more complicated. I was hoping that narcissistic walking alligator bag would keep his nose out of this for once, but it doesn't look like that."

"Why would he appear here?" Epona asked, looking at the starry sky, but the scout ship was no longer anywhere to be seen.

"Because Bres told him that he's going to give Enlil not one but two enemies on a silver platter. That snake-face has wanted to take a big chunk out of my ass for a long time, and I'm pretty sure he's annoyed by the presence of Colonel Thrush back on Earth," Kane explained. "This scale of emergency is enough to draw the egotistical bastard's attention because all of this is focused on him."

Epona frowned. "And here you'd wanted an alliance with us because we could keep an eye on the Appalachian range in case Enlil needed to use this as one of his hiding places."

"That's part of it," Kane said. "Another part is trying to reunite a country that has been scattered and fragmented. The mountain folk are part of an American tradition, and you can provide aid to us, and we can reciprocate."

Epona studied Kane, evaluating the champion of the ages as he checked a belt laden with loops for .50-caliber rounds. "This will not be the last time we work together."

"I sure as hell hope not," Kane answered. "But I don't put much faith in destiny or foresight."

"One battle at a time," Epona said. She whistled, and the old feral cat who had been Kane's link to the witch trotted into view.

"Hey, old boy," Kane said, kneeling to scratch the feline's ears. "My comm link to you?"

Epona nodded. "I have eyes and ears in all the trees.

There is not a part of this mountain that will not be looking out for you, warning you."

"But you'll still be here, a sitting target," Kane said.

"You are risking yourself. It would be dishonorable to hide. Besides, I would be worthless if I retreated down the other side of this mountain," Epona answered. "We need to work together, which is basically what you had wanted when you came to us."

"*E pluribus unum.* 'Out of many, one,'" Kane spoke, remembering an old phrase. "We aren't here to steal your culture, to take advantage of you. There's something about teamwork at its best that makes the combined force far more than the sum of its parts."

Epona nodded, then pulled in Kane for a tender embrace. "You have sold me already, hound of Cuchulainn."

Kane hadn't had much of an opportunity to repair the radio destroyed by the Fomorians, but he activated his Commtact in another attempt to reach his Cerberus colleagues. It worked.

"What happened to the radio we gave to the Appalachians?" Bry asked as soon as Kane raised the Cerberus tech.

"Busted," Kane explained, "so we'll have to use my Commtact. We don't have a lot of time for small talk. What's going on?"

"Well, you're probably aware that a duplicate Kane came back to Cerberus," Lakesh spoke up. "However, we've neutralized the body."

"The body," Kane repeated. "Let me guess—his robot brain's doing something right now."

"Well, he saw something over the mountain range where you are," Lakesh explained. "And he's trying to launch a salvo of ICBMs at you."

"He wants Enlil, and that something he saw was a scout craft," Kane replied. "ICBMs?"

"Three of them, rated at between 90 and 150 megatons of yield," Lakesh confirmed.

"I hope your techs are keeping him from initializing launch," Kane said.

Lakesh sighed. "We're recovering from a mainframe crash, so we're far behind the curve. The only thing keeping Thrush from engaging in a full launch is…you."

"He doesn't want to kill me?" Kane asked.

"I'll let you explain it to yourself," Lakesh returned.

A tinny, electronic version of Kane's voice spoke up. "Kane, I am the behavior program that was designed to facilitate Thrush-Kane's impersonation of you. I was constructed through considerable research to be as perfect a duplicate of your personality as possible."

"And they did their job a little too well?" Kane asked his electronic mirror image.

"I knew you'd understand," E-Kane replied. "I don't have a lot of energy or time left, as I'm battling the core Thrush programming, but I just wanted to speak with you."

Kane swallowed. "You'll be around later, kid."

E-Kane allowed a small chuckle. "Not if your

Cerberus friends are smart. I told them how to dispose of the Thrush cyborg. I'm not going to survive that disposal process."

Kane winced.

"We never surrender." E-Kane said. "But if we have to, we will give our everything for those we have sworn to protect. It's a fair trade, isn't it?"

"You don't need my answer to that question," Kane told his electronic counterpart. "Thank you for watching out for my people."

"Just get back to Cerberus and keep them safe," E-Kane told the original. "And make sure you let them know how much we really do love them all."

The line went silent, and Kane grit his teeth. "Lakesh? Bry?"

"Just a glitch," Lakesh answered immediately. "The Thrush entity is tapping mainframe resources in an effort to dislodge that program."

"Is there anything you can do?" Kane asked.

"We've got some of our best people up here," Lakesh answered. "Programmers, mathematicians, sharp minds. We'll see what we can do to separate the electronic entities, but E-Kane may be right. We have to destroy the brain of the cyborg, and once we do that, he'll be irretrievable."

"Kane," Epona spoke up as a word of warning. "The Fomorians are closer."

"Lakesh, what about some backup here?" Kane asked.

"We're battering away at some constructs that Thrush

put up over our mat-trans controls," another technician spoke up.

"Morganstern, right?" Kane asked.

"Yes, si— Kane," the mathematician replied.

"I can give you ten minutes before the Fomorians overwhelm me," Kane offered. "Anything longer than that, don't worry."

Kane turned to Epona. "Find someplace out of the way."

The witch woman nodded and slipped off to search for cover.

The cat pointed Kane in the direction of an oncoming reconnaissance team of Fomorians who assumed that they moved with such stealth that they could evade detection from human eyes and ears. As Kane closed in to intercept the trio of mutant hunters, he had to admit that they were skilled. If it hadn't been for the overlay of imagery from the local wildlife, Kane wouldn't have known they were there. Lining up the sights of Erik's big rifle, Kane triggered the five-foot-long cannon. The muzzle-flash was the size of a pumpkin, and as bright as the sun, but Kane was braced for the rifle's mighty kick. It was a sharp spike of pressure on his shoulder, and had he not been kneeling in a stable position, he'd have staggered off balance from the recoil.

Downrange, two Fomorians screamed in dismay as their partner's skull detonated under the impact of a half-inch-thick spike of copper and lead. The decapitated creature crashed through some bushes, and the two remaining Fomorian scouts opened fire with their AKs sweeping the mountainside where they'd seen the fireball issued from Kane's shot.

The Cerberus warrior was already in another position, tucked behind a toppled pine tree where it leaned against the trunk of a still standing tree. Kane lined up the shot, pulled the trigger and the chatter of one Fomorian's rifle went silent. Through the eyes of an owl, sent by Epona's network, Kane could see that he'd struck one of the panicked hunters in the chest. The mutant coughed blood and clutched his wound with his sole arm. Agony was scrawled across his already twisted features, and Kane fed another long .50-caliber cartridge into the open action of his rifle. A slam of the bolt shut, and he pulled the trigger again. The suffering monstrosity jerked as Kane's next bullet took him through the heart. The Fomorian's eyes rolled lifelessly up and he collapsed.

The last Fomorian let out apelike grunts of alarm as he struggled to reload his assault rifle. Kane sent a message to Epona, asking whom the scout was trying to contact. The image from the owl's eyes shifted, hurtling down the mountainside fifty yards to five of Bres's foul mutants who were being watched over by an alert fox. The superbly acute sense of smell and night vision of the canine blended in Kane's mind's eye. It was a heady rush, akin to when he first donned the Magistrate helmet, except this felt more visceral, more familiar. There was a flash of memory of an Indian forest, a prior incarnation of Kane running naked alongside a pack of wolves, all of them working together in concert in a hunt. Old, familiar senses that had been instilled in that life rushed to the surface.

Kane pivoted and fired another .50-caliber slug toward the encroaching Fomorian intruders. The echo of the supersonic bullet as it zipped past trees sounded like an arc of lightning crackling on a hot summer night. The fox forward observer smelled freshly spilled blood as it sprayed over two Fomorians, jetting from the severed aorta of Kane's target. The bestial hunter's solitary eye was wide with horror and he coughed, trying to clear the blood from his throat so he could beg for help from his kinsmen.

The Fomorians ignored him. They scrambled, scurrying into the trees to avoid their brethren's fate. Closer to Kane, the owl's senses overwhelmed Kane's, informing him that the last member of the scouting party had reloaded his weapon and was on the charge.

Kane let the Fifty hang on its sling, and he whipped up his confiscated assault rifle. The Fomorian growled angrily, holding down the trigger but not bothering to aim. The strategy seemed to be to cow Kane until the hunter was close enough to bludgeon the lone defending human. Kane held his ground and his fire, bullets ripping into the dirt off to his left. The impacts of the gunshots thumped the air, their heat uncomfortably close, but Kane waited until there was no way that he could miss. The Fomorian unleashed a challenging bellow, a last-ditch effort to force Kane to flinch.

Instead, Kane stiff-armed the rifle and held down the trigger, dumping a dozen rounds through the creature's open maw. Face and skull came apart in a bloody, chunky mist and the mutant stumbled out of control, tripping past Kane's form. The Fomorian's head, torn to pieces by the close-range burst, resembled the petals of a grisly flower, folded away from the gory stump of a neck.

The urge to move flooded Kane's mind, and the lone warrior leaped over the fallen trunk and dropped to his bottom. The slope's slippery surface allowed Kane to skid ten yards downhill, just as a storm of Fomorian rifle bullets crackled through the night.

"He's moved!" a resonant, childlike voice called. "There! He's closer to you!"

It was Balor, his baleful eye put to use tracking Kane. From the sound of his voice, the titanic Fomorian was at least a hundred yards downslope, directing traffic. Kane felt fortunate that he was out of range of the sizzling beam that had burned through the forest after him earlier. Its range was obviously limited, beyond which the energy it projected lost its lethality, probably due to the potential for backlash or overload. Whatever the case, Kane had a cushion of safety before having to deal with Balor. Even if Kane managed to avoid the powerful optic beam of the Fomorian prince, there was still the factor of arms as thick as tree trunks and possessing monumental strength.

"Epona," Kane spoke aloud. Since the need for stealth

had evaporated with the first exchange of gunfire, he used verbal speech as a focus for how he communicated with the Appalachian witch. "Where's Balor and Bres?"

"Balor's carved a perimeter of death around his father and himself," Epona answered. Unrestrained by having to communicate under the noses of her captors, now she was able to transmit more than just emotions. "I'm not sending any animals in closer to those two."

"Which will make precise targeting difficult," Kane muttered to himself. Fox senses flashed across his consciousness once more. The Fomorian group he'd scattered were reassembling, their rifles primed and ready to chew at Kane now that Balor had told them where he was and what direction he was heading in.

Kane shouldered the big Fifty again and put one of the mutants out of his misery, the half-inch, two-ounce bullet shearing through the Fomorian's throat and destroying neck bones on its exit. Shreds of skin and muscle still held the head dangling from the creature's shoulders, but the flopping head pulled him off-balance, dragging him to the ground in a grisly mess.

So far, Kane had used up one of the ten minutes he had provided for the Cerberus computer team to save the day, and he'd accounted for five of the enemy. While that might have been good news, Epona's forest eyes informed him that he'd barely taken care of one-tenth of the raiders' numbers.

Kane remembered the sheer carnage that the Silver Hand of Nadhua had wrought when it had been used against the Cerberus staff by Maccan. Brigid had explained that the Silver Hand was Nadhua's chief weapon in war against the Fomorian hordes. The immortal warrior had Kane's respect and envy. Respect because Nadhua had battled these beasts alone, perhaps in odds this strenuous, and envy because Kane didn't have a high-energy force projector to supply an edge against the superior numbers and strength of the Fomorians.

All he had were another twenty rounds of .50-caliber BMG rounds, and three magazines for an AK-47. He'd expended six of the big bullets in killing four of the creatures, and a third of an AK-47 payload in taking out the fifth. That kind of math meant that he wouldn't have enough firepower to deal with the fifty-plus remaining mutants. If Balor proceeded closer, the faint advantage of sensory ability that Epona had given him would be taken away, making things much more difficult.

"Lakesh, I'm being pressed too hard. The numbers aren't with me," Kane said. "It might be a good idea to let Thrush drop an ICBM on this mountain."

"We've already got one Kane sacrificing his existence for us," Lakesh responded. "You adding to the carnage isn't going to do anything for the Appalachians. The kind of firepower Thrush wants to bring to bear is going to render the rift valley running through Pennsylvania an uninhabitable wasteland, and there's no guarantee that Enlil will let his ship sit still long enough to take a hit."

Kane grimaced. "That's not going to end well for Epona's people."

"No, it's not," the witch interjected. "Even if I could reach all the animals within the blast radius, I won't leave you behind."

"Kane," Bry spoke up, "we've recovered control of the mat-trans. Grant and CAT B are en route."

Kane did the math. It'd take about five minutes before his partner would join the battle. "Did Grant bring me some gear?"

"Of course," Bry answered.

"Friend Kane, we're still trying to eject Thrush from the mainframe," Lakesh informed him.

Kane fired another half-inch bullet at a Fomorian. This one missed, but only because of Balor's cry of warning to his warrior. Balor's vision had to have been sharp enough to spot him even from a quarter of a mile away, because there was no way that the muzzle-flash would have given Balor enough time to shout an alert. That didn't make Kane feel comfortable, even with the knowledge that he was out of the optic beam range of Balor.

"Epona, pull back. Once Grant and the others arrive, we're still going to have to fight these things, and they're getting smarter the more of them I kill," Kane answered.

He fed another cartridge into the breech of his rifle. The old warrior cat yowled a warning, and Kane barely had enough time to dodge the slash of an AK receiver at head level. Had it not been for the cat's alert, Kane's head would have been cleaved from his shoulders. Kane pivoted with the five-foot-rifle and jammed its muzzle into the belly of the attacking Fomorian. A pull of the trigger and the rifle discharged into the creature's stomach. Not only did the bullet punch through his abdominal wall, but also the flaming belch of burning powder and superheated gasses were injected into the Fomorian's thoracic cavity. Roasted from the inside out, a puff of steam emerged from the monstrosity's lips as he clutched his shattered belly and collapsed to his knees.

Kane staggered away from the mortally wounded creature, but the cat meowed again. Two more of the towering monstrosities had lurched into view, rifles barking. Kane grabbed the dying Fomorian's arm and hauled him up as a shield. The dense musculature of the patchwork mutant absorbed a volley of steel-cored rifle rounds, stopping them cold. Kane unsheathed his AK and returned fire, but the Fomorians he hammered with a burst only grunted under the onslaught.

Yes, Thrush would be smart enough to give the Fomorians a rifle that won't be useful against their own kind, Kane thought.

The creature he'd wounded laughed spitefully.

"So much for the champion of Cerberus," the man-beast snarled.

Kane raised the rifle to eye level, knowing that even if he blew the head off the laughing Fomorian, the other creature would flank and kill him.

But Kane wasn't the kind of man who gave up.

Chapter 21

Cyberspace

Thrush hurtled through the empty void of space, hurled there by the might of the electronic Kane personality construct. Frustration pulsed through every part of the infiltrator's being. It had crossed dimensions and half a country, only to be stopped by the trappings of a disguise.

"This is not logical, Kane," Thrush growled. "What benefit do you seek from opposing me? Even if I fire the ICBMs, no one here at Cerberus will be harmed."

"Too many innocent people will be caught in the fallout of the explosions," E-Kane replied.

"But they aren't people that Kane would care about," Thrush countered. "Be reasonable. With this launch, we eliminate the single worst menace that humanity has ever known."

E-Kane shook his head, rejecting the argument. "It's not the kind of trade Kane would make. He's fought too hard to make the world a better place to sacrifice thousands of lives on one threat."

Thrush grimaced. "Damn idiot…"

He looked at his arsenal of saved programs and withdrew an antivirus that manifested itself in cyber-space as a wicked sword that crackled with a sheath of flames. "Move aside."

E-Kane stood his ground. "No. You'll have to fight your way through me."

"You're battling a god, fool," Thrush warned.

E-Kane managed a chuckle. "And how exactly are you so different from Enlil?"

"Because I'm not some scale-faced freak of nature from another world. I am a god of the Earth," Thrush told him. With a lunge, the artificial intelligence lashed out with its flaming sword.

E-Kane moved with the speed and skill of the original, lithely avoiding the slash. The copied personality countered with a punch to Thrush's head, a consciousness-rocking impact that drove the entity to his knees.

"A lot of people keep calling themselves gods, but all of them seem to drop when punched in the head," E-Kane said. "That's a very interesting trend in my original's life."

"Your original," Thrush said, struggling back to a standing position. The entity hadn't expected to be con-fronted by a force that could dish out pain so readily, but then, he hadn't anticipated part of his own multitiered identity to rebel against him. He was certain that some part of this equation had to do with the monster bullet that had crashed into his skull. The blob of plasma matrix contained within the reinforced head had to have taken significant damage, and the Kane construct's betrayal was symptomatic of the head trauma. It was only logical, considering the number of blows that had rained on his head in the past few hours. Bres's attack, Brigid's gunshots and now the antitank rifle's impact had created a split personality. "You are a set of behaviors with delusions of reality!"

"You wanted a means to be indistinguishable from the true Kane, and you made me. I am not going to betray the programming I have, which is full of the man's ideals," E-Kane responded.

Thrush felt all manner of minor impacts against his electronic body, and knew that E-Kane's attempts at logical disagreement were an attempt to distract him. Thrush tried to shake off the urge to stand and debate with the idiotic program. He had a nuclear missile launch to engage.

A robotic form leaped out of the darkness, a massive creature that looked as if it were a computerized three-headed dog. Thrush watched as the lumbering titan charged toward the control node for the ICBMs.

"No," Thrush called out. He hurled his antivirus at the robot, the flaming sword transforming into a lightning bolt that split the darkness. The program staggered under the impact and collapsed.

"What the hell is that?" Thrush asked, summoning his antivirus anew.

E-Kane grinned. "That's the Cerberus computer staff attempting to sever their link to this redoubt."

"Why can't you just die?" Thrush asked.

E-Kane leaped and grabbed Thrush in a headlock. Though they were only programs, both existed on a similar plane of existence. Here, their bodies were solid, and they stood as equals, despite the fact that the Thrush identity was supposed to be the primary influence. It was then that Thrush came to the realization that the sheer volume of data that he had put into copying Kane, right down to duplicating every inch of his flesh down to the smallest bit of scar tissue, had been pushed into the Kane construct. By dint of volume and complexity, the Kane personality had become stronger. Thrush thrashed in an effort to free himself from E-Kane's grasp, but their strength was too evenly matched.

Thrush remembered the antivirus program he had formed into a sword. With a desperate surge, he flung it at E-Kane. The headlock disappeared, and Thrush withdrew the blade from his body. The two entities staggered away from each other as the robotic canine gathered its strength once more. It swatted at the ICBM control module with one massive paw, and the electronic structure blurred for a moment.

Thrush glared at the monstrous dog with desperation. If the Cerberus program kept attacking that node, he would never get a chance to launch his nuclear attack on Enlil. Once more, Thrush hurled the flaming sword, and the Cerberus program howled from its three mouths as its paw disintegrated into a rain of lights and splinters.

E-Kane crashed down on Thrush's shoulders once more, fists hammering about the entity's head. Thrush twisted in an effort to get out from under the assault, but E-Kane stuck to his back. Thrush clawed at the Kane personality's arms, feeling his own limbs come under assault.

Thrush suddenly realized why it had been almost impossible to hit the other entity. Here in cyberspace, its perceptions were externalized, but the other personality was still a part of Thrush himself. He was batting at illusions. The only real opponent on this playing field was the program sent by Cerberus to sever the connection to the ICBM-equipped redoubt. No wonder Thrush felt as if his entire being was being continually pummeled. The battle was from within, and while it had been directing its energy outward at an opponent that was safely tucked away between his ears, the expenditure of energy and processing power was drained drastically.

With a leap, Thrush grabbed at the Cerberus program's neck joints. The program twisted and writhed, fighting to keep Thrush off balance, so much so that Thrush was unable to respond. The sword would not extend or ignite, but Thrush knew why his efforts at summoning the blade were inconclusive. E-Kane was still fighting. In growing frustration, Thrush hammered his head against one of the giant canine skulls it was battling. The impact jarred everyone involved, and the electronic entities sprawled away from the control node.

Trying to draw his strength, Thrush took a look back toward the redoubt. It was lit again, which was no surprise. If the techs were able to interface with the mainframe again, they would also be able to interfere with Thrush's plans against Enlil.

Thrush peered through a security camera. Philboyd and a team were bringing the inert duplicate body down a hallway. There was a brief glimpse of a sign on the wall reading High Voltage Security Precautions, and Thrush cursed.

"You told them how to shut down this brain," Thrush said.

"Without activating your self-destruct mechanism," E-Kane added. "Sorry, but it seemed the only way to stop you."

Thrush sighed, looking back at the control node. He had battled the Cerberus program to a standstill for now, but if it continued to penetrate the command node, there was a chance that it could deactivate his brain. His only options was to return to his body at Cerberus and awaken it. With one final vengeful kick to the Cerberus program, collapsing more of the great canine's structure, Thrush hurtled back through cyberspace to the redoubt.

Once Thrush was done tearing the humans apart, he would launch the ICBMs and eliminate Enlil once and for all.

The Appalachians

GRANT RUSHED to his friend's side, his long, powerful legs propelling him down the side of the hill. On his heels, Domi, Sinclair and Edwards were a bit more reserved in their descent down the slope, but the three members of CAT Beta were fully aware that lives were at stake. Grant was laden with an extra war bag for Kane, and he was clad from head to toe in the black polymers of the shadow suit. His eyes were as sharp as an owl's. The terrain before him was as clear as if it was illuminated by daylight, and the shadow suit's protective qualities kept his legs and feet from being carved up by bumping against rocks.

What Grant hadn't anticipated was the formation of squirrels that led the way down the slope. When the animals had rushed up to the CAT Beta team without a hint of trepidation, performed their dance and formed an arrow pointing in a certain direction, Grant wasn't about to look a gift horse in the mouth. Somehow, Kane had either developed the ability to command rodents, or more likely he had found an Appalachian granny witch with that ability. If the witch had been the woman he'd been thinking of, suddenly the whole song and dance of Kane having to go off alone to prove himself made sense, but it was in the wrong kind of way.

Why the hell not? he asked himself. Thrush had managed to make a copy of Kane, so why couldn't Bres, someone known to mutate people into monstrosities, make a woman look exactly like Epona?

Gunfire boomed from just beyond the tree line and Grant pushed himself harder. The Barrett was hardly a compact and easily maneuverable carbine, but in the hands of the massive ex-Magistrate, it was "normal" sized. Grant slalomed through the trees, following the rattle of weapons fire when he came upon a clearing.

A lone figure, AK-47 in hand, dressed in the ragged tatters of a tent, had just turned a gut shot Fomorian into a living shield. Two more of the creatures were firing on him, and the human, smaller than his enemies by a head, fired an ineffectual blast of automatic fire at them.

One of the bestial hunters cackled a threat toward the outnumbered man, and the two creatures charged simultaneously.

Grant shouldered the big Barrett rifle and fired off two rapid semiauto shots. The jolt of the steel-girder stock recoiling against his shoulder was blunted somewhat by the shadow suit. It didn't hurt, but it was a significant push. Were Grant any less powerful, the violent kick of the big rifle would have thrown him wildly off target with his second shot. Instead, Grant summoned up every ounce of stubborn determination and strength to hit both of the Fomorian marauders in rapid fire. The creatures jerked under the thunderbolt impacts, their bodies crashing to the forest floor and tumbling partway down the slope.

Kane pulled back his hood, and Grant could see the bloodied bandage wrapped around his head. Domi and Edwards and Sinclair hard on his heels, Grant ran to the small clearing and handed Kane his war bag.

Epona entered the clearing, as well, eliciting a moment of heightened alertness among CAT Beta while Kane was in the process of stripping out of his canvas wrappings.

"Right now, I'm distracting the leading edge of the Fomorian assault front with the great flock. We don't have much time," the witch said.

"Grant, Epona. The real Epona," Kane introduced.

Grant nodded to the woman. "Granny Epona, a pleasure to finally meet you."

Epona returned the nod. "I didn't think Kane could summon a force…"

The witch's gaze moved from the massive Grant and Edwards to the decidedly smaller Sinclair and Domi. "Well, half imposing works."

"Don't let Domi's size fool you. There's more fight in her than in the three of us big, strapping he-men," Kane said as he pulled the shadow suit top over his torso. The body-hugging fabric conformed to his lean, muscular physique.

Epona looked over Domi, receiving the woman's unsettling ruby-red stare.

"So, you're a witch?" Domi asked.

Epona nodded. "More or less."

"Cool," Domi replied. "How much time do we have before the Fomorians decide to ignore your birds?"

"I'm giving it ten more seconds," Epona said. "I've already tried this ploy once today. The Fomorians aren't stupid."

Kane slid into the forearm holster for a replacement for his Sin Eater. With his arm once more complete, he was ready to fight. Inside the bag were grens, as well as a pump shotgun.

"Heads up, people!" Domi shouted, dropping into a crouch and shouldering her rifle. Both Sinclair and the albino woman had traded in their less powerful Copperhead rifles for the much more authoritative SIG AMT rifles. More powerful by far than the relatively sedate AK-47, at close quarters the 7.62 mm NATO chambered rifles had enough punch to bring down a good-sized black bear, while having almost no recoil due to its ingenious bolt design. Domi sighted a Fomorian marauder over her sights and triggered the AMT, punching two rounds into the bestial mutant. The creature staggered backward, mortally injured by the high-powered rifle rounds. "SIGs work!"

"Glad for that," Sinclair replied as she targeted another monstrosity lurking in the trees.

Kane, Grant and Edwards slipped into the woods, the hoods on their shadow suits up and their faceplates gone completely dark. Domi and Sinclair also had darkened their hoods, rendering themselves nearly invisible in the darkness.

Kane spoke over the Commtact, "Team, make sure to engage the thermal baffles on your shadow suits. There's one large Fomorian down there named Balor. He has a bionic eye that has been tracking me and Epona for the past twenty minutes. He's able to coordinate the rest of his forces with his thermal and telescopic vision."

Grant grumbled. "Bionic eyes. I thought we were done with cyborgs once we deactivated Thrush's infiltrator."

"Grant, quit being a crybaby," Edwards returned.

"Besides, he has a bionic eye, how much worse could he be?"

"He's about the size of a horse and built like a gorilla," Kane answered.

Edwards hung his head, crestfallen. "When am I going to learn to stop tempting fate?"

"I dunno. We've been doing this for years, and we still don't know when to shut up," Grant told him.

The three men fell silent as a squad of Fomorians stalked into view. During Grant's and Edwards's banter, Kane heard Balor inform the marauding mutants that he was no longer able to see Kane, but ordered an attack force to go after Epona, who didn't have the benefit of a body-heat-concealing uniform.

"Domi, Sela, did you hear him?"

"We're already covering Epona," Sinclair answered. "Anyone going after her is going to get a head full of lead."

"Do you mind being bait, Epona?" Kane asked.

A telempathic chuckle reverberated through the five Cerberus warriors.

Edwards followed up that chuckle by clearing his throat. "I think we can translate that as 'come and get me.'"

Kane grinned and pointed at Grant. "It's women like her who keep me from settling down with anyone, partner."

Grant sighed. "Keep your mind on business, not pleasure. I've got a team of Fomorians trying to get up that wash over there."

"And I've got a silver flying saucer hanging about three hundred yards straight ahead," Edwards warned.

Grant and Kane looked up at the Annunaki scout ship as it hovered, silent and ominous over the valley. While neither of the Cerberus warriors had determined the full sensory capacity of the alien craft, the technology wielded by the alien overlords was significant. Their only saving grace was that the weapons apertures along the sides of the mirror-skinned saucer were not active. Having been bombarded by the powerful beam guns of the scout ships before, they were all too familiar with how such a ship appeared when it was on a war footing. Whoever was in the cockpit, and Grant had a suspicion that it was Enlil, was there solely as an observer.

"We could take a shot at that ship," Grant whispered to Kane. "We take down the big bad Dragon King, and Thrush quits trying to take over Cerberus and goes home."

Kane's grimace under his faceplate was evident when he replied. "As much as I want to see that snakeface go down in flames, we can't spare the effort to take the down craft. We'll deal with the bastard in our own time."

Grant nodded. "Yeah. Why do Thrush any favors?"

"Then we hit the Fomorians," Edwards asked.

"Or blow them kisses," Grant answered.

Edwards shouldered his multichambered grenade launcher. "Smooch on this, mutants."

A series of 40 mm shells erupted from the muzzle of the oversized revolver, their payloads arcing down into the group of Fomorians who were on their way to war.

The blazing explosions of the grens launched bodies into the air like ragdolls, Grant and Kane cleaning up the monstrosities that their partner had missed.

The war for the Appalachians between human and Fomorian was ending this night, and the Cerberus warriors were going to take every ounce of fight out of their inhuman enemy.

Chapter 22

Bres grimaced as he heard the thunder of grenades and heavy weapons clattering above. The rattle of the rifles that Thrush had supplied him seemed puny in comparison to the coordinated firepower focused on his magnificent Fomorians. He turned to Balor and slapped the creature across his face.

"Where are the humans?"

Balor winced from the attack. "Father, they are cloaked against my infrared vision. I can only get a few brief glimpses of them as they fire their weaponry. Other than that, they are like ghosts."

Bres's mouth twisted into an ugly sneer. "I give you the finest weapon of all, and you are like a blind infant!"

Balor rose to his full height. Never before had Bres been so insulting and condescending. The godling's patience had been something that had endeared Balor, and with this disappointment, a floodgate of scorn and bile had been unleashed. "You told me to stay back, to allow the other Fomorians to run roughshod over Kane and Epona."

"Because he shot you in the eye," Bres said. "He found what could be your weak spot."

Balor frowned. "Or he could deprive you of a toy that you'd grown fond of, no?"

Bres's eyes flashed with anger. "You will respect your father, you sniveling little brat. I made you—I can unmake you!"

Balor's twisted mouth turned down into a frown. "You can try."

Bres clenched his fists. "Keep directing our forces against the humans!"

Balor nodded. "But from someplace where it matters."

With a swat, Balor knocked Bres violently against a tree. It was a casual exertion of strength, with enough power to pulverize Bres's spinal column into fine powder. Agony speared through the immortal being as he twisted on the ground.

His eyes fell upon the silvery saucer above. "Enlil…"

With a rustle of thoughts, the words of the Annunaki overlord resounded in Bres's mind. "You called me here to witness the destruction of my enemies. All I see is rebellion within your ranks, and the humans turning your freakish foot soldiers into corpses."

"Master, I have also given you warning, about the Thrush Continuum," Bres gasped.

"Yes. Yes, you told me that," Enlil replied. "I've been listening to their radio communications, and it appears that they have a means of dealing with the android's infiltrator. And yet, you seemed to promise me that you would crush Thrush himself, not a constructed minion. Even then, you haven't done much to slow him."

"I damaged his robotic brain," Bres pleaded. "It was how I sabotaged him. If not for me…"

"If not for you, the ruse of his disguise would actually have lasted more than a few hours," Enlil returned. "Instead, you managed to bungle everything. You bungled Thrush's operation. You couldn't capture a wounded and nearly naked Kane. Yes, I've been watching ever since you first contacted me."

Bres swallowed. His spine was rebuilding itself, but it seemed slower. "Master? My gift…"

"Yes. You wanted the opportunity to feel again," Enlil answered.

As the shattered bones of his vertebrae stitched back together, Bres became aware of the prickling of pine needles against his cheek, the chill of night air, the shifting of chunks of spinal column and cord grating against each other. Bres broke out into a sweat as muscles spasmed and nerves tore. He had been battered and crushed so many times, but he had never experienced the sensations of the rebuilding process before. His guts were on fire, and tears poured down his cheeks as he bit ragged holes in his lips. The brief caresses of agony that had penetrated the numbness of his being were simple kisses, moments of sensation in a sea of nothingness. The pain stayed with Bres this time; it didn't go away as swollen and overstressed tissues contracted again, torn sheets of muscle tugging violently back together.

Being rebuilt hurt far more than he ever conceived it would. Now he understood the soul-piercing howls his "children" had emitted when he molded them into the mighty Fomorians.

"Oh, it will still be fun to see you as an immortal, re-constituting yourself from every injury," Enlil said. "I gave you a gift, the power to ignore every bit of pain in your life. The true gift wasn't that you healed, but you didn't feel it when you were hurt."

Bres whimpered. "My god…"

"Remember that honorific, my son. Don't be such a complete and utter failure the next time we meet," Enlil told the Fomorian king.

The scout ship shimmered for a moment, then rocketed straight up into the night sky.

Cerberus

BRIGID BAPTISTE wasn't surprised when Thrush-Kane sat up suddenly on the table. The compact motors built into the bones of the cyborg were powerful enough to shatter the steel chains binding him to the table. But utilizing the photocell technology built into the skin of the shadow suit she wore, she made certain that when Thrush-Kane woke up, she'd surprise him.

The infiltrator had snapped the chain wrapped around the main trunk of his torso and biceps, but that was about all he managed to get broken before Brigid grabbed Philboyd by the arm and shoved him out of the central transformer station for the redoubt. The other staff members had abandoned the rolling gurney at the door of the electrical junction. Philboyd and the rest slammed shut the armored doors, sealing her in with a superstrong cyborg with murder in its heart.

"Baptiste? Are you trying to hide from me?" Thrush asked. The android had dropped any pretense of duplicating Kane's voice, and even the sloughed section of face that remained on the reinforced skull of the infiltrator sagged and deformed under its own weight. No one would ever mistake this being for human.

"No. Not anymore," Brigid said, tapping the wrist control for her shadow suit and disabling the camouflage feature.

"Only because your gun harness hadn't turned invisible with you," Thrush said. He shrugged again, another link of steel chain falling away, another loop clinking to the floor. "Of course, I'm pretty certain that we've established that I am immune to any small-arms fire you could hope to bring against me."

Brigid smiled as Thrush hopped off the table, his bindings clattering to the floor in a musical rain of metal clanging against metal. "Yes, I was wondering what I'd do about that."

Thrush's eyes scanned the room. Though he had no forehead, no brow to wrinkle in confusion, Brigid knew what had happened.

"This particular area of the redoubt is not equipped for wireless computer access," Brigid explained. "You won't be able to hack into the Cerberus mainframe from here."

Thrush laughed, a mechanical bark coming from an electronic voice box situated on the artificial bone structure of his neck. "Those doors don't look strong enough to deter me, Baptiste. And there is no way on Earth that you could force me into the transformers to overload my plasma matrix brain."

Brigid shrugged, circling the rag-fleshed skeletal android. No longer was he a cyborg, a mix of living and mechanical. He was an articulated robot, wearing rotting flesh that dripped and sagged.

"You really should do the smart thing and stay out of my way, Baptiste. You'd be a worthy addition to the Thrush Continuum. I'm sure the prime unit would be glad to have you," Thrush said.

"Thanks, but I like it here," Brigid answered. She pulled off her faceplate and peeled the hood off her head. Thrush's eyes once again swiveled, looking around the room in a form of robotic paranoia that would have been comical.

"What are you doing?" Thrush asked.

"Killing time until any chance of you gaining access to nuclear missiles is completely gone," Brigid replied. "Of course, if you want, I could shoot at you, but that's not really my favorite solution to a problem."

Thrush chuckled. "It'd also be a waste of ammunition."

Brigid screwed up her face, as if she had somehow forgotten the android skeleton's invulnerability. Thrush took a step back. "What are you doing? Don't lie to me!"

Brigid withdrew a pistol from her shoulder holster. It was a compact device that only nominally resembled a conventional handgun, with a long, slender pipe for a barrel and two smaller tubes running parallel to it. Thrush looked closer at it.

"A gauss pistol from Manitius," Thrush muttered. "I knew you weren't stupid. Maybe a magnetically accelerated pellet could punch through my head, given the right material."

"Oh, I've got the right ammunition in this," Brigid said. "It's an easy choice—slain by me, or you can deactivate yourself by overloading your brain."

"Or option three, I tear your arms off, beat you to death with them, and then I kick open those flimsy doors and use your severed limbs to kill as many of your friends as I can," Thrush answered.

"I was afraid you'd say that," Brigid responded.

Thrush lurched as if to disarm the archivist, but froze in place. His limbs had seized up, and he was an easy target. "The Kane personality—"

Brigid nodded. "I thought that maybe if we deactivated you, we could somehow salvage him."

Kane's voice issued from the speaker box. "It's not going to happen. I can barely control Thrush as it is. He's gone insane with rage."

"Damn it," Brigid cursed.

"Baptiste, let me die as a free man," E-Kane replied. "I know you don't like listening to his suggestions, but show *me* some respect."

"I respect Kane," Brigid told the construct.

"Then let me free," the rotting doppelganger said. He lowered his head, closing one eye as the other had no lid.

Brigid raised the gauss pistol, making sure to aim at the flat portion of the skull. She didn't relish the idea of a ricochet bouncing off the curved bone at hypersonic speeds. "May your soul soar freely, *anam-chara*."

"Thank you," E-Kane whispered.

Brigid pulled the trigger, and the plasma matrix brain exploded out of the base of the android's skull in a mist of lime-green froth.

Taking a deep breath, trying not to let the tears come, she pushed the gauss pistol back into her belt. The skeleton folded and dropped to the floor, the semiliquid brain that controlled it churned up and shattered by the force of a piece of titanium accelerated to five times the speed of sound.

Brigid concentrated on the fact that the thing that had spoken to her was not real, but she couldn't buy it. Somehow, though, she managed to keep a lid on her emotions.

She wasn't proud of herself, but she kept her composure as she unlocked the transformer station doors.

The Appalachians

LAKESH'S VOICE RANG OUT in Kane's ears. "The nuclear threat has been disarmed. Thrush is no longer a problem."

"Did my friend's plan work?" Kane asked.

"Your counterpart…yes," Lakesh replied. "Brigid destroyed the android's brain."

A rustle of thoughts, and Epona was in his mind. "He will be mourned."

Kane fought to concentrate on reloading his shotgun. Two dozen Fomorians had already fallen in battle since Edwards lit up the night with high explosives, but the feeding of shells was a simple enough matter that he couldn't resist a moment of philosophical contemplation. "Does that make sense? He was a soulless construct."

"No. He had a soul. I could feel it from your memories of your brief conversation with you," Epona answered. "If he could love enough to sacrifice himself for others, then he had a soul."

Kane reeled at the implication. He wanted to say

more, but the Fomorians scattered as a bounding form crashed into the side of the mountain. Balor had arrived, no longer held back as a director. Muscles shifted on his muscular chest, shoulders the size of boulders flexing as he stretched out his arms, bellowing a challenge.

"Hound of Cuchulainn! My weakling father no longer holds me on his leash! It is time!" Balor bellowed.

"He sounds like a kid," Grant muttered.

"Sounds fused out," Domi added over the Commtact. "Do we hit him?"

Kane slung the shotgun over his shoulder. "I've got this."

"You sure, man?" Edwards asked. "Because I've got twelve rounds of high explosive ready to blow up in his face."

"Let Kane do his thing," Sinclair interjected.

"What time is it?" Kane called out in challenge. The sickly green eye turned to regard the shadow-suited warrior who rose to the challenge.

"It is time to set history right," Balor said.

"I think you'd want to talk to Lugh, not Cuchulainn," Kane mentioned. "But what the hell. I'm getting tired of blasting second-stringers."

Balor's lips twisted in a perversion of a smile. "I'm not too particular. Either way, like Lugh, you're a beacon of hope for these pedantic little apes infesting this planet. Bres felt you were his sole obstacle to everything he wanted, to the point where he was more afraid of confronting you than doing what needed to be done. I am not a sniveling coward like my father."

"You need to learn to respect your elders, even if

they are heartless, genocidal maniacs," Kane offered. "So, am I going to fight you bare-handed?"

Balor shook his head. "No. Lugh had a sword when he battled my grandfather. You can have those puny popguns."

"Thank you," Kane replied, circling the muscular titan. "So what happens if I kill your ugly ass?"

"The slaughter continues as before," Balor said. "I just want my crack at the legend. I want to see if you live up to the hype."

Kane unslung his shotgun. There was a round already in the chamber, and the magazine tube was fully loaded. The fat chunks of lead had proved their worth this night, tearing through Fomorian bodies like bricks through tissue paper, but Kane wasn't dealing with a half ton of monstrosity that moved with unnerving speed. "How about a compromise. I put you down, and anyone who walks away from this fight, I let live."

Kane looked around. Through the trees he could see dozens of Fomorians, wielding assault rifles, watching in uncertain concern. None of them cheered at the prospect of the duel between the legendary figures before them. They'd seen too many of their own felled by the might of the man in black.

"What say you, my brothers?" Balor asked.

"Crush him!" one managed to snarl defiantly.

"They don't think I'll lose," Balor said.

Kane shrugged. "They've been wrong about me before."

Balor raised both fists and slammed them down into the slope. Kane could feel the mountain shake beneath his feet, and he tightened his grip on the shotgun handle. A few rough voices grumbled now, excitement starting to spread through the Fomorians.

"When you are ready," Balor taunted.

Kane raised the shotgun and fired a blast into the titan's chest. Skin ruptured and muscle rippled under the mighty impact, and Balor grunted. An arm the length of a log whipped around, and Kane threw himself to the ground to avoid being struck. The monstrous fist of Balor would be more than sufficient to crush him. Luckily, when Kane went to the dirt, he did so in a forward roll, his sleek and agile form tumbling so quickly, he avoided Balor's other wrecking-ball fist as it crashed to the ground behind him.

Speed was going to be Kane's best ally, but he still triggered the semiautomatic shotgun once more. As the weapon cycled a new round into the chamber under recoil, Balor howled as Kane's slug hit him square in the groin.

"Bastard!" Balor screeched.

"With that face, you're not going to be using those anyway!" Kane returned, pivoting the barrel up and blasting away. His shot went high. He'd been hoping to catch Balor in his baleful eye, but instead of catching the cybernetic orb, the fat bullet carved a crease into the titan's forehead. With a frustrated howl, Balor lashed out again. This time, massive knuckles grazed Kane's rib cage. Had he been an instant slower, the full force of the unstoppable fist would have hurled him hundreds of feet through the forest. As it was, the impact hurled Kane onto his back.

Balor sneered and stomped toward the fallen man. Kane triggered two quick shots out of the slug gun, heavy bolts of jacketed lead stabbing into Balor's sternum. Fetid breath escaped the monstrosity's lungs, and one hand rose to cup the bloody wounds in his belly.

Balor's other hand darted out and grabbed the barrel and tubular magazine of the shotgun. Fingers as fat as Kane's forearm squeezed and crumpled metal as if it was cardboard. With a shrug, Balor hurled the mangled lump of weaponry into the woods. Kane tucked his knees to his chest and speared both feet into the Fomorian's wounded belly. The impact elicited a groaning creak from Balor's lips, and gave Kane enough time to roll out of the way before a massive foot smashed the ground where he'd lain a moment ago.

"Get over here," Balor snarled, a massive paw reaching out and wrapping around Kane's leg.

With a flex of his forearm, Kane launched the Sin Eater into his grasp and the machine pistol bellowed authoritatively. A volley of 240-grain slugs punched through Balor's forearm, tearing through muscle and ricocheting off bone. The massive hand released Kane's thigh, and he toppled to the ground. Kane felt as if his hip had been dislocated, but he had no time for self-diagnosis. Smearing the blood off of his forearm, Balor glared angrily at the fallen human.

The sickly green eye suddenly blazed, and it took every ounce of Kane's strength to leap out of the path of the burning beam. As if the pain of Kane's left leg hadn't been enough, now his right calf felt as if it had been left out in the sun too long. His skin had dried out and cracked from the sudden, oppressive heat from Balor's eye, and Kane knew that if it hadn't been for the radiation-dampening properties of the shadow suit's environmental controls, his leg would have been seared off by the Fomorian's dread gaze.

"Baleful Eye monkey!" Balor howled. "I'm gonna cook you good!"

Kane triggered his Sin Eater again, bullets chewing through a slab of chest muscle and forcing the titan to flinch. This time, instead of using the deadly radiation blast of his eye, Balor backhanded Kane.

Kane was thrown against a tree trunk, where he slumped, struggling to regain his breath. As soon as he inhaled, Kane was delighted to realize that his ribs hadn't been shattered, but his brains had been scrambled by the sudden acceleration and stop.

"Fuck this noise, Kane. Let me put some fifty into this monster," Grant growled over the Commtact.

"He's mine," Kane rasped.

Fingers wrapped around Kane's shoulders and he was lifted into the air.

"Trying to be noble, Kane? I'd take the advice of your friend and let them come into this. The more, the merrier," Balor taunted.

Kane speared his elbow right in the Fomorian's fist-sized eye. The lens cracked under the brutal surprise attack, and Balor dropped Kane, clutching the orb.

"You son of a bitch!" Balor screamed.

Kane landed on his feet, but the sudden jolt to his injured hip lanced a spear of pain into his side. He was red-faced under the shadow suit hood and faceplate, but he was glad that no one could see the agony written across his features. He managed to summon enough strength to rise to his feet again.

Balor righted himself, tears pouring from the bottom lid of his oversized eye. "That hurt, you miserable little monkey!"

Kane turned and brought up his Sin Eater, triggering the machine pistol only a foot from the Fomorian's face. The cybernetic orb sparked and flashed, cracking under the onslaught of a dozen slugs. Balor staggered away from Kane, coughing and cursing in pain. A blind flail missed Kane, but the breeze unbalanced the Cerberus warrior.

His footing unsteady, Kane tumbled a dozen feet down the slope as Balor continued to wave one arm about while his other hand cupped his damaged eye.

"You did it now!" Balor yelled. "I'm gonna boil the skin from your bones!"

"Balor! No!" Kane shouted.

Even from where he'd landed, Kane could see that the sickly green glow of the cybernetic eye was pulsing with an odd new color. The Fomorian wasn't hearing any of it, and the intensity of the glow increased. A red smear of radiation pulsed along with the green ring of the iris, and a cone of light sprayed from the center of Balor's face. The tattered rags of Balor's nose ignited from the spillover heat, and trees burst into flames in a wide arc.

Balor screamed as the backlash of heat seared the inside of his skull.

"My head! It's on fire!" Balor called out. "Father!"

Kane grimaced and struggled to his feet. Though he

had been fighting the Fomorians to the death, to see an opponent racked by so much pain was something he couldn't stomach. "Turn it off!"

He shouldered Balor in the abdomen, but his weight and momentum weren't enough to even elicit a grunt from the agonized titan. Balor's screams increased in pitch and volume, and Kane looked up to see the poor creature's hand and forearm had been charred to a crisp. He'd tried to close his eye and put a clamp on the searing energy that bled out of his face.

Instead, Balor had shorn off the limb as charred bones disintegrated and poured into the dirt.

"Stop the pain!" Balor pleaded as he stuffed his face into the dirt. The stench of roasting soil assailed Kane's nostrils as Balor's eye continued to burn out of control, blazing a circle of ground.

"I'm sorry, Balor," Kane whispered. He fed the Sin Eater a full new magazine, then fired through the back of the Fomorian's head. Twenty rounds thundered in the night on full-automatic, smashing the creature's skull and blowing the cybernetic eye into splinters out the other end.

Balor rolled over, his empty, smoking socket staring emptily into the night sky.

For the first time since Kane had first seen the Fomorian, the creature seemed to be at peace.

Kane looked up, but once Balor's eye had burned out of control, the other mutants had broken and ran for their lives. The battle had been too gruesome for them, and too many of their brethren had been felled by the Cerberus defenders.

The scourge of the man-eaters had been broken.

"Enlil's ship took off just before you began your fight," Domi said. "I think he wasn't impressed."

"What about Bres?" Kane asked.

"He's all the way down in the valley," Grant said. "But I have a feeling that none of his little muties are ever going to listen to him again."

Kane shook his head, grunting in agreement with his friend. "So we're done here."

Grant nodded.

"Lakesh? Brigid?" Kane called over the Commtact.

"Thrush is still dead, if you're asking," Brigid's voice came over the radio implant.

Kane groaned. "Yeah. In all the excitement with Balor, I forgot what happened."

"Grant, is Kane okay?" Brigid inquired.

"The fool already had his head wrapped up in bandages when I got here. Then he decided to play pattycake with some mutie who made me look like scrawny little Domi here," Grant explained.

"So Kane's got a concussion," Brigid said. "Just like the fake."

Kane winced as he pulled off his hood. "Yeah. Just like the fake. But this time, do me a favor and shoot me in the head before going through all this shit again."

Grant hauled Kane to his feet, supporting his friend.

"Not a chance, partner," Grant replied, smiling. "Misery loves company."

Kane cracked a smile of his own, but the pain and fatigue were clear on his features.

The most recent threat to Cerberus had been neutralized, but the Cerberus veterans knew that it was only a matter of time before Thrush or Enlil launched another offensive.

Together Kane and Grant trudged through the darkness to meet up with the other Cerberus personnel. The return trip to the redoubt beckoned, and the warmth and sanctuary it offered would be welcome indeed.

The Don Pendleton's
Executioner®
FRONTIER FURY

The Executioner is caught in no-man's-land... with no way out!

An informant has leaked vital information to the Stony Man Farm—the location of two of the highest-ranking members of al Qaeda. Bolan lands inside the brutal northern Pakistan border territory, facing government troops determined to protect the terrorists. With time running out and the enemy closing in, the Executioner must do what no one else has—settle the score.

Available March 2010 wherever books are sold.

GOLD EAGLE®

www.readgoldeagle.blogspot.com